SERUM

SERUM

A NOVEL BY
DENNIS OGDEN

OGDEN IMPRINT

https://ogdenimprint.com

Ogden Imprint respectfully acknowledge the Traditional Custodians and the original sto-
rytellers of the land on which we live and work, and pay respect to all Aboriginal and Torres
Strait Islander Elders, past and present.

Author bio and more:

www.ogdenimprint.com

For
Dorian
and
Bayliene

CHAPTER 1

Seventy-five-year-old Marine Biologist, Professor Sir Marcus Glasson knows he's dying. He knows why, and he knows there's no cure. It's not cancer. Nor has it anything to do with his heart, despite being under constant stress and strain.

He is a victim of his own research.

Sir Marcus has over the years discovered many treatments and cures. One particular discovery that changed burn victim's scar tissue back to smooth healthy skin without grafting, awarded him a knighthood in 1998.

A year later, the government that nominated him came under pressure from the anti-euthanasia lobby to have his knighthood revoked.

He had developed an undetectable drug to assist end of life.

However, burn victims, their families, and the medical profession provided overwhelming support, allowing his title to remain after he signed an agreement assuring the drug would never be released.

He could easily end his suffering. A lethal dose of the drug is always with him, concealed inside the platinum and gold signet ring embossed with the Glasson coat of arms and worn unaccompanied on his wedding finger.

He looks down at the ring as his hands tighten on the wheel of his twelve-metre cruiser as it slices through the waves of the Savu Sea towards Dili, the capital of Timor-Leste. Does he need to endure the pain, the nausea and the increasing loss of energy any longer? After all, he is about to keep a promise made eighteen long years ago — the rescue of Noi de Jesus!

***

In 1991, Australian born Professor Marcus was celebrating with his diving partner in the then Portuguese Timor capital, Dili. Paulo de Jesus' wife had just presented him with his second child — a cute baby girl named Noi.

Paulo, a twelfth-generation Portuguese Timorese, has an inherent understanding of and an uncanny connection to the unpredictable activities of the many volcanoes beneath the Banda Sea north of Dili. A quality that proved invaluable.

His discovery of strange and rare sea species provided a rich source of medical opportunities for the fledgling Glasson BioMarine research company.

But the succeeding years proved far safer to be in the deep volcanic waters than on land.

In 1975, Operation Komodo led to the merciless invasion and subsequent occupation of Portuguese Timor. In less than a year the 27th Provence of the Republic of Indonesia was declared followed by fifteen years of strong-arm rule.

As the country was once again opening up to the world, a dramatic event that occurred on November 12, 1991, changed the course of the island's history.

A large gathering of peaceful protestors had converged on the Santa Cruz Cemetery to pay tribute to the fallen. Without warning, Indonesian troops stormed the area and opened fire, killing over two-hundred innocent men, women and children.

This allowed the military, with the help of the secret police and pro-integration militia, to strengthen its control.

Torture, rape and murder became terrifyingly regular.

As Timorese resistance groups carried on their fight for independence, the world watched with conflicted support for the Indonesians.

After President Suharto's resignation in 1998, the incoming president, B.J. Habibie, paved the way for a referendum to be held the following year, intending to gain Indonesia's total control over Portuguese Timor.

In fact, the result went the other way, as the people of East Timor voted overwhelmingly for independence.

The Indonesian military refused to stand by and allow that to happen. A campaign of brutal devastation followed.

Around 1,400 Timorese died and 300,000 were forced into West Timor as refugees, leaving their country almost demolished until an Australian-led peacekeeping force brought the violence to an end.

It was during the September 1999 murderous rampage that Marcus held the shot and dying Paulo in his arms. Paulo's wife and son lay dead beside him. With rifles trained on him, Marcus could only watch helplessly as the ruthless leader of the militia group, Djan Muhammad Aswar, dragged away Paulo's eight-year-old daughter, Noi. Her kicking and screaming struggle to free herself was useless in the powerful arms of her abductor. Her plea to be allowed to die with her family brutally ignored. As she is driven away and her screams refuse to fade, Paulo pleads in his final breath for Marcus to find and bring his daughter back to his grave.

Over the years, it was a promise he found difficult to fulfil — until the day just passed!

CHAPTER 2

Sir Marcus is among many attending a ceremony to announce the completion of Indonesia's new 4,000-hectare salt farm in Kupang Bay, West Timor.

He had a minor role in the early planning stages of the Salt Farm, reporting on the effects on marine life. While dismissing his concerns, out of respect, they invited him.

Sir Marcus usually turned down invitations to such events when his input was minimal, or in this case, rejected. But this invitation offered a slim and rapidly fading opportunity.

With so many senior government ministers attending, he hoped that Djan Muhammad Aswar — now head of a security unit — would attend in a protective capacity.

Sir Marcus accepted it was no certainty, as Aswar rarely sets foot on Timor Island, as he is still wanted in the eastern half for atrocities committed during the invasion. With the grotesque image of the man dragging eight-year-old Noi de Jesus away from her slain family permanently etched in his mind, Sir Marcus had to take the last chance he might ever have.

Over the past year, reports filtered through that Aswar had married — not unusual as he has two wives already — but it's said this new wife is young and attractive.

The photo of the de Jesus family Sir Marcus keeps in his wallet shows a pretty, dark-haired and bright-eyed young Noi.

She'd be twenty-seven now and likely grown into a beautiful young woman — just the adornment Aswar would want to be seen with on an occasion such as this.

***

A 5-star beachfront hotel overlooking Kupang Bay is the venue for the official launch. Its broad sea-facing pool and alfresco dining area is chosen for the early evening formalities, allowing the media to capture sunset over the location of the Salt Farm. A celebratory function is to follow in the ballroom with guests to dress formally.

Sir Marcus is not one for dressing formally.

Nevertheless, he presents himself as a handsome, greying, mature gentleman in his only suit of khaki linen. A plain navy silk tie hangs loosened from the collar of his cottage blue chambray shirt with a matching handkerchief casually resting in the breast pocket of his jacket.

The only formal adornment is the Order of Australia pin on his lapel — a small gold convex disc of bursting wattle with a dark blue gemstone in the centre.

Expecting the other guests to be dressed in dark business attire, Sir Marcus is not concerned that he'll stand out. In fact, it is his intention.

Then, despite what he had long hoped for, the speed of recognition came as a surprise. Surveying the crowd in all his grotesque bulk, suspicious, threatening stance and severely pock-scarred face is Djan Muhammad Aswar.

Marcus' heart rate quickens at the possibility his long-held promise may be one step closer to fulfilment. But are his wives here?

Expected that the moment Aswar locked eyes on him — inevitably in his khaki suit — he'd be remembered as the one who witnessed his abduction of Noi and the murder of her family. From then on, Sir Marcus will be under his watchful, bloodshot eye.

Any suspicion Aswar may have that Sir Marcus was at this function intent on taking his new wife away from him, made it easier for Sir Marcus' accomplice to do just that.

Though there was one matter that needed sorting out. Sir Marcus was sure Noi would want to be free and return to her own people on Arturo Island. But after so many years, who would she trust? There is also the possibility that the years of suppression and mistreatment rendered her unrecognisable.

One item he was sure would offer that trust is a small wooden spoon she had made with her own hands and given to her father when she was seven. Once she had tried to carve her name on the spoon, but the wood chipped before she could finish and she cried for two days. Sir Marcus has kept that spoon for this sole purpose. Confirming her identity brought back memories of how he explained to the very young Noi that the small birthmark on her neck, under her left ear, was the mark left by a fairy's kiss.

At the end of a drawn-out series of official speeches and the explanations of various maps and charts on display, guests retreated into the cooler function room for refreshments while the various ministers see to their media duties.

Fame precedes Sir Marcus on occasions such as this. There's much money in medical royalties and an endless stream of those wanting a slice of the pie. Hence, thrusting hands and untrusting introductions are an unwanted distraction. He diplomatically cut short each attempted conversation so he could keep moving, hoping to spot Noi. Once the ministers have satisfied the media, they join the others in the function room where the many lobbyists in attendance compete for their attention. This allows Sir Marcus the freedom to continue his search.

It is not uncommon for wives to be isolated while ministerial husbands and their keepers do business. As Sir Marcus spotted no one who could be Noi after several circuits, he hoped that was the case. But if so, where could she be? If indeed she is here at all.

A waiter approaches, balancing a tray of primed glasses of champagne. Without being asked, he hands Sir Marcus a glass. Not the done thing, but neither is the waiter the real thing. Accepting the offer, he notes the direction the waiter's index finger is pointing. There's a mutual nod between the two before the waiter continues his rounds.

With the glass to his lips, Sir Marcus casually turns to study the closed door of an annexed meeting room just as a man exits. It's not Aswar, but someone just as heavy and just as threatening. He pauses at the open door, allowing Marcus to see a group of women dressed in expensive evening wear lounging around inside. He studies each face until fixing on an attractive young woman staring back at him. She raises her hands to hide her expression of surprise — or is it recognition? She looks back at the other ladies in the room, hoping they had not noticed her reaction, and in doing so reveals her fairy's kiss.

The connection ends abruptly as Aswar's broad, towering figure joins the other man to block the doorway.

Sir Marcus turns his back on the two men so as not to show his interest in the room. Convinced he has found his friend's stolen daughter, he beckons the hovering waiter to take his glass and asks directions to the restroom.

The rescue has started.

CHAPTER 3

J ude Yimenes returns to the kitchen dressed in his waiter's outfit
and places the tray of empty champagne glasses down beside
others waiting to be washed. The kitchen staff are busy cleaning
up after the function and preparing for the evening dinner service
and fail to see a small foil-wrapped wad of paper impregnated with
potassium nitrate tossed into the flame under a large simmering pot
of chicken rendang curry.

Meanwhile, Sir Marcus is making his way down a corridor leading
to the restrooms. Pausing at a door indicated by the waiter as the rear
entrance to the room housing Noi and the other wives in isolation,
he waits until a shadowy figure at the end of the hallway signals all
is clear. He opens the door just enough to spy the women talking
among themselves or playing games on their mobile phones. Noi sits
to one side, isolated from the group, her back to Marcus.

As if the smell of freedom has entered the room, Noi turns her
head and sees Marcus peering through the sliver of open door.
Confusion washes over her face. Satisfied that the other women have
not noticed, she looks back to Marcus with an unsure shake of her
head. Marcus takes the spoon out of his pocket, slides it on the floor
inside the room, then closes the door.

The fear of being caught twists at Noi's gut. The man she glimpsed
earlier and now at the door stirs a distant familiarity, but over the
years she's come to distrust everyone. She looks down at the object
on the floor. Her heart pounds as her mind floods with distant
memories. Carried in an invisible mist, she rises and drifts to the
door, picks up the spoon, and runs her fingers over her engraved
name. Can it be true, she wonders, pressing the spoon to her chest.

She has to believe and reaches out to open the door. Suddenly, a shrill, screaming alarm creates instant panic as smoke fills the function room. Guests rush to the outside patio while security units surround their appointed minister and look for a safer area to move them. Meanwhile, hotel staff usher the wives outside to join their government partners...all but Noi.

The possibility that a fire in the kitchen was not an accident but a diversion to cover a terrorist attack adds to the confusion and lack of direction. In their panic, hotel and government security personnel shuffle the ministers around, unaware of two figures running away, blanketed by smoke, and heading to the water's edge of Kupang Bay.

Nervous bodyguards manhandle ministers, separating them from guests. Aswar stands rigidly in the middle of the confusion. His arms by his sides and fists clenched. With no weapon in hand and a cold, suspicious glare in his searching eyes belies the threat of assassination or terrorism. A sharp twist of his head towards where all the ministers' wives stand ignites his rage. His young wife is not among them. He scans each individual in the confused huddle until his eyes rest on Sir Marcus Glasson. The smoke drifting over the area takes him back among the fire and devastation of Dili and the man cradling the dying father of his new bride. Again he strains his eyes to catch sight of her. He approaches the other women who, in their panic, cannot remember if his wife was with them. Aswar's body distorts in a fireball of rage as reality sinks in. His head lowers into hunched shoulders, and he looks around from under stressed eyebrows. Then, in an outburst that startles everyone, he bellows, "This is not an attack...it's a kidnapping!"

A stillness comes over the confusion, forcing ministers' security personnel to check on all their charges. No one is missing. If Aswar were more important in the government, then all resources would be called on to hunt down whoever has taken his wife. But Aswar did not want that. This was something he had to handle himself.

Aswar calls on his personal bodyguards, Fauzi and Afif, who are quickly at his side. He points to the bay. "My wife! They have my wife! Get her back!"

The two rush down the patio steps to the water's edge and peer into the darkness for any sign. All they hear is the sound of a jet ski heading out into the deep water. With their own speed boat moored at the marina further down the beach, the only choice is to grab two of the hotel's jet skis parked on the shore. Aswar watches from the patio in utter rampaging rage as his two henchmen disappear into the night.

Jude Yimenes had expected this, but the hotel jet skis are no match to his two-seater, four-cylinder, four-stroke, eighteen-hundred cc Yamaha with extended fuel capacity. The only danger is crashing into one of the many fishing boats without flaming torches. Feeling the arms of Noi tightly wrapped around his waist, he stares ahead into the darkness. With no lights himself, trust in his sense of direction is his only guide.

The first unlit jukung outrigger they come across is narrowly missed by a sharp turn to the right, resulting in a spray of wash that drenches the fisherman. Aswar can hear his cries of protest from the shore. But as the protesting dies down, so does the sound of the high-powered jet ski. All that remains is the splutter of the hotel jet skis as they zig-zag around fishing boats without gaining any distance.

Aswar accepts that whoever has his wife will be well into the Savu Sea and most likely heading to one of the many Lesser Sunda Islands. A search will be difficult even in daylight. He turns away from the lapping waves on the shore and raises his eyes towards Sir Marcus on the hotel patio.

Despite Aswar keeping a close watch on him most of the time, he has no doubt Sir Marcus is behind his wife's abduction. He relays his belief in a death glare towards Sir Marcus, who stands calmly among the subsiding confusion. He turns his head towards Aswar with a nod and a shrug of sublime innocence.

Aswar calls on every ounce of self-control to head off a confrontation in front of all the ministers and dignitaries. He resigns himself to the fact that there's nothing he can do...for now!

CHAPTER 4

It has taken Jude Yimenes almost three and a half hours to reach his destination. With virtually no light from a new moon and intermittent clouds hiding the stars, he needed to stop now and then to check his wrist compass. Noi, who tightly clung to Jude all the way, also added to the time taken by the need to vomit several times. This surprised Jude as she had spent most of her childhood at sea with her father.

Despite being four years older, Jude played with Noi when his mother, Mira Yimenes, often cared for her when her father went diving with Marcus Glasson. When she was old enough, they would all dive together.

Now, eighteen years later, they're together again — eighteen years of absolute contrast in their lives.

While Noi remained an abused and tormented prisoner, Jude revelled in freedom and success. He became part-owner of Glasson BioMarine because of two long-held secrets.

He had discovered several unknown and unique deep-sea species that led to significant medical breakthroughs — the location they inhabit locked securely in his mind.

A handful of people know the other secret: he is the illegitimate son of Sir Marcus Glasson and Mirla Yimenes.

Sharing in the royalties of his efforts enabled Jude to live the life of a jet-setting, playboy bachelor. When he was not diving in the volcanic depths of the Banda Sea, he was swimming among the roulette tables of the world's casinos and wading through the rich and famous crowds in top nightclubs. Young, fit, rich, and handsome meant the world was his to enjoy while leaving broken hearts in his wake.

Noi also had riches and good looks, but the riches controlled and her looks exploited to open many doors for Aswar who threatened the lives of anyone who challenged him for ownership of her.

Her rescue from the sadist's harem was a blessing, but it also presented the chance to terminate another secret — she believes she's pregnant.

At the first opportunity, she would abort rather than carry the genes and a reminder of the person she most loathed.

As they drift past the southern coast of the small island, Rusa, Jude peers into the darkness searching for the entrance to a small cove where his dive boat is anchored. With high cliffs all around, it is accessible only by sea and difficult to locate even in daylight. It took another twenty minutes to find the entrance.

Cold and wet from sea spray, they climb aboard the dive boat. Jude secures the jet ski beside the rear floating dock. At first light, he'll winch it aboard so it's unseen from the air.

Noi is shivering and needs to get out of her drenched formal gown and into dry clothes. As she changes into one of Jude's tee shirts, track pants and hoodie, Jude brews some hot chocolate in the faint beam of a small penlight.

Noi left her hot chocolate unfinished, allowing sleep to take precedence.

Satisfied that she is warm and comfortable in one of the two beds below deck, Jude sits under the canopy at the back of the boat sipping his drink while contemplating what has been and what is to be.

As the rising sun welcomes in a new day, Jude finishes securing the jet ski onto the rear deck. He looks at his watch and reckons Marcus should be on his way back home to Dili after sleeping on his cruiser overnight. Once there, Jude believes, he'll make some business calls and for the next couple of days act normal and be visible around town. This will not be typical behaviour for Marcus. He prefers spending his days unsighted and absorbed in his research. But that is the plan.

In the meantime, Jude — who knows the islands around the Banda Sea better than anyone — will take Noi on an island-hopping course to keep a step ahead of any attempt from Aswar and his network to find them. Meanwhile, Marcus will monitor the Indonesian media for news of Noi's abduction, though he would not expect to see any, such was Aswar's control over the media and the need to save face.

When the time is right, Jude will take Noi to the graves of her parents and brother on Atauro Island. The people there will take her in and protect her, knowing that Aswar would not risk setting foot on the island or anywhere else on Timor Leste.

Marcus can then rest, knowing he has kept his promise to his dying friend, Paulo.

***

Marcus reaches for his satellite phone as he manoeuvres around fishermen returning to Kupang with their night's catch. It was time to contact Jude and make sure all went to plan and that they were hiding somewhere safe and well.

Jude had insisted on his father not knowing where he planned to take Noi, just in case Aswar had him arrested and questioned.

To his surprise, his sat phone buzzed in his hand before he could make the call. He recognises the caller's number and with a worried expression puts the phone to his ear.

"Red fish, this is blue fish here," he hears.

Marcus takes another look at the caller's ID to reassure himself, even though he recognised Jude's voice. "Red fish here. Just about to call you. Everything okay?"

"Can we talk?" replies Jude.

Marcus senses some panic. He looks around to make sure no boats are following. "Yes, go ahead, blue fish."

It was long understood that Jude never referred to Marcus as father, dad, pop, or any other form of paternal identity. They chose blue and red fish for this one event only.

"We may have a problem here, Red."

Despite a hit of anxiety, Marcus tries to stay calm. "Go ahead, Blue, is your catch okay?"

"Yes and no, Red. Safe but not okay."

"Go on."

13

"Catch throwing up. When I asked what's wrong, catch went troppo."

"Go on."

"Ranting, raving, sobbing and trying to...um, self-harm."

Marcus is now more than anxious. "Shit Red! Um, you're on the phone, so I take it catch has calmed down, right?"

"Not totally. Had to tie up. But I may have got more than one catch."

"What do you mean, Blue? More than one catch!"

"I think this catch has another in the belly. At least that's what I figure. Not happy with it and wants it gone."

Marcus' mind is spinning. "Are you sure?" he asks.

"Not absolutely, Red. No sign of it. In fact, catch looks great...I mean, if it's true, then it must be very early."

There's no reply from Marcus as he considers what this could mean.

"You there, Red?"

It shakes Marcus out of his thoughts. "Yes, Blue. You said self-harm. How much?"

"Not much. I tied catch up before there was. Not happy to keep it like that, so can we meet asap?"

"Yes, of course. I still need to stop at the base. Where can I meet you?"

"VP25 top end, understood?"

"Understood," replies Marcus, knowing the codes they have given to all the volcanic islands in the Banda Sea. "I'll meet you there before nightfall."

"Roger, Red, understood...out."

Marcus cancels the call and, with renewed urgency, increases his speed towards Dili.

CHAPTER 5

~·~·~

S ir Marcus Glasson has much to think about before reaching Dili. If what Jude is saying is true and Noi is pregnant, this unexpected news has invigorated a depth of self-interest in Marcus. He can understand why she'd want to abort if Aswar is the father, but nothing can stop Marcus contemplating the incredible opportunity this presents?

It was around nine months ago when Jude came back from one of his deep-water searches with the most unusual-looking worm he had ever seen.

He discovered it among the chemical-rich hydrothermal vents that litter the sea floor of the Banda Sea volcanic ring. Earlier research using the unique fish, slugs and coral of the area has led to cures for many medical ailments in humans. But this one was more than unusual.

It was only by luck that Jude noticed its head poking out of one of the black ash-spewing tubes. The heat inside these tubes is around eighty degrees Celsius — a place where nothing should live.

They thought it to be an Alvinella pompejana or Pompeii Worm variety — interesting, but yet to deliver anything medicinally worthwhile.

But after further examination back in the Glasson lab in Dili, this worm proved different in several exciting ways.

It was smaller in length at seven centimetres and had twice as many red tentacles protruding from its head. The mouth had a covering of soft, down-like feathers, and what looked like two eyes were nipple-like extensions.

The grey, beard-like stubble covering its pink body is a form of bacteria. While it was like the Pompeii version, the bacteria proved different. So different that this worm could possibly be the genesis of the most significant medical discovery ever.

Despite extensive searching, all attempts at finding another worm of the same species failed. With only one specimen to work with, Marcus hesitated to do anything that would kill the worm. But something drove him to try. A small incision may not kill it, but could provide a sample of tissue for analysis. This turned out to be far beyond anyone's expectations. The small incision healed in just over an hour, whereas the tissue sample decomposed in minutes.

Marcus already knew the hairy bacteria was symbiotic — a benefit to both it and its host. The discharged mucus from the body fed the bacteria, which protected the worm from infection. But more than that, it had a reversal role.

Marcus ran the decaying sample over the bacteria to test his theory, and at once the colour and texture reverted to the original.

But it was short-lived. Within an hour decomposition began again — the symbiotic connection needed to be permanent.

This finding proved a blessing, for there was no need to dissect the worm. The secret was in the mucus and bacteria. As long as Marcus kept the worm alive in the nutrient-rich water collected where they found it, at the same temperature and under the same pressure, the mucus and bacteria were readily available.

Intravenous and oral testing on mice followed. All cases of induced infections healed, lacerations and broken bones mended in a short time, chronic ailments disappeared, and cancers vanished. Nothing put up to test the healing effects of this mucus/bacteria mix failed. Marcus knew he was on the verge of something great. Then, over the next two months, his hopes were all but dashed. All the mice, except one, reverted to their individual problems. Healed injuries became infected, and the mended bones became brittle and snapped. Cancer returned and became fatal.

While it devastated Marcus, there was one last hope: the only mouse that remained healthy was pregnant. He introduced other pregnant mice to the treatment. Some with current ailments and cancer responded positively. As the baby mice were born and examined, all were healthy and showed no sign of any inherited illness. In fact, their gene pattern had removed all defects evident in the mother before her treatment. It became clear to Marcus that the only way such a cure for all ills can work is through the mother.

It all sounded great until reality hit. There was no way of manufacturing the formula on a mass scale unless Jude can find more worms. All efforts failed. The one they had would not survive once it consumed all the nutrients in the water. But over the years, Marcus did not succeed by giving up. There had to be an answer.

Marcus saved and tested the umbilical cord after the birth of each baby mouse. The small cords contained concentrated amounts of the mucus/bacteria composition, providing an ample dose for four other pregnant mice. By Marcus' reckoning, every baby born from a mother who had taken the formula provided at least four doses for another four mothers-to-be. Within one or two generations there could be enough doses for every mother on Earth.

Further extensive research showed that one significant problem remained. As it's the mother who takes the compound — and so purifying her body — it is only her genes that pass to the baby. Removed are all traces of the father. In fact, of all mice tested, not one male mouse was born.

Marcus decided very early in his career that any moral dilemma should not interfere with research.

Society will deal with it as with his euthanasia drug.

In future defence of his life-changing discovery, it could be possible at some stage, and with further research, for males to benefit from taking a form of the compound and their bodies rejuvenated and purified. But that was far from his priority at this opportune moment.

With the first two stages of testing, the now-called SERUM AP80GBM/17 showed positive results. But, like any medicine or drug, it is required to pass the third stage of testing before release — the clinical trial on humans.

Unfortunately, unless more worms are located, time and the life of the only available resource will run out before someone suitably pregnant and willing to volunteer can be found.

Marcus thought of trialling the compound on himself. It could reverse his ailments and give him a few more years, but he decided not to waste on him what little was available.

He needed someone to volunteer, and fate has handed him Noi!

CHAPTER 6

A whiff of smoke carries the aroma of grilling fish across Dili's Avenue de Portugal. Cars and scooters peel off from the traffic to stop beside makeshift barbecues dotted along the beachfront for hungry drivers and riders or passengers to buy a midday meal. Barbecuers barter for the freshly caught fish hanging from poles balanced across vendors' shoulders. The mood is friendly as children play in the water to cool from the Dili heat and refresh from the humidity.

Opposite, among the row of houses, is the Sunday Roast Bar with its trickling water feature, greenery and a flickering neon sign inviting in over-the-yardarm drinkers.

Next door, separated by a covered carport where a white mud-splattered 4WD rests, is a featureless, cracked-plaster wall high enough for only the tall palm trees behind to be seen.

Inside the renovated house beyond, there is a different world. Entry via the carport leads into a large office accommodating furniture suited to a modern penthouse. There is no reception desk, but a large, solid carved wood table with one high-end computer on top. There are no filing cabinets, no brochure stands, and no company branding. In fact, the tonally subdued walls are clear of anything corporate. Instead, photographs of underwater coral, colourful sea life and valleys of submarine vegetation hang. The only hint of the world-renowned activity operating beyond the high wall.

Beside the large table with its four matching chairs is a tanned leather two-seater lounge, two matching armchairs and a coffee table from the same designer as the larger table. At the far end of the room is a closed doorway with a key-coded lock. The door has a small one-way window at eye height that can only be seen through from the inside. There, seated among purpose-built research equipment, is fifty-five-year-old Mirla Yimenes.

She looks up from the trinocular biological microscope to the wall clock. Her semi-dark attractive features and black, gently waved hair are clues to her Portuguese heritage. Her skin is smooth and sculpted, her lips full, her eyes dark but tired and betray a worried expression.

If Marcus Glasson is away for more than a day, she gets restless. For a good reason. She is more than well aware of his failing health and the easy way out to end his suffering. Being a partner of Glasson BioMarine, she helped develop the euthanasia drug he carries around on his ring finger. But as a secret intimate partner to Marcus for the past thirty-one years and mother of his equally secret son, Jude, they have a clear understanding that she will be by his side when the time comes.

Marcus made it clear to Mirla he'd be back around mid-afternoon. In fact, he repeated it several times, which seemed odd, and when the call came from someone wanting to know if Marcus had returned from Kupang, it sent a shiver down Mirla's spine.

Whether it was the caller's accent, or not giving his name, unsettled her, for her hatred towards the Indonesians still raged.

***

Mirla was born on Atauro Island, twenty-five kilometres north of Dili. In 1975 she was only twelve when the Indonesians invaded her country. She and her family worked hard to provide shelter and food for the growing number escaping the brutality of the Indonesian army and the pro-Indonesian militia.

Soon the island became overcrowded, water became scarce, and despite Mirla and others fishing and diving every day for food, there was never enough.

Overcrowding led to a lack of hygiene and illness spread. Mirla then spent more time tending the sick. Because of the lack of medicine, she studied natural remedies and what secrets the creatures of the sea could offer.

But this was not enough. In 1984, at the age of twenty-one, she joined Fretilin; the Revolutionary Front for an Independent East Timor.

She started as a medical assistant, but as tensions grew, she took up arms. This took her into action and into a world of sadistic brutality that proved her medical knowledge was far from adequate. Gathering all the medical books she could find, Mirla studied at every opportunity.

Two years later she met, by chance, Marcus Glasson. Initially, she was unimpressed with him as he was dealing with the Indonesians to help develop his fledgling marine research company. Despite this failing, it was his research that interested her.

Marcus Glasson was twenty-one years older. Yet to divorce his estranged Sydney-based wife, he became attracted to this fearless, strong-willed, inquisitive, and beautiful dark-haired girl.

Mirla felt the attraction but resisted, choosing to remain a student to his knowledge only.

The more Mirla asked about Marcus' research, the more it impressed him with her questions. They started as expected. "What are you doing?" to "Why are you doing it?" to "But what if...?" She reminded him what he was like at her age — asking the same questions and never satisfied with the answers.

She had a good understanding of medicine, but better still was her understanding of the Banda Sea, the volcanic seafloor, and the creatures that lived there.

Their relationship quickly became both professional and intimate.

As Indonesian control intensified, she also became his eyes on the ground and under the water and encouraged Marcus to keep his connection with the Indonesian agencies so she could use him for her revolutionary aims.

As more people fled to Atauro Island for safety, Mirla felt she needed to return and help in any way she could. It was then that she found out she was pregnant. Marcus wanted to take her to the nearest Australian city, Darwin, and away from danger, but she would not leave her family or those now classified as political prisoners. During the following months of invasion and turmoil, their son, Jude, was born.

***

Footsteps in the outer office alert Mirla to Marcus' return. He unlocks the door to the lab and enters. Her relief at seeing her beloved quickly turned to confusion. He cuts the usual kiss and embrace short as an air of urgency fills the room.

"Mirla, dear, I'm sorry, but I have to leave again." He looks around and, as an afterthought, asks, "Is everything okay? Any calls or visitors?"

His actions mystify her as she struggles to answer. "Umm, no...yes...I mean...Marcus, is everything all right? Where are you going?"

Marcus is busy rummaging through papers and the medicine cabinet. "Look, I'll fill you in, but first, go to the store and buy enough food for...I don't know...maybe two or three days." He pauses and turns to her. "Please," he adds, more as a hurry-up than out of politeness,

Mirla is about to stand her ground and insist on more information, but sensing the urgency and trusting him for an explanation when she returns, she grabs her purse and leaves for the nearby store.

Marcus waits to hear the outer door close before unlocking the atmosphere-controlled storeroom. Inside, among tanks containing an assortment of exotic sea life, biological specimens, and more laboratory equipment, are two solid steel safes of equal size. A key code opens one. Inside is another smaller steel compartment with its own security-coded keypad. He takes a quick glance back before opening it. Inside, the temperature is a constant three degrees Celsius, with four small stainless steel canisters side by side. Each has its own temperature control unit built in, powered by four internal rechargeable batteries. Marcus runs a finger across the individual codes etched on their outer surface and removes the chosen one. He locks the internal safe, then the outer one, and quickly adds the canister to a waterproof duffle bag.

Marcus checks he has what he needs, then looks through the diary on his phone. There are appointments and meetings scheduled over the coming week. Despite the change in plans, they won't be cancelled.

Mirla is usually frugal with her food buying, but this time she has bought more than enough. She places the shopping bags on the floor and turns to face Marcus.

"What's going on, Marcus?" she asks with an intended insistence.

Marcus places his hands on her shoulders. "I'll be away for maybe a week or more and don't want you to worry."

That's like a red rag to a bull, and Mirla shrugs away his hands. "Tell me Marcus, and no bullshit. Tell me, what is going on!"

"I can't. Not right now. I..."

He's cut short by Mirla. "When? You've just returned from some function in the West, that even you said would be boring, and now you're acting as if the world is about to end."

Marcus would love to respond with the words spinning around in his head — that the world is about to start. He changes the subject. "Jude will be back tomorrow. He'll tell you then. I'm sorry, darling, but for your sake, you must wait till then."

Mirla knows a threat when she hears one. "For my sake...or for my safety?"

Silence is her answer.

"Tell me one thing. Tell me the truth, then I'll trust you to go." She looks deeply into his eyes. "Is it time? We made a promise to be together."

Marcus squeezes her hands and shakes his head. "No, it's not time. I have too much to live for."

Mirla releases his hands, throws her arms around him, and they kiss.

CHAPTER 7

It's late afternoon and Marcus is in a cautious hurry to meet up with Jude at the arranged location. VP25 is some distance away from, but in sight of, Atauro Island. This worries him, as that is where Noi's family lies buried and the promise Marcus made to her father will have to wait. He's sure she'll insist on being taken to her island, back among her people and to the graves of her family. A battle Marcus is expecting to convince her otherwise.

He eases his cruiser beside Jude's dive boat and throws him a line. Any other time, he and Jude would sit back with a beer in hand and marvel at the sunset. Not this time.

"Where is she?" he calls out.

"Below deck. Locked in so I could get here without worrying about her all the time. Sorry, Marcus, but I also had to tie her up to stop her from hurting herself."

He offers his hand to help Marcus get on board. "Why the change of plans? I thought we were dropping her off on Atauro."

Marcus steps onto the deck and looks to the closed hatch leading to the sleeping quarters. He replies in a hushed voice, "I'm taking her with me. It's far too dangerous to have her anywhere near Indonesian waters. I bet his network is already spreading word of her kidnapping all over the islands. If, as you say, she is only just pregnant, Aswar may not know. But if he hears she is, he'll be more determined than ever to get her back."

"Where are you taking her then?" he asks with a frown.

"Best I don't tell you. Look, the sooner Noi is off your hands the better. I'll be in touch in a few days. In the meantime, I want you to go about your business as usual. We still have our little creature to find, right?" A grip on his arm and a shake call for confirmation.

"Yeah, sure...but..." Jude considers for a moment whether or not to bring it up. He does. "If this change of plans is because she's pregnant, then it's only her word that she is. She certainly doesn't look it."

"I'll confirm it later. I know the people on Atauro will care for her. But if she's pregnant, the stress of one day being found and returned to Aswar could affect both of them."

Jude shakes his head. "One thing I know for sure is that she does not want this baby and will do anything to get rid of it." He glances back to where she's locked away. "Maybe it would be for the best. How could she care for Aswar's kid after what she's been through?"

"Yes, I can imagine, and you're right. That's why I need to take her far away for a time. If I can't talk her out of an abortion, then best it's done someplace better suited."

Jude understands what Marcus is saying, but senses there's more to it. He decides not to pursue it further. "I'll go get her."

Marcus uses the time to compose himself. Many years have passed since he spent happier times with her and her family, and there's a need to reinforce her confidence in him again.

With apprehension, he waits as a heated conversation takes place beyond the hatch. When Jude and Noi emerge, Marcus stands back with a broad smile so as not to be too overpowering. Noi needs a moment to register Marcus, then looks around suspiciously.

"Have you still got your spoon I left for you?" he asks, hoping it will fill in some doubts she must carry.

She stares into his eyes while touching the spoon in her borrowed pants pocket. The dark fog of years of horror fragments into hints of happy childhood gatherings and her father enjoying the company of this man. A shiver ripples through her at the possibility her nightmare may be over. Tears fill her eyes as she rushes into his open arms.

"You're free, dear Noi. Safe and free," he says to reinforce her hopes.

Despite the urgency to get underway, Marcus holds the trembling Noi close. When he feels her relax, he eases her back from their embrace.

"Come, we must get you further away before it gets too dark."

He goes to steer her to his cruiser, but she resists, looks around, takes a step back, and with a shake of her head says, "No, that is my home, my island," she says pointing to the distance hill above the horizon. "There is where I want to be."

"You will, Noi, I promise. The same promise I gave your father. I'll bring you home...but not now. It's too dangerous to be within Aswar's grasp. I need to hide you far away for a short time, that's all...a short time."

Marcus sees her face drain of colour at the mention of Aswar's name. She takes another step back, grabbing at her stomach. "Mister Glasson...I have his baby in me, and I want it gone. I want him gone, and I want his baby gone. You can do that for me, Mr Glasson, yes?"

"Come Noi, we'll talk about it later, but we must get going as it's getting dark. I will help you, I promise...please believe me."

Noi looks to Jude, who responds with a nod that all will be fine. With little choice, she agrees.

Marcus gets Jude to hold the line tight so he can get Noi aboard his cruiser. As soon as she's seated, Marcus turns back to Jude and in a whisper says, "Mirla will want to see you tomorrow, Jude. She doesn't know what I'm doing, and I want you to tell her only what we've said now...and not what you think, understand?"

Jude nods but does not hide his worried look. "Get in touch with me soon, hey?"

Marcus takes the line from Jude and pushes away from the dive boat. Noi looks back at Jude with a silent thanks as the cruiser is reversed before turning due east to merge into the fading light.

CHAPTER 8

Marcus struggles to keep his cruiser at a steady twenty knots as his tired eyes peer into the increasing darkness. The day has been long and tiring for the weakened professor. He'd hoped to have travelled further, but decided the next few days would require all the energy he could gain from at least one decent sleep.

With Noi below deck, he silences the twin 480-horsepower engines and drops anchor 500 metres off the far north-eastern tip of Timor Island. Far enough away from any villages and fishermen. The silence allows him time to think about the many hurdles that lie ahead. Hurdles that will rely on favourable weather, timing, contacts and, of course, Noi.

She comes on deck after rummaging through the shopping bags, looking to satisfy her hunger and offers Marcus a nut bar.

"When can we talk?" questions Noi with a determined tone in her voice.

"Tomorrow," replies Marcus. "It's been a long, tiring day. I need some coffee and sleep."

He passes Noi to take the steps down to the gallery, but dizziness and nausea come over him and he grabs at the handrail to stop falling. Noi reaches out to grab his arm, but he brushes her hand away in frustration.

"What's wrong, Mr Glasson? You don't look too good."

"I'm fine, Noi. Just tired, that's all." He makes a mental note to keep his failing health a secret from her, for she is the one who will need support. "The coffee will help. Do you want some, or maybe tea?"

"Coffee will be fine, thanks."

The sun is yet to rise, but a hint of light in the eastern sky signals its arrival. The vibration of his wristwatch rouses Marcus from a restless sleep. He stretches the kinks out of his aching body, having chosen to sleep on the cockpit lounge on deck just in case...he was not sure, but Aswar needs to be constantly on his mind. The sleep has returned some energy, though his nausea is becoming a constant annoyance and not helped by the aroma of bacon and eggs sizzling away in the galley.

"I hope you don't mind?" asks Noi as Marcus approaches. "We could both do with a big breakfast, and seeing bacon there, I couldn't resist it. I hated the food they forced me to eat."

"Not at all," replies Marcus, heading to the bathroom. "I'll have mine on deck."

After some time trying to silence his heaving over the toilet, Marcus finds Noi waiting for him on deck as the sky shows a rim of pink on the horizon. She's seated on the small lounge to the left of the captain's chair. Her plate of bacon, eggs and toast on her lap and Marcus' on the small cockpit table, yet to be folded back to full size.

"Thanks, Noi. I'll have my breakfast after we get underway," says Marcus, needing a coffee first to settle his stomach.

Noi was hoping their talk would start over breakfast, and her kind deed of cooking it would give her an edge over telling of her plans. But Marcus wants to be far away and out of sight of Timor Island before the difficult task of talking her out of an abortion and convincing her to become a human guinea pig.

Marcus kept his cruiser at a speed that was fast yet economical on fuel. When satisfied he was far enough away from the island, he finally turns to Noi with the most crucial question that'll decide how the following conversation will go...if at all!

"Noi, I'm sure you know your body and what is happening to it, but I have to ask. How positive are you that you're pregnant?"

Noi's dark eyes tighten, and a frown creases her forehead. To assume she is making this up is not only infuriating but a tremendous disappointment coming from someone she had hoped would understand her better.

The lack of an immediate reply and the hurt in her eyes suggest two things: he doubts her belief in being pregnant, and Marcus has lost ground in gaining her confidence.

"Look, Noi, I'm not questioning your honesty. It's just that if you go ahead with aborting, there will be more questions and tests. If what you believe turns out to be an honest trick of the body, you would have put yourself through all that stress and embarrassment for nothing."

Noi remains silent.

He continues to explain himself. "Noi, you may not be aware of what I've been doing since your abduction, but I assure you I'm very familiar with the human body, what it can do and the tricks it plays. My medical research has helped change what many thought unchangeable." He pauses before laying the ground-work for his proposal. "I will never doubt your sincerity, Noi, or pretend to imagine what you have gone through over the past years. Your silence is understandable and respected, but Noi, as a doctor of sorts, I would like an answer before we can talk further."

No one has spoken to Noi like that for so many years, nor shown the slightest respect or understanding. All she has ever known is total control and violent abuse. She lowers her head and, in a barely audible voice, answers. "I just know I am."

Marcus asks, "Did you do a pregnancy test? One you could get from a pharmacy?"

Her painful past brings tears to her eyes. "It was impossible. They never allowed me to shop. If I went outside, it was never alone. The other wives and his bodyguards covered me with veils and watched me all the time. They tell me what to wear, how to look, and when to speak."

"Then, to remove any doubt, would you agree to do a test now? It's painless and quick, and then we can talk about what's to be done."

"Now? You mean right now?" Noi asks with a hint of hope she's not pregnant and it will remove a major problem.

"Yes, I have a test with me. I can explain what to do, or if you prefer, you can read the instructions yourself. But first, I must ask if you are taking any medication or drugs of any kind."

She lowers her eyes. "They forced me to take some drugs. I don't know what it was, but it made me sick, so they never gave it to me again. Will this mean the test will not work?"

"Was it over three months ago?"

"Yes. I was when..." She goes quiet as one of the many ugly memories surface.

"Then it'll have no effect."

Marcus hands her a packet taken from his jacket pocket. She studies it without taking it, then looks up at Marcus, unsure of the next step.

"Go to the bathroom, and when you've done the test, I want you to show me the reading straight away...understand?"

Unsure, but she gives a slight nod, then takes the package and slowly turns toward the hatch.

"Take as much time as you want. If you need help to understand the directions, I won't be going anywhere. Just show me the test as soon as it's done."

CHAPTER 9

Marcus has let the boat drift while Noi does the test. It is taking longer than he hoped, and time he did not have to waste. But since learning she could be pregnant, the wait allowed an unanswered question to surface again.

Finally, Noi emerges from the hatch and hands the test to Marcus with lowered eyes and no hint of the result.

Marcus remains detached from his feelings as he checks the result and checks it again to be sure. Now was the time to ask that question.

"Am I telling the truth? Am I pregnant?" she probes, unsure of her feelings.

"Noi, before I tell you, there is something I need to ask. It will be unpleasant for you to tell me, I'm sure, so if you find it too difficult I'll understand."

Noi is unsure what to say.

"Noi, is Aswar the only who has had sex with you?" The words come out as blunt as they sound.

Noi gives a shiver and recoils at the question. But before she can do or say anything, Marcus continues.

"Were you taking a contraceptive of some sort and only recently stopped?"

She tenses up and shakes her head wildly. Marcus is about to tell her not to answer when her shaking stops and she looks back into Marcus' eye with a new intensity.

"Look, why don't you sit down. There's no need to answer," suggests Marcus.

But Noi remains rigid until her voice bellows loud and shrill. "It was not sex! It was continuous rape!"

Marcus steps back as if the voice came from someone else.

Noi turns away from him and rests on the handrail looking down at the deep water.

"In the beginning, he passed me to others as payment for debts he owed. Then, when all his debts were paid, they still wanted me. That is when he decided I was just for him and no one else. From that day he continued to punish me for being with other men. Men he forced me onto."

She turns back to face Marcus with a look of weathered maturity, as if she had aged a couple of years in the minutes she had turned away.

"Yes, I was made to take things, use things, do things to stop becoming pregnant — until recently. I don't know why or what happened, but suddenly he desperately wanted a son. He went mad. Sex became more urgent and rougher than..."

"Stop!" Marcus interrupts. "You've said enough. Sit down and try to forget I asked," knowing that would be impossible.

"Did he make a son?" Noi asks in a cold, icy manner.

"I don't know about a son, but yes, Noi, you're pregnant."

The rage she has controlled erupts. "I want it gone. I want it gone now, and if you can't help me, I'd rather die with it than have any part of that monster around to continue his poison."

Marcus looks at his watch and realises how much time has passed. He knows he should sit with her for the next step in his proposal, but there is a plane they need to catch from Darwin and time is now against them.

"There is another solution," Marcus offers as he starts the engine and kicks the cruiser into gear.

"How can there be? You do not understand. I have inside me the seed of a monster. How can I let that seed grow into another monster to inflict more cruelty and brutality?"

"I understand, Noi, believe me. If there were no alternative, I would not hesitate to help you abort. But there is, and if you allow me to explain, you can rid the monster you carry and keep a baby that could change the world."

Noi senses Marcus is about to spin her an unbelievable story just to change her mind. "Nothing you say will stop me from what is right. You, of all people, know I am. You watched as this baby's father murdered my family and many others."

"Yes, I did, and one day he will pay for what he has done and continues to do. But you can have the last word. You can change the course of the baby inside you to rid the world of the disease that creates people like Aswar."

Noi shakes her head. "No, no, you're talking rubbish just to change my mind. How can that ever be possible?"

"The means are right here, and you alone can make it come true," he calls out over the sound of the revving twin engines.

"You lie, and now I must do what has to be done."

Suddenly, without warning, she jumps over the side of the speeding cruiser.

One leg of Jude's oversized, loose-fitting pants snags on a mooring cleat, interrupting her fall enough for Marcus to take his hands off the wheel and grab the waistband. Noi wrestles to free herself as the steering wheel spins, sending the cruiser on an erratic course. Water slaps at her face as the cruiser's momentum lurches to the left, forcing Noi back into the side of the boat. Marcus wraps both arms firmly around her waist and pulls her back aboard.

"You damn fool!" calls out an enraged Marcus as he turns off the ignition and yells into her face. "I will not let you destroy the only chance of presenting to the world my greatest discovery!"

The boat drifts as Marcus waits for each to calm.

"Now listen Noi, and listen good. I have with me one chance and one chance only of ridding the world of disease forever. I have the serum, and I have you. The serum will start losing its effect within a few hours and it's becoming unlikely more can be found. I could tie you down and force you to take the serum, but I won't. Unless you understand what a huge benefit you could bring to the world, you will only try what you just tried again and again until you succeed. So, I'm giving you one last chance to listen to me. If you still refuse to be part of history...well then, you are no use to me. I'll place you under protection once we get to Darwin. You'll be out of Aswar's reach and free to do whatever you choose regarding the baby."

Noi is finding it hard to understand what Marcus is saying, except that he's prepared to give her over to others. She knows the vast reach Aswar has around the world and his network of corruption.

Despite attempting to talk her out of an abortion, she still feels safer with Marcus than anyone else.

She eases her struggle and looks searchingly into his eyes. "Tell me, but understand this is my body and I'll be the only one to decide what to do with it and the baby."

Marcus nods and relaxes, but is ready to reach out to grab her again if need be. Noi sits down on the side lounge and wipes tears and sea spray from her eyes.

Marcus sits at the wheel and corrects the direction the boat is drifting. When Noi has calmed enough to concentrate on what he has to say, he begins.

"What if I told you, Noi, that you can rid yourself of the baby inside you and replace it with a different baby?"

Unbelievable as it sounds, it raises her attention level.

"Below deck is a serum that will remove all traces of Aswar's DNA. The baby will then carry only your genes and your DNA, and added to that, she will be immune to all known illnesses."

"She?" Noi interrupts. "You said she. How do you know this?"

"At this early stage in your pregnancy, the serum will change the male Y chromosome to an X chromosome resulting in two X chromosomes of a female as opposed to X and Y of a male. Do you understand?"

"I think so. Keep going."

"Well, if it's a boy you have, the serum will remove all traces of the father, and you'll give birth to a new baby girl."

He studies Noi to make sure she understands. She is looking at him, but her mind is struggling to come to grips with what he's saying. Before she can raise questions, Marcus continues.

"Now there's another element to this miracle, and one I hope will benefit not only your baby but many, many more future babies. By using the jelly in the discarded umbilical cord, maybe up to four doses will be available for other new mothers. They will give birth to immune girls, and the process repeated. When your daughter and all the others grow up and have their own babies, they also will be immune girls. As the process continues, most of the world will end up being free of disease and deformity."

Noi shows no reaction until a question she asks convinces him she understands.

"If all babies will be born female, then how can more babies be born without men?"

"A great question, Noi, and one I will leave to the morals and needs of the parents. It will be their choice to take the serum knowing the outcome. But I predict a future serum will not change the chromosomes and yet still pass on the immunity to males."

Marcus has nothing further to say and waits to answer any further questions.

"Will it hurt?" is the one surprising question.

Marcus cannot hide his relief and takes Noi into his arms. "Not at all, Noi. Just a simple injection. The only person hurt will be Aswar. You, Noi, with be the Eve of a new race and a slap in the face to that man."

CHAPTER 10

Noi harboured no fear of the needle. Pain had been her companion for many years. It's the moment the serum started spreading through her body and the onset of drowsiness that triggered panic. She had learnt through many brutal incidents that staying awake and aware was the only way to survive. She senses her self-control slipping away. Past injuries, both physical and mental, flash through her confused mind. She turns her head from side to side as her surroundings become blurred. She tries to get up, but her body is uncoordinated. Has he tricked her? Has she again fallen into the trap of trusting someone only to discover it was all part of their subservient game? The shadow of a looming figure over her is her abductor, her abuser, her controller, her manic husband she thought she had fled. She lashes out at him, knowing his response could be fatal — but that is what she hopes for.

Marcus is keeping an eye on her while steering a course to Darwin. His intense observation of the erratic and violent effect the serum is having on Noi's body needs to be written down later. Nothing like this ever happened to the lab animals. Is it because only humans carry so much emotional baggage that the serum makes them react this way? Was he putting this girl through further torture? He has never questioned his research before, but has he gone too far, too fast this time? Has his opportunistic greed made him like the monster he saved her from?

Marcus reaches out to stroke her head in the hope it will calm her, but she slaps his hand away and lunges at him. Forced to fend off her rage while keeping the cruiser under control, he wedges the steering wheel between his knees and wraps his arms around her. With one last struggle to free herself, she goes limp. Her breathing slows, her eyes close, and she is asleep.

Marcus makes her comfortable on the lounge beside the captain's chair and stays watching over her. The sleep is deep. Her face is now relaxed with a hint of pleasurable dreams. He sits back at the controls and kicks the engines back into action. There is now a desperate need to make up time. Keeping a watchful eye on her, he accelerates to the fastest cruising speed that would get them to Darwin, four-and-a-half hours away without running out of fuel.

Marcus is sure Aswar will have his network of informers keeping an eye out for them. Unavoidably, the airport is where it could happen.

***

Noi stirs from her deep sleep as the boat approaches Darwin. Marcus studies her while keeping up the pace. She looks calm and drowsy as she sits up.

"How are you feeling?" he asks, more in a researcher's tone than genuine concern.

She just nods.

"Have a drink of water. It'll make you feel better," he says, handing her a bottle.

She takes it and chokes on the first thirsty mouthful. She consumes a third of the water before handing the bottle back.

"Where are we?" she asked, looking around.

"Approaching Darwin," he replies, eager to get a better idea of how she feels.

Noi looks around without comment as the coastline comes into view. Now is the time to explain what he has planned.

"Noi, I need you to be invisible from now on." He pauses, not knowing if he should mention Aswar's name and trigger off another violent outburst. "Do you understand how important that is?"

"He'll find me no matter what you do. You know that, don't you?" she replies, aware of what he omitted to say. "You don't know how many people he has in his pocket, but I do. They're not on his payroll. They either owe him, or he has something on them and would do anything to keep hidden. The first person you meet could be on the phone back to him before you know it."

Marcus looks at her, wondering just how much knowledge she has of this man.

She reads his face and replies, "There's a lot I know about him he wants to keep hidden. It's not that he wants me back, Mr Glasson...he wants me silenced."

Marcus has no answer to this, and as Darwin Harbour is fast approaching, he needs to prepare her.

"Keep Jude's clothes on. I need you to look as much like him as you can. People at the marina where we'll dock know him, and I want you to fool them, understand?"

Noi nods, thinks for a moment, then, unsteadily, makes her way below deck.

Marcus cuts back the engines as he eases across the port of Darwin, around the lagoon with its sweeping jetty, and into the East Arm towards the mouth of Sadgroves Creek and the third marina. Noi is told to stay below deck with the hatch closed as Marcus steers to his permanent berth, secures the cruiser and returns pleasantries with other boat owners he knows. He checks to make sure the hatch is closed before checking in at the marina office. A glance at his watch quickened his step. Time is running out fast.

Marcus returns to his boat after arranging for a taxi to wait outside the marina. He knocks on the hatch to hurry Noi up. When she opens it, Marcus is amazed by her transformation. She has cropped her long dark hair and rubbed coffee grounds into her face to look like stubble. He gives her an accepting smile, grabs his overnight bag and locks the cruiser. On their way to the taxi, a boat owner waves and calls out a hello to Marcus and Jude. They both wave back. The deception appears to be working.

There is only one direct flight from Darwin to the northern Queensland city of Cairns, and little time to catch it. Marcus will need to book seats at the airport, confident he'll get two in business or first class. He has a gold pass to the Qantas lounge where they can be out of sight from the public area.

Her ticket is in Jude's name, and she's told to stay in the men's toilet until their flight is called.

First class passengers are last to board, and as they walk from the lounge to the boarding gate, they're observed.

An airport cleaner is one of many from overseas on a questionable working visa that Aswar illegally issues out to be his eyes and ears around the globe. Messages carrying photos of Noi, Marcus and Jude were sent to all their phones with instructions to report back if they see any of them.

As soon as the cleaner reports his sighting of Marcus and Jude, it's relayed to Aswar. He knows damn well it's not Jude. He was seen tying up his dive boat at Dili only an hour before. That leaves only one explanation of who is with Sir Marcus Glasson — his abducted wife!

Aswar at once orders the two members of his Darwin network to take the next plane to wherever they're heading. He is not pleased with the answer he gets back. Their plane is the last direct flight to Cairns. The next flight is in two hours via Sydney with a long stopover. The earliest they can get to Cairns is ten in the morning. Aswar cancels the order. He'll organise something else when he has a better idea where they're heading.

***

It's a different story in Dili, but no less urgent. As soon as Jude enters the Glasson lab office, Mirla attacks him with a barrage of questions.

"Jude! What's going on?" she says before he drops his bag. "Marcus came back from Kupang acting strange, rushed off and wouldn't tell me anything."

"He's got Noi."

"Who?" asks a bewildered Mirla.

"Djan Muhammad Aswar's new wife once called Noi de Jesus."

Mirla's face drains of colour at the sound of Aswar's name. She clenches her fists as her mind races back to 1999.

"You remember Noi, don't you? We used to play together."

"Yes, I remember little Noi," Mirla says through her growing rage. "And I'll never forget that ugly bastard, Aswar."

38

"Yes, well, she was only eight years old then. Marcus promised her father before he died at the hands of Aswar that he would one day bring her back to his grave. Kupang gave us our only chance."

"You were in on this and didn't tell me...why?"

"He made me promise not to involve you until we saved her."

Mirla is not happy with the answer, and her look does nothing to hide it.

"Yeah, well, Marcus stayed there overnight in his boat acting innocent while I took Noi by jet ski to Alor. We stayed in a hidden cove, then met up with Marcus the next day. That's when the plan changed."

"What do you mean changed? Why?"

"Well, Marcus was to take Noi to Saumlaki on Yamdena Island for two days to allow things to cool down before taking her back to Atauro..."

"Watupo," interrupts Mirla. "She was born at Watupo on Atauro Island."

"Yeah, well, that was the original plan. She will remain hidden and cared for there and..."

"And what changed?" Mirla interrupts looking into Jude's eyes for any untruths. "And where is she now?"

"With Marcus."

"And where is he now?"

"I don't know."

She glares at him for more information.

"When Marcus found out that she was pregnant, he..."

"Pregnant?"

"Yeah, though you wouldn't know it. Anyway, Noi was dead-set on getting rid of it as Aswar was the father. I sort of don't blame her."

Mirla is trying to understand what all this means. She looks around the room, back at Jude, then the thought enters her head. She rushes into the back lab and fumbles getting the code entered to open the safe. There's more nervous fiddling with the inner box. She looks back at Jude who has followed her into the room.

"He's taken the serum. The only serum, and he's jumped at the opportunity."

"You mean to use on Noi? But she won't take it. She wants to abort so badly I had to tie her up to stop her from hurting herself until Marcus took her."

"Where? Where has he taken her?" she asks, grabbing his arms.

"He mentioned something that if she wants to abort, the best place would be somewhere reliable like Darwin."

"If I know Marcus, he'll talk her out of an abortion and into taking the serum."

Jude shakes his head. "But was it ready to try on a human? I mean, you've only tested on mice."

"Yes, but that's the last dose of serum. Once out of the atmosphere regulated safe, the portable unit is good for maybe two days. Then the serum changes its structure...and we never got to find out what effect that would have."

CHAPTER 11

I t's nine o'clock at night as the Qantas flight from Darwin approaches Cairns Airport. Noi slept most of the way in a window seat with Marcus struggling to stay awake in the aisle seat next to her. It wasn't only to keep an eye on her; he also needed to plan out the next few days. And there were so many things to think about.

The primary concern is keeping a close eye on Noi for any changes that may signal unknown and potentially dangerous side effects. Whether or not there is, her progress needs to be recorded and regular medical checks done.

Then there is the matter of keeping her hidden and safe from Aswar. While confident in his medical research abilities, being a strategic, defensive bodyguard he is not.

The jolt of the plane's wheels touching down wakes Noi out of her drowsiness and for a moment brings on another panic attack. Marcus is quick to reassure her that there is nothing to worry about and to get ready to disembark.

Noi pulls down the 'Top End' cap purchased at Darwin Airport to hide her face as they hurry through the arrivals hall to the terminal exit. They take the first cab in line, instructing the driver to go to the marina as fast as possible.

Before leaving the Darwin Qantas lounge, Marcus called a marine biologist friend in Cairns, whom he often accompanied on trips to the Great Barrier Reef. It took some convincing, but he has a loan of a boat for several days, fuelled up and ready to sail on their arrival at the Cairns Marina.

Behind the marina office is an area of dense trees with hardly any light from the marina lights penetrating the darkness. Noi is told to stay out of sight among the trees while Marcus goes to the marina office to sign the required papers and register that he will be the sole skipper/passenger on the boat.

Beggars can't be choosers, as the saying goes, and a retired 8-metre pilot boat of 1980s vintage falls well into that category. A quick check shows a 250-horsepower outboard with 200 litres of fuel. Enough to get some distance before refueling. It will have to do.

Looking around the marina for a way to get Noi onboard, he spots a CCTV camera facing the moored boats scanning the area in a wide, slow arc. Marcus times the movement from when it faces his boat until it loops back.

It will be tight, but doable. He runs to get Noi.

With Noi tucked behind him, the camera has returned to face their boat. He waits for it to do another swing around before rushing to board the boat. Noi is told to crouch low in the wheelhouse while Marcus throws off the mooring lines and gives the craft a gentle nudge away from the jetty. The outboard comes to life. The navigation lights are turned on, and they ease out of the marina into the darkness.

Noi remains quiet and pensive as she sits beside the skipper's chair as if disconnected from reality. She takes in the immediate surrounding of the boat in a seemingly dreamlike state and ends up focussing on Marcus at the helm. The age of the craft revives lost memories of when she and her father dived off the coast of Atauro Island. It was a time when they shared the serenity below the waves, then cheerful company above. The full force of this memory and what has happened since brings on a flow of tears.

Marcus glances at her while navigating his way out of the marina. Once assured she's not in physical pain, he makes another mental note of her reactions to the serum. From her first angry outbursts, she's now taken on a more emotional attitude. He chooses not to pry and turns to the task ahead, for he has his own worries. Lack of sleep and the effort of getting as far away as possible from the tentacles of Aswar is wearing down his resistance to what's killing him. He takes another glance at Noi. Her crying has stopped; her head bowed as she looks at her hands wrapped around her stomach and the new life she carries. A life that will give Marcus his greatest gift to humanity, and the fear that he will not be around to see it.

After almost four hours of navigating in the dark, Marcus anchors off the coast a little north of Townsville. The calm sea will allow sleep until first light when he'll refuel at the marina before heading further south. He sends Noi to sleep in the cramped forward cabin while he makes himself as comfortable as he can on deck under the canopy. Lack of comfort does not stop an exhausted Marcus from plunging into a deep sleep.

A shake of his shoulder awakens him with a start. The depth of sleep had taken him to other places and other times. For a moment he's disoriented and confused at the sight of a cropped-haired young girl shaking and staring at him. She's mouthing words, and as they become audible, she becomes recognisable.

"Mister Glasson, Mister Glasson, wake up! Should we be on the move again?" she says.

Marcus shakes the haze from his head and looks to the sky and the sun well over the horizon. He's over-slept and needs to get himself together fast.

"I found some coffee," she says, handing him a steaming hot mug. "There's no food, or I would have made something."

"Thanks, Noi," he replies, taking the mug. "I'll get some when we refuel."

After a quick stop at Townsville's Breakwater Marina, the old pilot boat heads back out into the Coral Sea with a heading due south.

Noi is cooking up a simple omelet in the cramped galley. The smell and thought of food bring back Marcus' nausea. He accepts the plate handed to him, hoping he'll keep some of it down as he needs to build up much needed energy.

Both ate in silence. Marcus takes it slow, but is pleased Noi has found an appetite.

The cloudless sky allows the sun to glisten off the moderate waves. There's a sense of calm. On any other occasion, this would be a relaxing pleasure trip with fishing, diving, and pleasant chatter.

But it's not!

Noi studies Marcus at the wheel, then turns to look back towards Townsville where they came from. It is well out of sight, yet a shudder ripples through her body at the thought of the lengths Aswar will go to get her back — or have her killed — unaware two are already in the chase.

CHAPTER 12

A nother stop at Mackay for fuel and Marcus is becoming so exhausted the next stop will need to be the last. His heart is working hard to fight off the attack on his body, and the increasing cramps, pain, and nausea are clouding his mind. He kicks the boat into top speed, for there are two things he needs to do that cannot wait another day.

***

Like other coastal towns along the North Queensland coast, Yeppoon is a link to some of the many islands that dot the length of the Great Barrier Reef. It's a place that is working hard to modernise and revamp its attraction as a tourist stepping-stone to island hideaways.

Marcus contacts the Yeppoon Marina for a berth before passing around the breakwater and orders Noi to stay hidden in the cabin and not to come out. To all concerned, Marcus is on a solo voyage to the islands.

He finishes securing the line to the jetty and stresses once more for Noi to stay hidden while he attends to some business in the town. Her worried look at being left alone has Marcus promise he'll only be a couple of hours and bring back some decent food.

A taxi has pulled up at the marina office to unload some passengers on their way to one of the islands. Marcus secures a ride into town after a look back to make sure Noi is unseen. He gives the driver the address of a solicitor, and twenty minutes later he's walking into their office.

In less than an hour, Marcus emerges feeling relieved, yet increasingly ill. His next obligation will be the most challenging.

Opting for a pay phone rather than his traceable mobile, he rings his partner, Mirla, in Dili.

Before he can add to his 'Hello darling', Mirla attacks him with so many questions that Marcus believes Jude has told her enough for her to fill in the gaps. But he did not ring to answer her questions; all he wanted was to hear her voice.

After stopping to buy some food, the ride back to the marina is in silence. The driver notices in his rearview mirror that his backseat passenger has tears in his eyes and asks if he's okay. He gets a nod back and assumes it's something personal and to mind his own business.

The sun is low on the horizon as Marcus steps onto the ramp that leads to the jetty and his boat. Suddenly he stops and gives a shudder. The bags of food drop from his hands, spilling their contents on the timber boards and into the surrounding water. He looks up, hoping to see Noi, but she is obeying his order to stay out of sight. He shakes his head and gives out a low, guttural groan as he tries to call out her name before collapsing onto the jetty unconscious.

A couple of deckhands working on a nearby yacht run to the falling figure. One is already calling for an ambulance.

A crowd gathers around the stricken figure, then told to move back as one of the boat owners with some medical training assumes a heart attack and begins CPR.

The commotion on the jetty is enough to bring Noi out of the cabin. Keeping low, she peers out of the wheelhouse window. It takes a moment for her to understand what is happening. But when the bystanders step aside, exposing the body on the jetty, she immediately drops back out of sight. This cannot happen! She cries out to herself. She takes another glance to confirm who is receiving attention. Shock sets in. He can't die...he just can't!

The distant siren of an ambulance increases until its arrival at the marina office.

Within seconds, the paramedics are in charge and checking all vital signs. Marcus had an oxygen mask placed over his face before they put him on a gurney and connected him to a monitor.

Noi is numb with confusion and shock. The promise to stay hidden suppresses the urge to rush to his side. All she can do is watch Sir Marcus Glasson being wheeled away through the marina reception area. Within minutes, the ambulance drives off with its emergency siren joining the screaming in her head and heart.

She sinks down beneath the steering wheel, curled up into a trembling ball. She is now alone in a strange place with no one to protect her. Something has to be done...and done quickly!

She rises from the deck and chances another look around. The jetty is clear of people in the darkening twilight. She can't stay confined to the boat, and what she sees is where she'll go.

CHAPTER 13

On the inland fringe of Yeppoon township is the single-story regional Capricorn Coast Hospital. The call has come through of an emergency and an ambulance is on its way. Alerted and waiting at the emergency entrance are a doctor and a nurse.

Immediately the ambulance stops, the motionless Marcus is wheeled into the Emergency Department. Then, during the triage process of determining the problem, a sense of familiarity bothers the doctor. He asks the nurse if the paramedics have listed a name of the patient in their report. The doctor then became well aware of who he is trying to keep alive.

Sir Marcus had featured in many medical papers because of his discoveries, and his knighthood was still a contentious issue in the medical world — depending on your view on euthanasia.

The doctor's initial appraisal was a heart attack, but after more tests and a second opinion, whatever caused their patient's collapse became harder to diagnose.

Was it a twinge of panic on the young doctor's part, having the life of such a respected man in his hands, or was it accepting the reality that a regional hospital lacked the specialists and equipment needed to give an exact diagnosis?

After consulting with his superiors, it was decided he needed more specialist examination and that Sir Marcus be transferred to the main hospital in the city of Rockhampton, forty-three kilometres away.

***

Meanwhile, Yeppoon Marina has taken on a fairyland appearance as pontoon lights dotting the jetties reflect sparkles in the gently lapping water. Rhythmic clinking from the rigging of all the boats moored at the marina masked the sound of Noi easing herself over the side of the ageing pilot boat and into the dark water. After taking a deep breath, she sinks below the surface and moves through the water, leaving no sign of her movement above.

Once past the rows of jetties, she surfaces to get her bearings and replenish her air. There is a stretch of water before she reaches the shoreline and the steep rise of a hill. The sound of voices ahead directs her attention to a Water Police boat moored a little to her right. Further along are two yellow Coast Guard boats. Being found by any authority is the last thing she wants. Taking another deep breath, she sinks below the surface and glides effortlessly through the water as if it were her natural environment. Coming to a rocky up-slope, she surfaces at the rear of a closed seafood outlet. After a look around to make sure she'll not be seen, she climbs out of the water, creeps around the side of the shop, then pauses for a moment before running across a roadway to the base of the hill. With the help of a streetlight and a glow from the moon, she makes out a hollow in the sheer rock face. A fence runs along the side of the road to deter climbers but ends to allow access to the ocean side. She carefully steps over wet rocks until she can climb up to the hollow. On reaching it, she discovers it's more of a cave. Not big, but deep enough to hide out of sight from the marina until the morning. Then she will have to figure out what to do with no one to help her.

As a child, she would hide from her brother in caves such as this back on Atauro Island. Such memories help to ease the current dire predicament. She removes her wet T-shirt and pants for them to dry in the warm tropical night. From the pants pocket, she takes out the small spoon, then curls up in the deepest corner of the cave. With the spoon held tight to her chest, she allows its childhood memories and the smell of the sea to carry her into the mist of sleep.

***

The multi-storied Rockhampton Hospital, with its green framework facade and overhanging helipad, takes on a majestic dominance of the skyline as sits high overlooking downtown Rockhampton.

In the intensive care ward, Sir Marcus Glasson continues to undergo various tests. His bodily functions are failing, yet nothing they have come across has identified the cause.

Because of his status, the uncertainty of his condition, and the awareness of his research on unclassified creatures, they moved him to an isolation ward where he's stabilised in a semi-induced coma.

A specialist in rare diseases has been called in to examine Marcus. He is well-aware of Professor Sir Marcus Glasson, having attended some of his lectures and keeping up-to-date with his research papers, and had a feeling that finding a cause will be challenging.

After his initial consultation with the treating medical staff and evaluating their findings, more blood, together with saliva samples, are to be taken and sent to the nearest lab for gene testing where the results will then be compared to known sequencing. This will take some time, so Marcus is to remain in isolation until the findings are known and a possible treatment agreed on...if at all!

CHAPTER 14

A fierce wind whips the national flag and ripples the grass-covered mound over the new Government House in Australia's capital, Canberra.

Inside the House of Representatives chamber, a fierce debate is raging over the export of uranium to China. The elected conservative coalition is arguing for mining companies to speed up their efforts in digging as much uranium out of the ground. This is to make up for the revenue shortfall from the previous primary export earner, iron ore.

The Prime Minister has his back turned to the shadow minister for the environment as he addresses the chamber. Despite delivering a strong and compelling argument in favour of the move towards renewable energy and the phasing out of coal power, the PM shows no interest. Preferring instead to converse with his minister for Export and Resources, the Honourable Conrad Glasson MP.

Minister Glasson is a recent addition to the front bench since a party room spill led to a change of leadership. A position some in the media and political commentators regard as a reward for his underhand and devious lobbying for votes to topple the previous leader of the party.

Glasson has youthful looks, a public school demeanour and a conservative appearance down to his short-cropped curly hair, a tight-fitting suit, under-sized shirt collar forcing constant flushing of the face.

His unpopularity in the public's eye is used to significant advantage by the new leader as the proclaimed whipping-boy. The one to spread the dirt without an iota of feeling or belief in the truth.

His sudden and questionable rise in power from a failed solicitor in the only law firm that would hire him, meant he could now inflict retribution on all who had scoffed at and devalued his abilities during his early school days, at university, at the law firm that dismissed him — but most importantly if the opportunity ever presented itself — his father, Professor Sir Marcus Glasson AO.

A clerk approaches and hands Minister Glasson a note. He reads it without a hint of emotion, then, after a pause, passes it to the Prime Minister.

Meanwhile, the opposition minister's time has expired, and despite the microphone being turned off, continues to make a point. The Prime Minister turns and rises from his chair, waits for the shadow minister to obey instructions to take his seat, then informs the Speaker of the House that due to a sudden and serious family illness the Minister for Export and Resources needs to leave the House. He therefore requests that further questions relating to his portfolio be placed on notice.

***

The afternoon editorial staff is halfway through a meeting to finalise the content for the next day's edition of a Sydney newspaper. It's been a relatively quiet news day, and a selection of filler articles are being discussed.

As usual, Harper Glasson — the older sister of Conrad — is sitting at the opposite end of the boardroom table from the editor with empty seats on each side. The dislike towards her is clear.

The self-belief in her superiority over everyone at the paper, including her editor, has forever been her signature along with her slicked, jet black hair, her blood red lipstick and heavy make-up that would crack if she ever smiled — which no one has ever witnessed.

But she has contacts who continually supply scoops and is, therefore, a valuable asset for the tabloid paper. The morning edition will be a testament to that. The front-page screamer will announce to the world that a wealthy corporate heavyweight, and chairman of the largest pet food manufacturer in the country, apparently has a penchant for pornography involving animals.

Outside the boardroom, a junior reporter takes a phone call, listens while writing down the information, then glances up at the closed boardroom door. The hairs on his neck bristled with dread that he would have to approach the most feared member of staff. With the phone back on its cradle, he ponders whether to interrupt the meeting or wait. He waits. Harper is always the first to leave and in a rush to get somewhere. She is then rarely seen in the office for the rest of the day.

The young man stands trembling with the note in his hand as the meeting ends and Harper exits the boardroom in her usual haste. He calls to her, but as usual, she ignores minions. The young man goes to follow but instead hands the note to another of the reporters leaving the meeting.

The reporter reads the note and, aware of its importance, catches up with Harper just as the doors of the elevator start to close. Seeing the urgent look on the reporter's face, Harper presses the door open button with a long, spindly, red-tipped finger. After reading the note, she asks who gave it to him. The reporter points back into the room at the young man trying not to look up. Harper pushes past her messenger and stomps back into the open office where she berates the young fledgling into a withering pulp. Her raspy, cigarette-toned voice would drown out all noise in the busy open office, but there was no other noise to drown out as everyone and everything, including the constant ringing of phones, fell silent.

Satisfied with her blistering demolition of the young man, she turns and cuts a path through anyone in her way back to the elevator. When passing the desk of another reporter, she slaps the note down for him to write a piece for the next day's paper.

CHAPTER 15

The warm, early morning tropical sun does little to stem the anxious shivering of Noi as she remains curled up in her cave. From her elevated position, she can see the boat she and Marcus came on still moored at the jetty while hoping to see her Mister Glasson return after being fixed up. After all, he's a medical man, and if he can come up with a serum that'll fix all illnesses, then sure he can fix himself.

With her eyes fixed on the marina, every movement gives her hope. There is plenty of activity around the many boats moored along the jetties. Some crew members are busy hosing down their boats while others chat in groups.

But the only people she sees coming out of the marina building are holidaymakers and day-trippers waiting to board ferries that will take them to the distant islands. The scene is peaceful and happy — for them! Not for Noi!

She follows a small group walking down the jetty as they pass the small pilot boat she left during the night, now empty and deserted.

By midday, Noi accepts that her Mister Glasson's collapse is more serious than she wanted to believe. Panic sets in as she has no idea what to do or where to go in this foreign land. If she sought help without identification or a passport, it could land her in a lot of trouble.

The thought of trying to find the hospital they took her Mr Glasson meant talking to people, and that meant revealing more than she wanted. The realisation that there is no one to protect her is a massive jolt. She looks down at her stomach. If what she has been told is true, nor is there anyone to protect the baby.

Without realising it, she calls out in anger, "If it is so special, Mister Glasson, why have you left me?"

"Who's there?" comes a voice from below.

Noi instantly backs deep into the furthest corner of the cave, grasps the spoon tighter in her hand and covers her mouth to stem any sound of her breathing.

"Is someone there?" comes the voice again. "You know you shouldn't be up there; it's too dangerous."

There's no reply.

"Who ya talking to, Stu?" comes another voice.

"There's someone up there in the bloody cave, Gaz," replies Stu. "Sounded like a girl."

"Yeah? No shit! Hey, you up there, come down. If not, we'll come and get ya."

Noi grabs her t-shirt and curls herself up in a tighter ball hoping they just go away.

"Come on, luv. We won't hurt ya," adds Stu. "We've just been fishing off the rocks here. How long ya been up there?"

The two look at each other after getting no reply.

"You're the lighter one, Gaz, you go and get her."

"Shit, Stu, why is it always me?" he snaps back.

"Cuz you're not only lighter but the prettier one," he answers back with a laugh.

Noi hears the scrambling over rocks as whoever it is gets closer. She quickly puts on the T-shirt. Her heart is pounding as a face appears around the mouth of the cave before she can grab her pants.

"Well, well, hi there pretty one," says Gaz with an unnerving grin.

"Whatcha got, Gaz?" is the call from below.

"Heaven on Earth, mate, Heaven on Earth!"

"Well, bring her down."

"Come on, luv," beckons Gaz, reaching out a hand. "No need to worry. We can help if ya lost or something."

Noi accepts she has no choice. If, as they say, they are just fishermen — and as fishermen back on her island are friendly and helpful — then they could be too. She uncurls herself and reaches out her hand.

Stu can't take his eyes off long, tanned, naked legs as Noi carefully steps down the strata layers of the rock face. Gaz follows with a broad smile and a flutter of a hand indicating how 'hot' she is.

"Ya right, Gaz. Ya just brought down an angel. You okay, darling?" asks Stu, wrapping a tattooed arm around her waist. He looks back at Gaz. "Did she have anything with her? Like a bag or something?"

"Nothing, mate. What you see is what you get. One very pretty Asian babe."

"Not wrong there. You speak English?" he asks, forgetting what language he had heard.

Noi is about to say she had left her pants in the cave, but realises an opportunity presents itself to play the non-English speaking Asian so she can get out of explaining who she is.

"No...spe...Angish," she says with a confused shake of her head.

Gaz butts in with, "No probs, luv, we're not much good at it either."

"Yeah, well, you look like you could do with some food, a cleanup and something to wear, hey?" suggests Stu.

Noi plays dumb. But she is hungry, and the way the two are looking at her, she could do with her pants back on.

"Look, our place is not far, and this is our car just here," he says, pointing to an old, dust-covered ute with fishing rods sticking out the back. "You drive, Gaz, and she can sit between us."

Noi hesitates and takes a hopeful look around the marina in case she sees her professor returning. Sadly, there's no sign of him.

Noi clutches her spoon to her chest as she's sandwiched between the two men on the single bench seat. They encourage the clapped-out ute back to life after a couple of attempts, then drive off with the trailing rattle of a loose exhaust pipe.

CHAPTER 16

Conrad Glasson arranged to meet his sister at Brisbane Airport before they fly on to Rockhampton to visit their father.

Harper has arrived early and, while waiting for her brother, checks out the Glasson BioMarine website on her tablet for an update on how it's travelling.

She had no interest in her father's business. They were both excluded from any share of the company's profits because of a messy legal battle after their mother died three years earlier.

Cancer sidetracked a divorce between her and Sir Marcus and did nothing to bring them together. Vera Glasson was an insufferable social climber with no graces to go with it. She doted on her husband's reputation, but out of the public eye showed fierce bitterness towards him.

As Harper and Conrad grew into adults, it was clear who they took after. For several years the three bled Marcus of every dollar they could to further their social standing.

Marcus found the relationship with his wife and children intolerable and spent longer periods away, devoting his time to research in East Timor — and to his secret family.

He structured the company into three parts: research, development, and distribution. Financial support for his family in Australia came from the development side, while sales and distribution, being the primary income for the company, financed the ongoing research.

Marcus shielded the research arm of the business from his wife by making sure she, Harper, and Conrad were financially comfortable and able to match socially with their peers.

When Vera learnt she had only a month or two to live, the children became concerned as their mother managed all their finances. As they had never shown an interest in where the money came from, it was vital they learnt...and quickly.

Vera struggled with the pain and side effects of her treatment, making it difficult for Harper and Conrad to get detailed information from her about their financial position.

During this period, Sir Marcus had his own worries. He'd started getting death threats because of opposition to the euthanasia drug he had devised. When Vera died, the press questioned if her husband's drug aided her death.

Before she died, Vera convinced her children to take all legal action necessary to gain control of their father's company. The premise being that the euthanasia drug and its adverse publicity questioned Sir Marcus' ability to run a medical research company.

Vera died before they took such action, and as a joint signatory to the development arm of the company, she failed to sign over her interest to her children.

It enraged them with untold fury, and through Harper's media contacts and Conrad's legal background, they spread rumours that their father's euthanasia drug contributed to their mother's death.

The coroner found no evidence of this, though the purpose of the drug was to be undetectable.

Conrad and Harper never accepted the coroner's ruling. Undaunted, they tried their hardest to discredit their father and have him jailed for murder.

It was because of their refusal to discuss the matter, together with their unrelenting obsession to see him ruined personally and professionally, that Sir Marcus disowned his children.

***

There was little conversation between brother and sister on the flight from Brisbane to Rockhampton. Each had their own thoughts about their father's death and what it may mean to their financial futures. In fact, there was no thought of the alternative that their father could pull through.

The taxi ride from the airport to the hospital continued in silent contemplation of all things possible. But as soon as the car stops at the hospital entrance, both transform into sensitive, heartbroken, devastated, and expecting the worst but hoping for the best adult children of the ailing Sir Marcus.

They're met by a doctor who escorts them to their father's private room. Both hesitate before entering for fear their father is conscious and lucid. Through the window in the closed door they see their father lying with drips and monitors attached, oxygen being fed through his nose, and with great relief, eyes tightly closed.

"Maybe we should not wake him," suggests Conrad.

"There's no fear of that, I'm afraid," replies the doctor. "He remains in a coma while we determine the cause and treatment."

"Cause?" snaps Harper. "What, you mean you don't know what's wrong with him?" Her sentimental veneer slipping.

The doctor takes her change of attitude as understandable under such circumstances. "Unfortunately, not at the moment," he says with some hesitation. "The blood tests provided some information that we treated, but there is something else causing his condition that is not showing up."

"I don't understand," utters a confused Conrad. "Are you saying there's nothing you can find wrong with him apart from the fact that he's dying?"

The doctor concedes. "At this moment...yes."

Conrad takes a moment to study his father before opening the door and stepping into the room. Before going any further, he stops and turns back to the doctor. "There's nothing contagious, is there?"

"No," replies the doctor in a tone to dispel any fears. "We isolated him and tested for everything and found nothing."

Harper joins in with her concern. "You are aware my father worked with strange and exotic sea creatures, yes?"

"Yes, of course," replies the doctor, sensing his need to defend the hospital. "All the doctors are well aware of your father's research and his remarkable discoveries. We checked for any sign of poison, disease, antibodies — everything we could think of. We called in an expert marine biologist, and he was sure that if your father were suffering from the result of a marine toxin, there would be signs such as skin eruptions, vomiting, a high temperature, any number of things. Your father showed no such signs."

Conrad takes a cautious step towards the bed and stops again. "He will die, though?"

Harper reacts quickly to dispel her brother's tone of hope. "We both pray, of course, that it will not be the case."

"I'm afraid at the moment the only thing keeping your father alive is the life-support he's connected to," confesses the doctor.

"And how long will that work?" asks Conrad, taking a quick glance at his sister.

"Are there other family members that we can call on your behalf?" asks the doctor in response.

"You mean, doctor, our father could die at any minute?" asks Harper clutching a tissue to her nose.

"I'm afraid you must prepare yourselves for the worst," the doctor replied in his practiced sombre tone.

Harper slides her arm into her brother's as an act of mutual support. "No, there's no other immediate family. Can we sit with him?" she asks caringly.

"Yes, of course," replies the doctor while nodding to a nurse to get another chair. "I'll leave you alone. If you need anything, the nurse will be just outside."

"Thank you," they say in sync. But just before the doctor leaves the room, Harper asks in the most caring tone she can muster. "Can we talk to him? Will our father hear us? Will he know we're here to comfort him?"

"I doubt it, I'm afraid," says the doctor, taking a step back into the room. "One thing we are sure of is whatever caused his condition has brought on a cerebellar stroke. His brain function has diminished considerably."

"I'm not sure what that means," Conrad asks as if he were cross-examining in court.

The doctor explains. "The stroke is a post consequence of the cause. This type of stroke is not overly common, so while he is in a coma, we cannot be absolutely sure of how much damage there is to the brain or what functions are affected."

Harper and Conrad both turn their attention to their father. Brain-dead is the thought shared.

"Well, I'll leave you to your privacy," says the doctor, backing up to the door. There's no reply.

It takes a couple of minutes of mind-churning possibilities before Harper decides to test for any reaction to touch. With some hesitation, she prods her father's hand with the tip of one long fingernail and immediately pulls back — a twitch of the fingers, perhaps — nothing. Conrad follows with a poke to the arm, also instantly retracted. There is no response, but they both watch the slow reversion of the dent left on the skin.

After a quick glance back towards the closed door to make sure no one would enter, they turned their attention to their father's face. The hiss from the oxygen supply is the only sign of life apart from a slight stream of dribble from the corner of his mouth. His eyes are tightly closed, and a small lump on the eyelids shows they have rolled back. Harper dabs at the dribble with her dry tissue, not out of concern for his dignity, but to test for a reaction. There is none.

Conrad leans closer and whispers into Marcus' ear, "Father, this is Conrad."

Harper has leant back into her chair with legs crossed. "Save your breath, Conrad. Even if he can hear you, what's he going to do? He's a vegetable."

"But don't you think...like...just in case?"

"Look, Conrad, the bastard gave us up years ago. If you want to shed a tear for the media, go ahead, but the fact remains: what are we going to do?"

"What do you mean?"

Harper allows time for it to sink into Conrad's mind. "You heard what the doctor said; he's basically brain-dead and about to die. So, what do you think I mean?"

Conrad looks from Harper to his father, fearing his father is listening. "You mean pull the plug?"

"You know, Conrad, you may have been a shit lawyer, and now an even worse politician, but you can't be that dumb always. Of course, that's what I mean."

Conrad looks around the ward, back to his father, then to his sister, and again around the room in confusion.

Harper pushes her chair back, stands with arms crossed, and spits out, "Shit, you're a weak prick! Absolutely hopeless without your minders and advisors and whatever other creeps you have deciding for you. Look at him, for God's sake. He could be dead already for all we know. Why don't you for once show some guts and make a case to the doctor to put the bastard out of his misery...and out of our misery at the same time?"

Conrad is feeling the heat and loosens his tie. "But...but..." he mumbled.

"But nothing! Look, the sooner he's gone, the sooner we can look at his will. I'm sure he's left some nasties for us, but there's got to be some reward for putting up with him all our lives. Shit, he can't give all his vast wealth to charity and us peanuts. Not good for his obituary, let alone his image, don't you reckon?"

"But, Harper...I mean...it's...it's like killing someone."

"So, you'd let a dog hit by a car suffer and not put it out of its misery, would you?"

"No, but he's our father, whatever we feel about him and..."

Harper is tired of his wimpish response. "Will you stop thinking about your fucking political image and think about how much of his wealth we'll get? Look at him. Shit, even he was pro-euthanasia and, well, both you and I still believe what he did to our mother is what he'd want us to do to him in this condition."

This gets through to Conrad. But before he can say anything, a stench rises from the bed. They both look at the ashen figure and notice a change in their father's expression and a flicker of movement under his eyelids.

"Shit, Harper, what's happening?"

A beeping monitor has the nurse in the ward and beside the bed in an instant. Conrad and Harper move back as the doctor also enters. He checks for a pulse with his stethoscope, then peels back both eyelids to shine a light into the eyes.

"We didn't do any..." Harper interrupts Conrad and gives him a fierce look that would halt a herd of stampeding cattle.

After a moment of frantic action by the doctor and nurse, the doctor unplugs the stethoscope from his ears and slings it back around his neck, looks at his watch and makes a note of the time for the nurse to record then turns with lowered shoulders to Conrad and Harper. "I'm afraid your father has passed away. I'm sorry."

***

Sir Marcus Glasson is aware of his surroundings as he lay in his co-matose state. His research into the effects and progression to death of his euthanasia drug was close, but not quite as he thought. While there's no way of getting to his ring and taking his own discovery, death was now being realised and understood.

He knew, despite the doctor's honest and thorough attempt at finding the cause, he never would. It was a side effect of his experiments and, like the euthanasia drug, it had no known example for comparison.

He doesn't want to die. His mission is unfinished, and he desperately regrets leaving Noi without his protection. But with no choice, he can only allow things to take their course.

He knows Conrad and Harper are in the room beside him. He can hear everything they say, even the whispers at the door with the doctor. If he could have smiled at their false concerns, crocodile tears, and pompous snobbery, he would have. As his body accepts the time has come and there is nothing he can do about it, he can only regret dying of his own accord and that Harper and Conrad would never go through the process of pulling the plug. Even they, with their selfish, cold-blooded attitudes, would, he believed ever so briefly, have a moment of soul-searching.

As he merges into eternal darkness, he focuses on the image of a pretty pregnant young girl with bright eyes and once flowing black hair, and hopes with his last breath that she and her baby's freedom will last.

CHAPTER 17

On the fifth floor of a six-story renovated 1930s building, sandwiched between two much taller modern structures on Sydney's North Shore, is the unassuming head office of Glasson BioMarine.

Set in white plastic letters on the foyer's simple directory are the names of the tenants. Glasson BioMarine occupies the entire fifth floor.

Despite its low-key image, forty-two staff occupy four departments: legal, distribution, accounting, and marketing. Each department has its own manager, with a CEO overseeing the entire operation.

Most have never met or laid eyes on Sir Marcus Glasson. Such is the intended separation from the research arm carried out in Dili.

It's late afternoon and the day's work is almost over when a call comes through to reception from a reporter wanting more information on Sir Marcus Glasson. When questioned by the receptionist for what purpose, she is told it's for an obituary he is writing.

The news of the death of their secretive founder comes as a great shock, despite having never met him. Flustered at receiving such news, the receptionist transferred the call to the CEO.

***

The front door to the Dili lab opens, flooding the room with a warm glow from the setting sun, only to be once again blocked out by a figure of massive proportion.

"Hi, Mirla. Been away for a few days. The prof in?" asks Evelyn Sunday, closing the door behind him.

Mirla Yimenes has just got off the phone and slumped over her large desk. A wet tissue in trembling hands is wiping tears from her eyes.

"What is it, Mirla?" asks the hulk of a man as he comes to her side. "What's happened?"

The need for instant support is overwhelming. She pushes back her chair to stand and wrap her arms around his broad body.

"Everything," she says as tears drop on Evelyn's shirt. He gently eases her back to look into her eyes. Her head lowered for an instant before looking up into the brute of a face.

"It's Marcus and..." Her voice breaks with the quiver of her chin. "I don't know what to believe." She reaches out for Evelyn's hand. "Evelyn, I don't want to believe any of it."

Evelyn Sunday — named by his father as a joke — is a massive, walking contradiction.

With a stubbled beard, a poorly corrected broken nose, shaved head and the ever-present Perdomo Slow-Aged Lot 826 Glorioso Maduro cigar protruding from his mouth, Evelyn is one tough American from the Deep South.

Ex-shipyard worker, ex-military, ex-boxer, ex-salvage diver, ex-InterFET peacekeeper during the lead-up to East Timor's vote for independence, and now Dili bar owner since the beginning of the millennium. He is also a loyal, compassionate friend to Mirla, Marcus, and Jude.

"Details?" he asks in his customary no-nonsense, direct-to-the-point manner while chewing on his cigar.

Mirla can't speak. Her body tense and quivering in shock. Evelyn slides an outstretched tattooed arm over her shoulders. "Come and sit on the couch with me."

When Mirla had settled onto the couch and calm enough, he asks, "Now what about the Prof?"

Mirla can only look down at her hands now clasped together on her lap.

"I got a call from the Sydney office." She clears her throat. "One of the managers, I think. I wrote his name down and called him back on the office number in case it was another hoax call." She looks up at Evelyn with fresh tears running down her cheeks. "Oh, Evelyn...Marcus is dead."

The arm around her shoulder tightens pulling the sobbing Mirla closer into his chest.

"How? Where? Where is he?"

Mirla takes a moment to compose herself. After accepting a dry tissue from Evelyn, she says with a shake of her head, "They're saying a heart attack, but I know differently. The strange thing is, he died in Australia. In the hospital at a place called Rockhampton."

"In Queensland? What the bloody hell was he doing there?"

"That's the strange thing. No one knows...no one in the office...not even Jude."

"Where is Jude?"

"I called him as soon as I got the news. He's on his way back from diving."

"Did Marcus say anything to you the last time you saw him?"

"No, but he acted strange."

"What do you mean, strange?"

"It was when he got back from attending some salt farm launch in Kupang. He was in such a rush to go out again that he asked me to get him food for a few days. I tried to get him to tell me what was going on, but he said that Jude would tell me."

"And did he?" breaks in Evelyn.

She ignores his question and continues. "You know how ill he was getting. Well, we had this pact that he'll not end his suffering without me being with him."

Evelyn knew what she meant by ending his suffering. He and Marcus often talked about the ever-present euthanasia drug over many beers and whiskeys.

"He said he would get in touch with me in a week and that he would keep his promise. Then he was gone."

Evelyn waited until Mirla was ready to continue.

"Jude was just as evasive. Seems when Marcus went to Kupang, Jude was with him as they'd planned to grab that bastard Djan Muhammad Aswar's latest wife if she was there."

Evelyn stands and walks around the room chewing on his cigar. "That bloody monster! What did he do that for? It'll get him killed...um...sorry. Was she there?"

It takes a moment for Mirla to remember the details.

"Noi de Jesus is her name. Marcus held her dying father in his arms when Aswar took her away. He promised her father he would one day rescue her and bring her back to his grave. I guess he realised his time was running out, and this was the last chance he would ever have."

"So he's taken this girl as far away as he can from Aswar. He should have told me. I would have protected her."

"I wish he had, Evelyn. I really do. But that's not all."

Evelyn joins her back on the couch. "What else?" he asks.

Mirla shakes her head. "He should have told me," she replies then stared into the distance.

"Told you what, Mirla? Told you what?" he insists.

She turns to face Evelyn with a stern expression. "When Marcus found out the girl was pregnant..." She pauses to get her words right. "Evelyn, he's taken a serum we've been working on and is using her as a test subject. Then, the day before yesterday, Marcus called me and..."

She breaks down into tears again as Evelyn holds her close.

"Oh, Evelyn, I was so angry with him; I didn't allow him to get a word in and he hung up."

"He hung up on you without a word?" asks a surprised Evelyn.

"I now understand," she says to stop Evelyn thinking the worst of Marcus. "He knew he was dying and just wanted to hear my voice. We had a pact to be together when that time came, and that was the only way he could keep his part of the promise."

They sit together without another word. Each in their own thoughts.

Evelyn is first to break the silence. "Where's the girl now?"

Mirla shrugs her shoulders. "I don't know, but she needs to be found."

CHAPTER 18

T he lack of late flights back to Sydney or Canberra forces Harper and Conrad to stay in Rockhampton. A media release announcing the death of the prominent scientist Sir Marcus Glasson AO led to the press being tipped off that his two children — well known in their own dubious ways — have booked to stay a night in a five-star hotel overlooking the Fitzroy River.

It's not a large media contingent waiting as Harper and Conrad arrive, but all major outlets in Australia and abroad will take their coverage up.

Conrad feels uncomfortable not knowing any of the regional reporters. He has become accustomed to the Canberra press gallery and has mastered the art of saying a lot with no substance to lessen the time for questions. There, the questions are based around politics. Here, they'll be personal.

Harper is far savvier with media manipulation and takes the brunt of the thrusting microphones. After a moment to dab at a supposed tear in her eye, she makes a brief statement.

"This has come as a grave shock to us both, and we just hope you will offer us the courtesy of privacy to mourn the loss of our father and the loss to the world of a great man. Thank you."

Fully aware that the short visual grab will come across well on the evening news, they ignore the flurry of questions and enter the hotel.

Harper accepts condolences as she checks in at reception and orders a bottle of French Cuvée to be sent to their suite — to make a toast to their late father, she adds.

Once inside the privacy of their spacious two-bedroom apartment on an upper floor, Conrad looks over the river winding below while his sister fills two glasses of champagne — at around two-hundred dollars a bottle it will go on Conrad's government expense account.

They raise their glasses, and with a smile, salute their 'dear departed'. They each take a moment to savour the expensive drop with thoughts of more and even better to come.

"I guess there's the likelihood of a state funeral," says Conrad, seeing political mileage in it for him.

Harper sees only the opportunity to rub shoulders with people she could possibly vilify in the following day's papers.

Harper refills the glasses before changing the subject to a more important topic — their father's last Will and Testament.

Conrad cringes at the need to explain to his sister the problem with that.

"Harper, there needs to be an autopsy to determine the cause of death before they can issue a death certificate. Until that time, no one can view the Will."

Harper finds this unacceptable. "Damn, Conrad," she says, thumping her glass onto the coffee table. "You're supposed to be a bloody lawyer; get around that stupid rule and demand to see it!"

Conrad is never good at standing up to his overbearing sister. In fact, the IOUs have mounted up for all the dirt Harper has given him on the opposition parties and their members. He, like most people she knows, fall into her debt, and she uses it extremely well.

"I can't tomorrow. Parliament is sitting, and I need to be there." His mind focuses on the more useful doorstop interview that will come across better on the evening news.

Harper knows of Conrad's desperate need for positive press.

"Well, do your doorstop, then make excuses that you're needed to sort out family arrangements," she ordains.

The compromise is barely convincing, but Conrad agrees.

Harper empties the remaining Cuvée into her glass without sharing it with Conrad.

"What did the old bastard have with him?" she asks, half-interested. "They gave you his belongings, right?"

"There was not much at all. I left his clothes for the hospital to get rid of. Just a wallet, his passport and this," he says, flashing the ring on his finger after placing the wallet and passport on the table.

"I guess you can have it if you'd bothered to ask me," Harper says in a snide tone. "Wouldn't suit me, anyway."

Conrad huffs on the ring and polishes it as confirmation that he is now the bearer of the family crest.

Harper looks through the wallet, finding only two credit cards and three hundred and twenty US dollars.

"That's what they use in East Timor," Conrad says, seeing the confused look on Harper's face.

"Timor Leste," Harper corrects him. "Your mob never liked the change, did they?"

While pocketing the US dollars, she asks, "So what was he doing in a place like this, anyway? Where was he staying?"

"Who knows?" answers Conrad with a shrug.

Harper's journalistic inquisitiveness wants to know. She downs the dregs in her glass and slides the wallet towards Conrad. "I'm sure you have ways of checking the activity on his cards. That's what you government people do, isn't it?"

CHAPTER 19

Doctor Frazer Goodwin is halfway through his night shift and taking in some refreshing air outside the Yeppoon Capricorn Coast Hospital emergency entrance. He enjoys these moments of quiet solitude when he can. The cloudless sky adds to his enjoyment with its astral display, and his mind wanders to more peaceful realms.

A slight breeze is pushing whatever nearby traffic noise there is away from the hospital. The brief break accomplished its purpose, and Doctor Goodwin is about to return to his duties when a distant sound attracts his attention.

He looks back at the roar of an approaching car. As it turns into the hospital entrance road, the car's headlights go off, yet the car maintains its speed.

At the driveway leading to the emergency entrance, it does a hundred-and-eighty-degree wheel spin before accelerating off, leaving the smell of burnt tyres, burnt engine oil, the fading sound of an unhealthy engine and rattle, and a body dumped on the road.

Doctor Goodwin calls out for assistance as he runs to the motionless figure.

He turns the head to check for breathing, then feels for a pulse. Both are weak, but there're signs of life. He looks over the body for a quick assessment as a nurse arrives with a gurney. Together they carefully turn the bloodied figure of a girl over. After an initial appraisal, they place her on the gurney and wheel her quickly into the hospital.

Further examination concludes she's the victim of a sexual assault and the police be called.

The fractures to her face need an X-ray to determine the extent and if there is any brain damage. But unfortunately, that will have to wait until the police arrive. In the interim, the doctor administers a dose of pentobarbital to induce a temporary coma.

It takes over thirty minutes for the police to show up.

This frustrates the doctor, and to add to his concern is the attitude of the two officers who appear rather put out at being called away from whatever they were doing to attend an assault on an Asian girl.

As the female officer begins her own examination, jotting down notes and taking photographs, her male partner takes a statement from the doctor.

"She been penetrated?" he asks, much to the surprise of the doctor and nurse at his blunt and insensitive question.

"My preliminary examination shows she hasn't. We took swabs, and I'll add the results to my report," replies the doctor. "I believe this girl put up a fierce fight in defending herself that deterred her rape." He then adds, "But there are signs of past vaginal trauma and lacerations."

The female officer adds an entry to her report and takes a close photograph.

"Any ID or personal items on her?" asks the male officer.

"Nothing. Only what she's wearing."

"The initial call to the station stated someone dumped her outside the entrance. Who found her?"

"I did," replies the doctor. "I was taking a break outside when I heard the car."

"What car? Can you describe it?"

"Not really, the headlights were off, but I think it was a red ute. It had a loose tailpipe or something that rattled. That's what got my attention."

"Could you make out a model or a number plate?"

"No, it all happened so quick. She was thrown out, and they sped off."

"Doctor?" asks the female officer. "What's the extent of her other injuries?"

"Apart from multiple scratches and bruising to her inner thighs, the worst are facial. I believe she has suffered a broken nose and cheekbone. No loss of teeth or fracture to the jaw that I can make out. The swelling on the side of the head because of some impact may cause bleeding in the brain. An X-ray will show us, and I'd like to get it underway as soon as you've finished."

"Of course," she replies. "I'll need to bag her clothes. Is this all she was wearing?"

"Yes. Just the t-shirt."

"If you could take it off without any further tearing, please? Was there any jewellery, wedding ring, anything at all?"

"No, nothing. What you see is everything. Oh, there is one thing," the doctor adds. "She's holding a small wooden spoon in her hand. Very tightly, and I prefer not to remove it at the moment for fear of breaking her fingers. Whether it's paralysis caused by some trauma to the brain, I can't tell until we do the tests."

"When you have it free, it needs adding to the evidence," says the male officer. He looks to his partner if there was anything further to do. She shakes her head with a slight shrug of the shoulders. "We'll get outta your hair then."

Returning to their squad car with the t-shirt in an evidence bag, the female officer turns to her partner.

"What do you think?" she asks.

"Not much to go by," he says, scratching his head after taking off his cap. "The doc couldn't make out the model of the ute or the number plate. She's got no identification on her. Unless she's able to talk when she recovers, we have nothing. If she doesn't recover, then it's over to homicide. So if you really want to know what I think, I can see a shitload of paperwork and knocking on doors for someone I suspect is an illegal Asian sex worker."

He looks to his partner, expecting she'll find his opinion offensive.

"So, what are you suggesting we do?"

"Give it to immigration. I reckon it'll end up there, anyway."

CHAPTER 20

T he media coverage of the death of Professor Sir Marcus Glasson AO dominated the morning's news.

Endless special reports, biographies, and interviews with scientists around the world showed how well-respected the man was. Though there were adverse comments from those who still find his attempt to provide assisted dying offensive and against God's will.

Politicians lined up to offer their insights into the man and confirm his importance to Australia and to the world. Though most had never met him.

Conrad Glasson relished the attention. In interview after interview, he greatly exaggerated his relationship with his father. Covering only his pre-teen years.

Harper refused all interviews. Even to her own paper. This encouraged the more inquisitive journalists to uncover what they could. Despite all their efforts, no one learnt of Mirla Yimenes' son.

Sky, CNN, ABC, BBC, Al Jazeera and all other international media networks took up the story, such as the global reach Glasson BioMarine had across the globe.

Burn victims from China to Chile cried into cameras over the restorative power of Glasson Derma158F.

Countries that allow euthanasia — legally or illegally — mourned his death.

But the people of Timor-Leste felt the shock most deeply.

Long before East Timor achieved independence, Marcus Glasson had an affinity with the place and its people. His father died there fighting off the Japanese in WWII. His remains lay buried on Atauro Island.

Marcus Glasson did everything he could to help and protect the people of East Timor throughout the occupation by using whatever political nous he carried with Indonesia in the hope of a peaceful solution.

His greatest disappointment, however, was his failure to convince politicians of his own country, Australia, to drop their support of the Indonesian invasion.

Not all mourned the death of Professor Glasson in the same way. While not sorry he's dead, it infuriated Djan Muhammad Aswar that it was not of his doing! But the taking of his wife had now become complicated. There's no mention of her in all the reports, though he knows they would have been together. Is she alone or being cared for by someone else? He must find her, and Rockhampton, where Marcus Glasson died, is where his hunt will begin.

***

It's one-thirty in the morning. The streets and laneways of the seedy back blocks of Jakarta are deserted. The evening strollers have returned to their homes, and any seeking a social outing headed to brighter lights in search of the sparkle and glitter of the city's karaoke bars.

Not so Aswar.

He prefers the dank and seedier establishments where the karaoke is there just to keep the girls happy between servicing customers. The lights are low; the heat is high, and only those known to Aswar may enjoy the fruits of the flesh on offer.

He's not the owner of this somewhat secretive 'club', hiding behind the street facade of a bicycle shop, but its protector. As he is of many similar businesses spread over Jakarta, Surabaya and Kupang.

When not in his official office as head of a secret department within the State Intelligence Agency, referred to as BIN, he is doing more personal business in any of these 'unofficial' places.

He sits in a secluded corner illumination by a single grime and cobweb-covered globe. The blades of a slow-rotating ceiling fan cast intermittent shadows over his pock-cratered face. His two henchmen, badged with the scars of battle, sat opposite.

Fauzi is the older, bigger and calmer of the two. Afif is a younger, smaller, higher-strung version. Both have dual roles under Aswar's control. One is the security assistant to Aswar in his official government role. The other is very unofficial. To carry out any of Aswar's dirty work.

A couple of girls approach wearing only the skimpiest of g-strings. With one sharp glare from Aswar, they halt, bow, and quickly back away. Aswar waits until they are out of earshot and continues outlining his orders to his henchmen. They are direct and to the point. "Go to Australia. Go to this place, Rockhampton, where Marcus Glasson died. Find my wife and kill her!"

He slides a bulging manila envelope across the table.

"There's enough there to cover your expenses." As Afif goes to pick it up, Aswar places a heavy hand over it. "You come back with a finger from each hand and a photograph of her body, hear me! I'll match the fingerprints to those I have on file and if it's not her." He pauses, then with the most threatening leer, adds, "You lose your own hands. Understand!"

Aswar leans back in his chair with arms crossed. With a sincere nod, he says, "Whenever it's announced, I'll accompany one of our ministers to the service of my dear friend, Professor Marcus Glasson. You must carry out this matter well before with absolutely no connection to the Minister or myself." He unfolds his arms and taps the table with a blunt finger. "If there is...it's not your hands you lose but your heads!" He takes a moment to study the grim faces opposite. Satisfied that they fully grasp his warning, he leans back and snaps his fingers. Immediately the girls reappear and rub their naked breasts into the cheap aftershave-scented faces of the two henchmen.

CHAPTER 21

C onrad's driver meets him on arrival back in Canberra and immediately drives him to Parliament House. He'd arranged a doorstop presser, and the media were waiting. Wearing the driver's black tie and a look of sorrow, he approached the mikes and cameras and gives a brief overview of his father's achievements with a few pauses to gather his composure. When the questions turn to matters of policy, he ends the presser with a "thank you" and disappears into the building.

Inside the Lower House, the Speaker has allowed time for expressions of sorrow for losing one of Australia's finest and noted medical researchers. Both sides of the house are generous with their accolades.

Conrad laps up their sentiment, and when the time allotted ends, his request for leave to attend to family arrangements is accepted.

There's a rush to get on the first available flight to Sydney. After landing, there's another rush for Conrad to meet Harper in the elegantly decorated and furnished office of Schultz & Anders Lawyers.

Sir Marcus' lawyer, Dignam Schultz, argued strongly against the premature sighting of their father's Will, stating there were legal conditions to be met, and a death certificate has yet to be issued by the coroner.

Despite his efforts, Conrad pressured Dignam that he and his sister had come across some inside information that could be embarrassing to the law firm, and it would be in his best interest to at least see them. Once in his office, Conrad would leave it to Harper to pile on the pressure using her cruel experience and venomous talents.

After due polite condolences, Dignam Schultz sits opposite Conrad and Harper across the vast expanse of a polished oak desk, clear of anything that looked remotely like a Will binder.

Harper is eager to get straight to the point.

"Mr Schultz, you have diligently represented my father and his organisation for many years." She pauses for effect. "My father chose you for your policy of only representing those of clean and green morals, right?"

Dignam Schultz gives a slight but worrying nod.

"Now I appreciate you have rules to follow regarding the Will, but..." Again she pauses for effect, adding a glare of 'wait for it'. "But I'm sure all your other clean-n-green clients would not like to hear that one of the major companies that you represent is deeply involved in importing cheap, asbestos-riddled building materials...now would they?"

Dignam Schultz's face takes on a pale hue.

Harper relishes these moments, and while she would love to play sink-the-boot-in longer, she is eager to get to the point of their visit.

"You know of my reputation, Mr Schultz, and you know how resourceful I can be. I can also accommodate a reasonable explanation that would placate your other clients."

The inference that Harper will publish her findings anyway is enough for Dignam Schutz to minimise any potential damage she could inflict.

He well knows of the rift between his client, Sir Marcus Glasson, and his two children. Sitting now face-to-face, he realises how right his long-time friend was in setting up his organisation to minimise the amount of money directed to them and closing any loophole that would allow them to take control.

For this reason, and given the veracity of Harper's threat, why not read the Will now? It will happen eventually, and there's still the need for an audit and a six-month wait for creditors to come forward before he can complete all conditions in the Will and distribute the assets.

Sweat beads on Dignam's forehead, fearing the response from the two seated opposite to what they are about to hear.

From a drawer to Dignam's left, he removes a binder, folded and bound. Without a word, he unties the ribbon and removes the parchment document. With a cough to clear his throat and loosen his larynx, he reads the Last Will and Testament of Professor Sir Marcus Glasson OA.

"You, Conrad and Harper, will continue to receive income from the family trust financed by one section of the Glasson empire."

This registers no excitement on the faces of Conrad and Harper, as it's a far more lucrative outcome they're waiting for.

"The Glasson Fund, set up to protect the diverse sea life in the Timor and Banda Seas, will benefit from an initial fifty-million dollars. Thereafter, a grant of twenty-million dollars each year after adjusting to the CPI. Glasson BioMarine is to come under the ownership and control of Mirla Yimenes and Jude Yimenes of Timor-Leste. A trust, set up for Jude Yimenes, will receive an additional ten million dollars."

Dignam senses a reaction from Conrad and Harper, but refuses to look up to see how fierce it is. He continues without hesitation.

"Five million dollars go to Conrad and Harper to cover payment of any mortgage still owing on each of their properties. All personal property owned by Marcus Glasson in Sydney, Darwin, Dili and one on nearby Atauro Island goes to Mirla and Jude Yimenes."

This is a massive shock to Conrad and Harper as their chairs creak under their growing unease. Dignam continues with haste. "The rest of the estate, comprising bank deposits, shares and investments estimated the previous year to total over twenty-five million dollars are to stay under the control of the nominated executor, Schultz & Anders, with interest shared each year between two orphanages in Timor Leste, a Dili hospital fund and a Dili dental clinic. Mr Evelyn Sunday of Dili is to take over ownership of the research cruiser, Banda One."

Dignam Schultz manages a glance up. Harper and Conrad sit red-faced and expecting more. But before Harper can explode into a fury of abuse and threats of a legal challenge to the Will, Dignam removes two sheets of paper clipped to the top left corner of the binder and smooths them out in front of him.

"Two days ago a local solicitor in Yeppoon, Queensland, contacted us. This is their letterhead that arrived by registered mail this morning." He turns the page to face the stunned pair sitting opposite. "Professor Glasson visited him to dictate a codicil to his Will. It has

changes and additions to the instructions I have just read to you."
After another dry swallow and a useless cough, he continued. "The
property in Sydney is to be auctioned, with proceeds added to the
trust fund set up for Jude Yimenes. This trust is now to be shared
equally between Jude Yimenes and Noi de Jesus and re-named ac-
cordingly." Dignam cannot continue without a sip of water to stop his
voice completely giving up.

Harper slams her fist on the solid desk with a loud bang, resulting
in more pain to her than an effect on the timber. "This is absolute
bullshit!" she bellowed. "Who the fuck are these people? We are his
blood descendants, and what do we get? A miserly five million on
top of what we already get." She points a shaking fist across the desk
at a cowering Dignam. "You prepare yourself for a fucking legal fight
over this piece of shit rubbish," she yells while pushing her chair back
in readiness to walk out. "Come, Conrad, we need to see our own
solicitors." She turns back to Dignam, pointing a threatening finger at
him as Conrad stands to follow. "So much for your clean-and-green
image, Mr Schultz!"

Dignam was waiting for this outburst, but it wasn't over. "There's
more," he utters.

Harper pauses, unsure if she wants to hear more, but Conrad does.
"Wait, Harper. Let's get the full story before we head off," he says, as
both remain standing.

Another sip of water and Dignam reads the last paragraph of the
Codicil. "If Noi de Jesus, Mirla Yimenes and Jude Yimenes pre-de-
cease me, all assets due to them go to my two children Conrad and
Harper." He pauses, hoping this will calm the air. Dignam knows
Mirla and Jude Yimenes are still alive, but Noi de Jesus was unknown
to him and that needed investigation.

The looks on Conrad and Harper's faces ease at the thought of
big dollars, but not knowing these people or if they're dead or alive,
their rage returns.

Before Harper can get a word out, Dignam continues.

"It goes on to read, if either Mirla Yimenes, Jude Yimenes, Noi de
Jesus or the baby she carries were to die because of suspicious circumstances after my death, and during the Will determination period
of six months plus two, all assets go to the survivors of the four. In
the extreme case that all four die under suspicious circumstances

within the time-frame mentioned above, all said assets go to the listed orphanages, hospital, and dental clinic in equal portions."

Dignam places the codicil down onto the formal Will and waits for the expectant outburst.

Harper is the first to cry foul. "This is outrageous," she calls out, stamping her foot on the loop-pile carpet like a spoilt child. "I will prove that you have been implicit in this attempt at depriving us of our due inheritance and will create such a media storm you will not be practising law or in a legal position to be the executor of this piece of shit."

This was more than Dignam expected, and it was to be a pleasure in informing his facing enemy of the last instruction. "Added to the codicil is a rider," he says, his voice clearer than it has been throughout the meeting. He continues. "Any challenge to the Will or this Codicil attached will cause the removal of the Conrad and Harper Trust Fund, and its value added to the overall assets. Signed, Professor Sir Marcus Glasson OA."

Dignam looks up from the paper and sees the horror mixed with rage on the faces leering at him.

The trust fund brings in a comfortable quarter of a million dollars a year to each of them. But their greed condemns this as an insult compared to the full worth of their father's vast estate.

"There are some minor items in the Will relating to funeral insurance and instructions for the service, but I feel these to be of less importance to you than what you both have requested from me today." He stands and directs a hand toward the door. "I bid you goodbye and will inform you through your solicitors when the death certificate arrives."

Dignam has already buzzed his secretary, who opens the door and steps aside so as not to be trampled by fired-up Conrad and Harper as they make their stampeding exit.

CHAPTER 22

Deep in the sombre bowels of the Immigration Department in Canberra, a small army of computer operators hunch over keyboards and peer into monitors.

They spend their working hours as if they are family tree genealogists, confirming or dismissing the identity of those wanting to come into the country, or those already here.

At the back are the junior staff, where the effects of the air-con struggle to reach, and the temperature can either be stifling in summer or freezing in winter.

Kailee Banks is one as her section overseer dumps a manila folder on her desk, causing her to mistype a word.

She glances at the case file number IC18/7993 added above a stock form printed on the cover with boxes to be filled in, signed and dated by all who see and add to the contents.

Except for the IC donating 'IN COUNTRY', it means nothing to her at the moment, but it will.

"Just decide on the girl's origin; another department will do the rest," comes the usual demeaning command from the supervisor.

At thirty-three, Kailee is older than the other juniors. It's rather cruelly assumed by many that she's a bit slow or impaired and employed to fill the equal opportunity quota.

The fact is, Kailee is very much the opposite — though her shyness and insecurity do nothing to help dispel that thought. Nor does her lack of interest in her appearance. Everything is functional rather than fashionable. She ties her auburn hair back in a ponytail and keeps her fringe long at the front to blend with the thick black frame of her glasses, which constantly slide down her curved, chiselled nose. The only makeup she wears is musk flavoured lip balm that she licks every time she pushes back her glasses.

But the lack of makeup exposes a natural beauty. She has shapely lips; her teeth are white and even. Her eyes are a greenish-blue that have a distant, enticing look. She is tallish but not tall; her slender body sees to that. Not that anyone could tell, hidden under a baggy, oversized blouse and an ankle-length skirt — all a dull shade of brown.

She dropped out of a medical degree after less than two years when her father died. Being an only child, she was alone in caring for her invalid mother. It was the least she could do since her father told her, at a much too young age, that her birth caused her mother's condition.

He loathed the responsibility of a house-bound wife. It interrupted his life's plans to travel the world, never set down roots, and become the bon vivant he was never born to be.

Kailee carried the unfair blame, and her introverted guilt made her shun anyone who tried to befriend her.

Believing she had a lifelong debt to her mother, Kailee started a medical degree hoping to become an obstetrician and one day shine a light on why her birth cursed her mother's condition.

When her father died, leaving no financial support, it was left up to her to provide one.

She dropped out of university and applied for a government job, hoping it would offer her flexible hours to tend to her mother. It did until her mother died six months ago.

If it hadn't been for one skill, she might not have got the job. She has an uncanny ability to recognise facial features that pointed to a person's country of birth — even to regions or towns.

Her success rate over a short time was ninety-five percent, but it was from photos of intact people, yet to decompose, unblemished or with no deformity from birth.

Out of interest to see what challenge her next case presents, she opens the folder. The photo of the person concerned fit none of those descriptions. Sure, she is of Asian descent, but with extensive bruising, lacerations, a broken nose and eye socket, she fitted into the defaced category.

But there was something to work with and more challenging than the current case she was closing the file on. She signs her name with the date and time on the folder and places it for the supervisor to collect.

She opens the new folder and studies the photo of the girl again with her usual search for detail.

The worst injuries are to one side of the face. Some swelling had spread, but possible to correct later. She prints out a reverse photocopy of the girl's face, folds it in half vertically and places it over the original photo to cover the injuries.

It helped despite no person being born with absolutely mirrored features.

She quickly dismisses Japanese, Chinese, or being from the subcontinent. South-East Asian, most likely, but there was something, some small trait that just didn't fit her short-list of Thai, Malay or Indonesian. It had to be European.

This opened the proverbial can of worms.

Traders throughout the centuries had spread their genes on their long and distant voyages, and these could have mixed with other origins over generations — a melting pot that threw up bits of everything. To decide this girl's identity will not be easy.

She expected her boss to be back later in the day for the result. She could make her best guess taken from her shortlist and leave it for others to fill in the gaps.

But something is urging Kailee not to give up on this case so quickly.

It stemmed from her father's racial intolerance of anyone who was not born white. A doctrine she had grown to loathe and reject, and after reading the attached police report, the stubbornness to her cause only grew stronger.

The inference that this girl could be an illegal sex worker was, she felt deep down, a false and foolish assumption.

She knows she's the best in the entire department at determining people's origins, but never credited for it. In fact, others take the limelight for discoveries she's made. But here's a case she is sure no one except herself could find the correct answer. One requiring more in-depth research that would prove her worth — and a promotion closer to the air-conditioning. This case is hers, and she knows deep down only Kailee Banks can tell this girl's story.

There are groans all around the department as an infinite number of files appear on desks. More supposed refugees need their backgrounds filled in, and Kailee has one more case added to her workload. With a sigh of annoyance at having her adopted case interrupted, she opens the new file and smiles to herself. The attached photo of a middle-aged man made it so easy to recognise his origin; she could have all the information required in less than an hour.

The middle-aged Sri Lankan man, who is most likely descendant from the Tamil Jaffna Kingdom regions to the north of the island, has delivered her time.

With the Sri Lankan file left open, Kailee reads through the girl's file and the police report again while keeping a wary eye open for any meandering supervisor.

Their assertion that this girl has entered the country to work in the sex trade is a common label pinned on girls of Asian appearance. This is a pure and deliberate case of racial profiling, and snaps something inside her.

She looks at her watch. Another hour and a half on a Friday, then the weekend is all hers. It may cost her job, but Kailee sees no other choice than to follow up this case in her own time.

She must see this girl in the flesh.

CHAPTER 23

Kailee Banks and travel, whether by land, sea or air, are relative strangers. In fact, the only flight she's been on was south to Melbourne and return. The farthest north she had travelled was to Sydney, and that was by bus. Now she's about to take four flights — north to Brisbane, change planes for Rockhampton and the same back — all in one day.

With only a shoulder bag to carry her laptop, a folder with copies of the girl's files, a notepad and her wallet, Kailee is already wondering if she's wasting almost two weeks' wages on seeing this girl.

She relaxes her white-knuckle grip on the armrests as the plane levels off after leaving Canberra. The urge to take out the file for another read will have to wait as she presumes most passengers — including the man sitting next to her — would be government people and to be seen with a file she should not have outside her office would be unwise.

Despite the early morning flight and no breakfast, the flight attendant's offer of a meagre snack and drink was refused, allowing more time for her stomach to settle while reading the inflight magazine.

The layover in Brisbane before her flight to Rockhampton allowed for some breakfast and the relief of seeing normal people waiting for her flight and not public servants. Though how they viewed her crossed her mind.

On this flight, she has an empty seat beside her, allowing a look over the file and prepare questions for the doctors, nurses, and police, something she fears will be confronting because of her lack of people skills.

Of course, there is the real possibility that no one will want to talk to her. She is cold-calling with no official status or relevant identification other than her employment tag displaying her mugshot, name, employee number 810566, and the Department of Immigration crest. Important as it may be to get her into her workplace, it's hardly official enough to be interrogating people.

Half-way into the flight she accepts there is nothing more to learn from the many readings of the files nor further questions to add to her list. She places the file into her bag and settles down by the window seat to watch the earth pass below. Thoughts of having one day the freedom to travel widely drift her into wild imaginations. Maybe, just maybe, Yeppoon is a start.

She opted to hire a car at Rockhampton Airport and drive to Yeppoon. With only about four hours before catching her first flight back to Canberra, she's pretty sure it'll be ample time to examine the girl in the hospital, talk to the doctors and drop into the police station.

By the time she reaches the Capricorn Coast Hospital in Yeppoon, almost an hour has passed. After parking her car, she steps into the compact foyer of the hospital and immediately attracts the attention of several elderly people sitting on two rows of chairs on her left. They study her closely as she approaches the timber-panelled counter.

The sole person manning the counter looks up with an efficient smile. "How can I help you?" she asks.

Kailee nervously flashes her employee ID, covering most of it with her hand so only her face and the seal of the Immigration Department are noticeable.

"My name is Kailee Banks from the Federal Department of Immigration, and I'm here to help identify this girl." She holds up the photo taken from her file.

"Do you have her name?" is asks as the woman scans her computer screen.

"No, that is why I'm here, to help identify her," replies Kailee, bemused by the question.

"Is this a police matter?"

"It was," Kailee replies. "It's now an immigration matter."

"Yes, well, take a seat and I'll get someone."

Kailee thanks her and finds an empty seat among her audience.

As her instinct is to determine people's cultural origins, she can't help being interested in two men as they enter the hospital foyer. Nor can those she's seated with.

Kailee determined almost immediately that they are both Indonesian. One definitely from Java, where the capital Jakarta is. The other, younger-looking one is harder to place precisely. Maybe Sulawesi is her initial thought. Feeling smug about her talent, she switches her mind back to her case and feels less smug about interviewing people.

She turns her attention back to the two men. The older one is talking to the lady behind the counter in a deep that carries. To add to her linguistic understanding of where people come from, she studies his accent. His English is not good, but it's how words and syllables are formed that can help identify people's origins. She believes every language uses unique sequences of muscles to form words. Often this makes some English words hard to pronounce for those from other countries.

Suddenly another voice interrupts her study.

"Miss Banks, is it? I believe you want to speak to me. I'm Joel Tillanson, one of the administrators here."

Kailee has to turn her attention away from the man with the deep voice who is having trouble with an English word.

"Yes, sorry, I was a little distracted," she says getting up from her seat and extending her hand. "I'm Kailee Banks from the Department of Immigration, and I'm here to see the unidentified girl that was admitted to casualty a few days ago."

"Yes, of course. Do you have some identification?"

Kailee shows the department's report first, hoping it will be a distraction from the quick flash of her ID. It worked.

"Please come with me," he says, leading the way.

CHAPTER 24

T he head nurse on duty is as broad as she is tall, with bosoms to match. She's introduced to Kailee and told to help in any way she can before the administrator bids his farewell, leaving Kailee wondering why he bothered to meet her at all.

Kailee senses a degree of disinterest in the patient, and she's left to explain once again her reason for being where she is.

"Hello, Julie," she says, spotting her name pinned to her uniform. "I'm here to see the unidentified girl left outside the emergency entrance a few days ago, and I'm hoping to speak to the doctor who attended to her."

Nurse Julie looks her up and down, unable to hide her wonder at the nerdy types they have in Canberra looking after Australia's welfare.

"He's not on duty," she snaps with no further help offered.

"Can I speak to another doctor who's familiar with the girl's condition?" Kailee's voice is losing its authority.

"I thought the police were handling this?" asks nurse Julie.

"They are," replies Kailee. "I've been called in to assist at the federal level."

"She's down here," she says, walking off down the corridor with Kailee at her heels. The thought of being accused of obstruction at a 'federal level' worked.

Kailee follows the nurse into a ward isolated from the rest. It is here she's introduced to JD, or Jane Doe tagged to unknown persons of the female gender.

The girl looks peaceful as if in a distant dream. The swelling and bruising of her face have spread. A thick bandage covers her head, a plaster strip is across the bridge of her nose, and six stitches close a cut on her left cheek. An intravenous drip is feeding fluid into her left arm. A monitor on a stand beside her trails her heartbeat.

"I'll see if I can find a doctor free to talk to you," offers the nurse in a less than friendly tone.

"Thank you," replies Kailee with a half-glance back.

Alone, Kailee moves closer to study the girl and take in every feature of her face that's not covered. There is not a lot to see as her head is turned so the least damaged side rests on the pillow.

She checks her ear for any piercings. Finding none, her eyes focused on a small birthmark that did not show in the file photo, nor was there any mention of it in the report.

The only other part of her body not covered by a blanket is her left arm and hand, showing defensive wounds. Kailee studies her long, slender fingers and fingernails. Apart from one broken nail, all appear manicured. An opaque pinkish flesh-coloured nail polish is wearing off, revealing congealed blood under the nails. Kailee hopes the police took samples. With her glasses sliding down the bridge of her nose, Kailee turns over the girl's hand to study the palm for signs of physical labour: scars, calluses, hardening of the skin, but nothing. The first impression is that someone has pampered this girl.

Kailee hadn't noticed a doctor had entered with nurse Julie. He watches her for a moment before speaking.

"Can I help you?" he asks, startling the prying Kailee, who lets go of the girl's hand, straightens up and steps away from the bed.

"Um, yes, sorry, I... I was just..." her words fading.

"I'm told you're from the Immigration Depar..." His words cut short by an over-eager Kailee offering out her hand.

"Kailee Banks..." she looks at the doctor's name tag on the breast pocket of his white coat. "Doctor Hadish."

"Have you washed your hands?" asks the doctor.

Kailee looks down at her hands and wonders if she's infected the patient, let alone spreading whatever she's picked up since leaving her home in Canberra.

"Nurse, take..." the doctor looks down at Kailee's ring finger. "Miss Banks out to the visitor's sink." He steps aside to allow nurse Julie to direct Kailee out into the corridor. "And hurry! I don't have all day."

A flushed-faced Kailee passes the doctor with her head bowed in embarrassment. Should I tick the nurse off for not telling me...I don't think so! But this admonishment, together with her shyness and lack of people skills, has left what little confidence she has somewhat battered.

The doctor is looking over the girl's chart when Kailee returns with sterile hands.

"Have you seen and read the police and medical reports on this girl?" asks the doctor without looking up.

"Yes, of course," answers Kailee, hoping the doctor had forgotten the hand episode.

"So, tell me, Miss Banks, what more do you think you can add?" The doctor places the chart back in its cradle at the base of the bed and turns to Kailee, doubting someone so young could have anything at all to offer.

Kailee understands his look, and for the first time, wonders why in the world she thought she could do something so far out of her depth and presume to add anything.

But deep down there is a drive that has pushed her this far, and she looks at the girl lying in need of someone. Someone to answer for her and someone to give her...

"A name," she replies with surprising confidence.

The doctor looks at nurse Julie, then back at Kailee.

"And that is?"

Kailee looks from one to the other as she searches for a suitable answer.

"I don't know...yet!"

Doctor Hadish slides both hands into his coat pocket — most likely to avoid shaking hands again. "Well then, until that day comes, I have rounds to complete. The nurse will show you out." He turns and disappears behind the breadth of nurse Julie struggling to cross her arms over her ample breasts.

"Doctor," Kailee calls out. "What's keeping this girl in a coma? And why is she in a secured ward?"

The doctor stops and turns back. "Nothing that will help identify her, I assure you. Because of complications surrounding her condition, we thought it best to keep her stable."

"Complications?" Kailee questions. "And what condition?" she adds, taking the report from her bag.

"She is pregnant," the doctor informs her, looking down at the paper in her hand.

"Pregnant? There's no mention of that in my report."

"Undetected at first. We estimate she is only in the first month and a half. There is so much past internal damage, we thought conceiving to be impossible."

"And the complications?" Kailee asks as she adds notes to her report. "Was there an attempt to abort?"

"Not that we could confirm. The foetus had not yet formed, and when we did further tests, they showed an anomaly."

"What do you mean, an anomaly?"

"There was something we could not explain. A trace element in the girl's blood was unrecognisable."

"Has she been awake at any stage?"

"No, and until she does, we won't know of any brain damage. She may not even remember what happened to her."

Kailee finishes writing a note and looks back up at the doctor. "Has there been any further clue to her identity?"

"I'm not aware of any. You'll need to talk to the police."

"That I will, thank you, Doctor."

"The nurse will see you out. Goodbye."

Despite sensing there's more to what is happening to this girl, she accepts she'll not get any more out of the doctor. With him out of sight, a flicker of something she learnt on another case crosses her mind.

"Can I examine the girl's body, nurse?" She asks as if coming from someone older and far more experienced.

"Certainly not," snaps the nurse. "You heard the doctor, come back when you have a name."

"There's some confusion between the medical report and the police report about marks on the body," suggests Kailee, knowing she'll be caught out if asked to show the discrepancies. "Some marks may appear as scars from injuries, but are ceremonial markings."

The nurse looks uncertain and in need of more reassurance.

"I've worked on many cases like this as an investigator for the Federal Department of Immigration and can contact my superior to direct you to assist me if that is what you need?" Kailee knows she has buried herself if the nurse insists she does just that.

The last thing nurse Julie wants is to be caught up in some bureaucratic hassle.

"You have five minutes," she conceded. "I need to stay here and I have another ward to run, so be quick."

Kailee nods with a rare sense of achievement.

The nurse removes the blanket and Noi's hospital gown, allowing Kailee to study her naked body.

There are no piercing marks, no tattoos or other birthmarks. Apart from lacerations and bruising because of the attempted rape, her body is perfect, leaving Kailee feeling uncomfortable photographing the girl's pubic region.

Her pubic hair is trimmed to her bikini line, and her natural dark olive skin tone shows no hint of a bikini shape. Does this girl sunbathe naked, or does she even sunbake at all? Tan is not something of beauty in Asia. And beautiful she is, leaving Kailee envious.

"What's that?" asks Kailee, seeing something clenched in Noi's right hand, covered earlier by the blanket.

"A spoon of some sort," nurse Julie replies, making her impatience obvious. "Her grip is so strong they decided not to force her fingers off it. Now I must get back to my rounds."

Kailee makes a mental note of it, as there's no chance of taking a photo before being pushed aside by the nurse putting Noi's gown back on and the blanket returned.

On being escorted out to the foyer, Kailee spots the two Indonesian men standing just outside the entrance in deep conversation.

Seeing the girl in the flesh confirmed her judgement that she is part Indonesian and wonders if these two have any connection?

Both men respond to a sense of being studied and look back at Kailee. Sprung, she grabs a brochure from the rack and pretends to read it. Chancing a glance back, she sees the two walk to a car in the car park and drive off.

Kailee is not ready to accept it's just a coincidence that two Indonesian men are at the same hospital where a girl with mixed Indonesian features lies unidentified and in a coma.

She tries to remember the difficulty one had in mouthing what could have been someone's name. Could it have been the girl's name?

"Hello, I spoke to you earlier, and I'm sorry to bother you again," says Kailee, approaching the reception desk.

"Yes, you're with the Immigration Department. Was there something else?"

"Well, it has nothing to do with my earlier request, but I'm curious to know who the two Indonesian men were asking about earlier?"

"Indonesian, were they? I wasn't sure. Anyway, they asked about Professor Glasson. He was admitted here three or four days ago, then transferred to Rockhampton. Unfortunately, he passed away there."

"Well, thanks," says Kailee. "I didn't mean to pry, but it was sad news about the professor. Friends were they? It must have been a shock to come and visit only to find out the professor had died?"

"More like associates of the professor, I reckon. They knew he'd passed away and wanted to know if he had other visitors while he was here. They said Asian, but probably meant Indonesian if that's where they're from."

"Yes, well, sorry to bother you again. Goodbye."

On her way out of the hospital, Kailee writes on the hospital brochure, Professor Glasson?

CHAPTER 25

As Kailee drives into Yeppoon township looking for the police station, she gets her first sight of the coast and the ocean. She pauses for a moment to take in the distant islands and makes a mental note to come back one day for a holiday.

She flashes her ID to the desk sergeant and introduces herself, adding, "Can I speak to the two officers whose names are on this report, please?"

The sergeant looks down at the names and shakes his head. "Both are not here..." He takes another look at Kailee's ID and only registers her name to her relief. "Miss Banks. Um, we didn't expect a visit from the department."

"Yes, well, the department decided this to be a special case, and I'm the one they sent." Then adds to direct attention away from her falsehood. "Have you caught whoever attacked the girl?"

"Not at this stage...it's ongoing."

"Has any more information on the girl's identity come to light?"

"Not that I'm aware of. Look, once this case went over to you, all we had to do was track down the assailant."

Kailee believes she's being given the brush-off.

"The report states that they bagged her clothes. Where are they now?"

"In the evidence room. If the girl dies, they go to homicide."

"Can I see them?"

The sergeant cannot hide his growing frustration at her questions, but if it gets rid of her, he disappears into a back room, then returns with a paper bag and places it on the counter.

"It's sealed. Can I open it?" asks Kailee, trying not to appear intimidated.

The sergeant takes out a pair of scissors from a drawer and cuts the seal. "You got gloves?" he asks, confident she hasn't.

"Sorry, no," Kailee confesses, kicking herself for not having thought of it.

He takes a pair of blue latex gloves from the same drawer as the scissors and hands them over with a questioning look.

Kailee puts on the gloves and removes the girl's t-shirt and checks for anything else inside the bag. "There's nothing else?" she asks. "No panties, jewellery, or anything?"

"That's all she had," comes the blunt reply.

She places the only item of clothing flat on the counter, takes out her phone and photographs the front and back. Holding up the t-shirt, she asks, "What size would you say this is? The label's faded."

The sergeant looks with a shrug of his shoulders. "Hard to say, but I see your point. It's much too big for a cute little Asian girl. Then again, kids these days want to look sloppy."

Kailee smiles at the sergeant's assessment of the girl and takes one more close-up photo of the t-shirt neck label before placing the clothes back into the evidence bag.

"Well, you have been very helpful, Sergeant. I won't keep you any longer from your duties."

"Yes, well, before you go, Miss Banks, you need to sign the evidence bag to show you opened the seal and viewed the contents."

This sends a nervous shiver down Kailee's spine. It will be evidence that she has acted alone on this case. To hide her concern, she puts on an act of authority and signs her name.

Kailee is in two minds about how she feels as she drives back to Rockhampton. She'll now be on the girl's police report, and that alone could get her sacked. Lying to the doctor and the police about her authority and using her employment ID card as false credentials could even see her end up in prison. But no matter how big the problems she's created for herself, the deep-seated belief that this girl has been wrongly pigeon-holed by the police officer's assessment and the apparent lack of interest in the case is disturbing.

After topping up the petrol and delivering the car back to the car hire, she enters the airport with little time to spare as her flight was boarding.

Did she notice them, or was it the hairs on her neck standing up that alerted her? She looks around and spots the two Indonesian men at the information counter. Just like at the hospital, one is doing the talking while the other is looking around as if he's expecting trouble. Kailee lowers her head, rushes off through security and to the gate where her plane is waiting.

Once the seatbelt sign is off, Kailee takes advantage of having an empty seat beside her and takes out the report, her phone, and notebook. She studies the photos taken of the girl, then adds comments into her notebook about what she has learnt this day and what she has not.

CHAPTER 26

C onrad Glasson leans on the balcony railing of his Potts Point townhouse as if mesmerised by the anchored boats dancing in the increasing swell of Elizabeth Bay.

But it's not the peaceful scene below that has his attention. He's waiting for his sister to arrive, and that always makes him uncomfortable.

The doorbell chimes, and Conrad opens the door for his sister to enter, exhibiting her usual aggressive manner.

There are no brother/sister hugs or kisses between the two, and never has been. Their relationship is more of a formality. Neither do they hide their dislike of each other. But in the current situation, their feelings need to be tempered.

Conrad pours a glass of Glaetzer Bishop Shiraz for Harper. It's the only wine he knows she likes and keeps a case in the cellar for her rare visits. He tops up his whisky and sits opposite her across the large glass-topped coffee table.

Harper takes a sip after swirling some air into the wine and judges whether her brother has cellared it correctly. Reasonably satisfied, she takes a long sip and places the glass down on the table.

"So, what do you want to talk about?" she asks, taking out a cigarette.

Conrad looks for the only ashtray he has. He abhors anyone who smokes indoors, but to ask his sister not to smoke would be unwise.

"Well, apart from the obvious," he says, opening the sliding balcony doors wider. "I thought you'd want to know there's talk of a state memorial service and you may want to have some input," he adds.

"All I want is that shit to be over so we can contest the Will and this bloody codicil."

She looks around the room, taking in all the art and family objects. "I'm sure you could do better than this if we get our full entitlement from his estate."

Conrad takes a glance back across the bay. He likes this place, but something else in the south of France would suit. "I agree," he says, wanting to return to the balcony for smokeless fresh air. "But I can't allow contesting the Will to get media momentum. It could damage my political advancement."

Harper blows smoke in his direction. "Humph! Your what? Dear brother, you're lucky to be in the cabinet. If it weren't for me, you'd be a backbencher hack with no portfolio."

Conrad is well aware of what she's talking about. She kept the media in the dark about several shady deals he made with unethical and dubious businesses and developers in return for government favours — and a not so insignificant monetary hand-shake that was never declared.

He turns back to face her with a rush of retaliation. "And I've leaked many a scoop to you from the halls of power that's made you look good as well. Don't forget that." He raises his glass to his lips as if toasting his rare riposte to his sister. "Anyway, what have you discovered about this girl with all your media-savvy investigative powers?"

Harper squashes her cigarette into the ashtray. Not taking kindly to being put down, she snaps, "If that's how we'll tackle this problem with tit-for-tat one-upmanship, then I'm off." She gets to her feet to leave.

"Wait," beckons Conrad. "Look, if we don't stick together contesting the Will and this codicil, we could end up with just the dregs. So, let's concentrate on the problem at hand and try not to argue." He reaches for the bottle of Shiraz. "Care for some more?"

As if the wine alone is worth the hassle of putting up with her brother for another few minutes, she relents and walks to the balcony, leaving Conrad to pick up her glass and follow.

Once seated on cushioned designer outdoor furniture, they allow a moment for the breeze off the water to clear the air.

"Obits," Harper says without taking her eyes off the array of yachts and cruisers dotting the water. "What?"

"Obits. I'll use our media scanner to get every obituary mentioning our father in every paper around the country and overseas. There would have to be hundreds, and with luck, at least one might mention this girl."

Conrad takes a sip of his Whisky annoyed he didn't think about it first. "Yes, that's an obvious thing to do, of course," he says, watering down her idea.

"And what will you do?" challenges Harper.

"I, um, I have contacts in Indonesia. Political contacts. Their connection to East Timor may dig up something."

Harper usually knocks back suggestions he comes up with, but this one could be worth a shot.

"Okay, so what's this about a state service?"

"The New South Wales Premier is seeking cabinet approval for a state memorial service. It's not dependent on the coroner releasing the body," he adds preempting her question. "It's sure to attract many important people from here and overseas."

Harper tries to hide her smirk, knowing those of importance will be more critical to his own image. But she cringes at the thought of attending a state gathering with so many attending. She'd rather hide behind her by-line than have the most unflattering photo of her spread across the media. Such is the disdain that those in the media have for her.

"Well, if you got me here for my input, then sorry to disappoint you, but I'll leave all that for you to sort out." After a moment, she adds, "All I ask is that when you have a list of those attending, I'd like to see it. Pre-event research wouldn't go astray."

She downs the rest of her wine and heads for the door. Before opening it, she turns back to Conrad.

"Who is this Indonesian contact?"

Conrad taps his nose. She gets the hint he's not about to tell and leaves.

CHAPTER 27

Since her mother died, Kailee has been free to spend every Sunday doing what she does every workday: looking into a computer screen. It was never work-related, though she wished it would be one day. It was building on what she'd learnt during her two years studying medicine and to one day attain her degree. This Sunday is different.

Eager to key in her notes and load the photos taken in Yeppoon, Kailee made a mug of coffee and a slice of toast with Vegemite before emptying the contents of her shoulder bag onto the table.

She places the notebook and camera neatly beside her open laptop, and after a bite of her toast and licking her fingers clean, she keys in her notes.

Almost two hours later, Kailee had entered everything onto her laptop and cross-referenced her notes to the Immigration Department's report, the doctor's report, and the police report.

Her final entry is loading the photos taken of the t-shirt together with captions and then all the photos of the girl. This makes her feel uncomfortable and slightly voyeuristic, but she needs to study them closely in case there was something she missed.

When all is done, she leans back in her chair, pleased with the data gathered. But her smugness is short-lived. Organising material gives her pleasure, but the ultimate satisfaction comes from finding answers to the questions raised. The journey to get to this point has fulfilled the first part, but has not led to any solution.

She flips through the pages of her notebook for something she might have missed. Nothing!

Whether through fatigue or disappointment, her mind wanders. She sees her wallet on the table and thinks of the credit card inside, bulging with a new debt to be paid. A problem if she loses her job. Then her eyes land on the hospital brochure. She has no recollection of saving it to her bag and picks it up out of interest. Scribbled on the cover is the name one of the Indonesian men had difficulty in saying — Professor Glasson.

She keys the name into her search engine, and the amount of material that came up was daunting. As a professor of medicine — of sorts — his life's work and discoveries may add something to her degree studies. She digs deeper and finds scattered among the articles, commendations, medical journal entries and obituaries that refer to Dili and East Timor, come Timor-Leste.

It's the spark that brings her back to the Yeppoon girl. East Timor had been a Portuguese colony from 1769 until the Indonesian occupation in 1975. This supports her theory that the girl had a mix of European and Asian features. Could her parents be Timorese and Portuguese? The more she thinks about this possibility, the stronger her belief in the girl's origin.

The image of two Indonesian men at the hospital also come to mind. She shakes her head. It's too much of a long shot to connect the girl and the professor. But the thought wouldn't leave her. Was she an employee of Glasson BioMarine at the Dili office? Was she a friend taken on a holiday, or more than just a friend: a sexual companion, maybe?

Kailee pushes her chair back from the computer and again shakes her head.

"What am I doing?" she asks herself. "I have to get out of the romantic notion I'm some sort of private investigator and stick to the facts. There is nothing I've seen that connects the two." Even thinking about what she overheard the two Indonesian men asking if the professor had any Asian visitors proved there was no connection. If there had been, they would have known she was lying in a nearby bed in the same hospital the professor was first taken.

She's half out of her chair to make another cup of coffee when the weight of her belief has her sitting back down. Coincidences need disproving before they're dismissed, and there's a growing number surrounding the girl and this professor to ignore. She sits back down and returns to searching Sir Marcus Glasson and Glasson BioMarine.

Among the many articles and condolence messages, Kailee comes across coverage of the launch of a salt farm in Kupang in Indonesian West Timor. Salt farms are of no interest to Kailee, but one photo taken at the official launch changes that.

By now she's familiar with what the professor looks like and picks him out among others in the photograph. He and the Indonesian ministers related to the project have their names in the accompanying caption.

It's those not listed in the caption that have her interest. Standing outside a closed door in the background with arms crossed is one of the two men she saw at Yeppoon Hospital.

While Kailee's time working in a government department is short, she's come to recognise protective services people. This man is one and raises a question. "If those two at the hospital are not business associates of the Professor, then who do they work for?" She takes a screenshot and adds it to her dossier.

The most important member of the Indonesian government hosting the launch is the Minister of Trade. She opens the Indonesian Trade and Resources website to see if this man was part of the minister's security attachment. The site is full of photos of the minister shaking hands with various government dignitaries from around the world. She scans the photos, focussing not on the government members but those in the background or to the side.

She's about to give up when the word 'Australia' in one caption catches her eye. The photo is of two men shaking hands and smiling awkwardly at the camera. The caption identifies the man on the right as Conrad Glasson MP, the Australian Minister for Minerals, Resources and Trade!

Kailee inspects the photo closer. Despite working for the government, she has little interest in politics and even less in politicians, so the thought of any connection never occurred to her.

She brings up the many notices of condolences for the Professor again, and there, most prominent, is one from his beloved son and daughter, Conrad and Harper.

Kailee spends a few moments staring at the screen. She is sure one of Australia's own ministers could have nothing to do with the girl, but it's another coincidence not to be dismissed. She adds the death notice to her growing file.

Then, as an afterthought, she copies all other death notices relating to the Professor printed, not only in the Australian press but also in some international newspapers.

As she expected, many are from people and government agencies in Indonesia, including a small and discrete notice from the research office in Dili, East Timor.

With great sadness
gone is our founder.
What is not gone
is so much he gave
and still giving
to a healthier world.

She takes a moment to question her next action. Then, with a decisive nod, she searches for the contact details of the office of Glasson BioMarine. Getting the Sydney office, she keys in Dili and enters the contact details into her phone.

The following day, Kailee settles herself into her office chair looking over a new case file that was waiting for her on her desk. Hoping it to be as easy to identify the origins of this person as it was the Sri Lankan man so she can continue with the Yeppoon girl case, her supervisor approaches.

"Miss Banks, I was expecting your case IC18/7993 findings to be on my desk first thing this morning. If you're having trouble identifying the person concerned, I'll give it to someone else."

Kailee was expecting this, but believed there was an answer within reach. Hoping it will show her dedication to finding the girl's identity and enable her to stay on the case, she explains her trip to Yeppoon.

Instead of being impressed by her initiative, and in her own time, the supervisor cruelly chastised her.

"Your actions went far beyond what you are authorised or qualified to do," he says, waving a finger at her. "Put together all you have, and I'll pass it on to someone else who has the proper qualifications."

"I know this girl," she protests. "Not her name...yet, but I will. I just need a little more time."

"You have another case to work on," he says, pointing to the new file on her desk. "Need I repeat myself? Put together all you have on this girl and get on with the new one. I'll be back in ten minutes to make sure it's done." He walks away from any further argument.

Kailee believes whoever takes over this case will not take the identity of this girl seriously. Her file will go into the pile of minor problems and, with a mountain of luck, dragged out in a couple of months and stamped identification unsuccessful. In the meantime, she'll be held in detention and forgotten. If she's found to have brain damage, what then? She ponders. Left to rot in some institution with no friends or relatives to care for her or the baby...if it lives? I can't allow that to happen.

Accepting she has no choice, she begins putting together all her findings for someone else. Immediately she realises that most of her findings are in her own dossier and it would take well over ten minutes to copy and transfer everything into the original file.

Accepting that going to Yeppoon could see her sacked, or even sent to prison, she decides everything she has gathered could, with luck, be useful to whoever takes over the case.

She uploads her full dossier to the department's portal.

During her lunch break, a despondent Kailee needs to get out of the building for some fresh air. She strolls down the neighbouring street and notices a sandwich board outside a cafe promoting their lunch specials. Normally she brings her own lunch of fruit and Greek yoghurt and eats at her desk. But the urge to break with tradition has her enter the cafe. Behind a glass display is a towering, untouched Black Forest cake. A slice with cream and a coffee might help to ease the pain of losing her case...and most likely her job.

From the first explosive mouthful of sweetness, her mind drifts back to the girl lying unconscious in a Yeppoon hospital

No other challenge to finding someone's identity has drawn her in as much. Try as she might, she can't dismiss the lingering suspicion that there's something far more mysterious surrounding this girl.

The last mouthful of cake is the sugar hit needed to boost her confidence. She opens her phone, goes to the contact details of Glasson BioMarine, Dili, and hits 'call'.

"Hello," comes a soft, sad female voice that surprises Kailee, expecting a receptionist to answer in the way receptionists do.

"Hello," replies Kailee. "Um, my name is Kailee Banks. I...um...first, I wish to offer my condolences on the death of Professor Glasson."

"Thank you," is a rather curt reply. "What media are you with?"

"Oh, no, I'm not with the media," she hurriedly dismisses any connection. "I'm with the Department of Immigration in Canberra and, I...sorry, who am I speaking to?"

There's a considered pause before answering. "My name is Mirla Yimenes." Then the tone of her voice changes to one of suspicion. "Department of Immigration? What are you calling about?"

Kailee recognises the suspicious tone and also a slight panic in her voice. Then, to her surprise, the voice calls out, "You have information for me?"

"I'm...I'm sorry, I'm not sure what you're asking," Kailee says, thinking the woman is still grieving. "Look, if it's not a good time, I can ring back later."

Kailee gets a hint of a sniff on the phone as if the woman is crying and is about to end the conversation when the woman comes back on the phone.

"I'm sorry. It has been a sad time for us here. I hope you understand?"

"Yes, I absolutely understand. Is it Miss or Mrs Yimenes?"

"You can call me Mirla...and you?"

"Oh, Miss," offers Kailee, far too quickly. "But please call me Kailee." She waits a moment but gets no reply. "Um, Mirla, this may sound an odd call, and please, I understand if you have too many other things on your mind, and all, but I'm calling hoping you may help me identify a man the professor may have known."

Another pause, and Kailee is certain something else is on the mind of Mirla Yimenes.

"If I can help, I will," comes the reply, and Kailee feels she was hoping for a more important call.

"I have your email address, and I can send you a photo of the man. He's in the background when the professor attended the launch of a salt farm in Kupang."

"Very well, send it and I'll reply by email. Is that all, Miss Banks?"

Aware she had intruded enough, Kailee says before ending the call, "I'll send it right away with the man circled. Please, I don't mean for you to reply straight away as I can only imagine what you're going through. I thank you for the time you have given me. Goodbye, and my condolences once again."

The only response is a click on the phone.

Kailee feels sick to her stomach at her careless intrusion at such a sensitive time and adds an apology in her email she sends containing the photo attachment.

***

Evelyn walks in as Mirla hangs up the phone. Seeing a confused look on her face, he asks, "What is it, Mirla? You okay?"

Mirla looks up at the big man and shrugs. "Oh, I'm sure it's nothing."

"Look, if the media is giving you a problem, just hang up on them," he suggests.

"No, it wasn't the media. It was a girl from the Department of Immigration in Canberra."

"Where? What did she want?" He asks, showing interest.

"Oh, she wants me to identify someone in a photo. She's emailing it now. I have no idea what it could be about."

A sound on her computer announces that an email has arrived. "Look, ignore it, Mirla. You look tired. Have a rest."

Mirla instinctively opens the new email. The text appears with Kailee's apology accompanied by the photo. Mirla chokes back a tear at the sight of the professor in the picture. Evelyn comes to her side and looks at the screen.

"That scumbag!" Evelyn snaps at the sight of the man circled in the background.

"You know him?" asks Mirla with little interest.

"I think his name is Afif. One of Djan Muhammad Aswar's bodyguards. An all-around nasty piece of work."

CHAPTER 28

C onrad is in a meeting with representatives of the mining and associated industries when he's passed a message that the Indonesian Minister for Resources is on the phone.

Presuming it may have relevance to the meeting, he excused himself and returns to his office.

Settling back into his leather executive chair, he presses the flashing button with the caller on speaker.

"Hello, Minister," says Conrad in his official voice.

"Minister Glasson, I hope your secretary did not misinform you I was the Minister."

Conrad instantly recognises the raspy voice of Aswar and quickly shuts off the speaker then places the handset firmly against his ear, surprised, as Aswar never calls him at his government office.

"Though I am calling on behalf of the Minister," Aswar continues, satisfied he has put Conrad on edge. "He offers his condolences on the death of your father, and will of course, represent our government in attending a memorial service when it is arranged."

Conrad is never at ease when in contact with Aswar and wonders why this message of condolence could not wait. He stiffens, expecting more.

Aswar continues. "I know it is premature, and no date has yet been set, but as I will be responsible for the Minister's security, I'm in Sydney at the moment and about to catch a plane to Canberra to assess security needs."

Conrad wonders why he's telling him this, having nothing to do with security in these matters.

Before he can comment, Aswar continues. "Can we meet at the airport? I wish to talk to you about a matter that I'm sure will benefit us both to a great degree."

Conrad looks around his office to make sure the door is closed. In past communications, Aswar has used the same words, 'will benefit us both to a great degree' — but never while he is in Parliament.

Of course he has benefitted from Aswar's advice, offers and inside information. Mostly financially, and always behind his government's back. Could this be another serious offer he can't afford to ignore?

"I'm in the middle of a meeting and need to be in the chamber for question time. Can it wait till later in the day, sir?" suggests Conrad, noting the time.

"No, it can't," comes the blunt answer.

"I see. It..." Conrad is about to question that it better be worthwhile but decides against it, picturing the face on the other end of the phone. "It's a quarter-to-ten now. I'll meet you in the Qantas lounge as early as I can."

He waits for a response, but Aswar has hung up.

Conrad would prefer to meet this man far away from prying eyes, but as there is little time, he orders his secretary to change his schedule and book a private meeting room at the Qantas Lounge then returns to the conference room where he raises matters that need greater detail before any further discussion. The meeting is adjourned.

Arriving at Canberra Airport, he orders his driver to wait at the VIP parking entrance to take him back to Parliament as soon as his meeting finished. The sooner the better, as he dreads being face-to-face with Djan Muhammad Aswar. What has he got for me this time? Conrad wonders. Nothing comes to mind that could be so urgent...and urgency and Aswar is not a mix Conrad wants to contemplate.

The arrivals board shows that the flight from Sydney is yet to land but is on time. Conrad was eager to get to the airport earlier to check out who might be in the business lounge and to inform the girl at the desk to send Aswar to the reserved meeting room as soon as he arrives. To be seen talking to Aswar by the press, or anyone else, in fact, is not a good idea. At least other ministers are back at the

House fulfilling their obligations, so they are of no concern. Despite an almost empty business lounge, Conrad remained apprehensive.

The board announces the flight from Sydney had landed. Aswar will be in first class, so first off, if he's returning to Sydney, he'll have no luggage to hold him up. Conrad readies himself in the small meeting room.

It's a brief wait.

Aswar enters the lounge, shows his ticket to the girl at the desk who directs him with a perfect smile to the meeting room.

"Mr Aswar," Conrad welcomes him with an outstretched hand. Aswar grabs it, then lets it go without a shake and sits. Before Conrad can resume his seat, Aswar thumbs towards the girl at reception. "Get her to bring me a whiskey, no ice," he demands.

"I don't think it's her role. I'll get it from the bar," Conrad says, rising from his chair.

"Her! She gets it!" he insists.

Conrad knows not to cross Aswar when he says something so forceful. He nods and walks to the receptionist. The girl looks back at Aswar after hearing the instructions. Before she can refuse, Conrad gives her the 'government VIP about to sign a huge contract' line. For the first time, she regrets her customer is always right commitment and agrees.

Conrad returns to the meeting room, unsure whether to start a conversation or wait until the drink arrives. Aswar decides for him.

"While a sad time for you and your sister, I'm sure you both will do well out of the inheritance," he says to a surprised Conrad.

"Um...well, I haven't thought about it," Conrad flusters.

"Well, you should!" says Aswar, as if berating a small child.

The receptionist arrives with the drink, and as she places it on the table in front of Aswar, he grabs her hand before she can return to her desk.

"Come back to Sydney with me. I fuck you good."

The shock on the girl's face mirrors the look on Conrad's. If it was only red before, it's now scarlet.

With a boisterous laugh, Aswar slaps her on the behind. "I make joke, ha."

Both the girl and Conrad are positive it was no joke. As soon as Aswar releases her hand, she retreats. Not back to her desk, but to the bathroom for some soap and water.

"She make good fuck. You should fuck her," he suggests. "I...I'm married," Conrad mutters, still in shock.

"Yes. One wife only, no?"

"Yes, only one," Conrad tries to make a joke of it, aware Aswar has several.

"I had three...now only two." Aswar's face turns sour, and he leans forward. "I want you to help me find my third wife. In return, I'll do you a favour that will secure your inheritance."

This has Conrad totally rattled. Is this it? No dealings with the government? No insider knowledge to take back as ammunition to his department? And why is he talking about inheritance? Is he aware of the Will and codicil? Impossible! How could he?

"Sorry, Aswar, but I'm confused."

"Yes, of course you are." He takes a sip of his whiskey and leans closer to Conrad. "Your father, the late Professor Glasson, kidnapped my wife. Does that make it easier for you?"

The gaping mouth of Conrad is the answer.

"No? Well, let me lay out what the situation is. Your father is dead. My wife is somewhere in Australia, and I want to find her. You are in contact with the authorities and the resources to do just that. I'm sure she came into the country with a false passport, so get your immigration people on to it. After all, she is here illegally, yes?"

"What...what do you mean my father kidnapped your wife? Why? That's impossible!"

Aswar slams his broad fist on the table. "I tell you. He took my wife and I want her back, or I want her dead!"

The words rebound around the room, and Conrad hopes they didn't reach beyond the meeting room.

"Aswar, please. Watch what you say."

"I know what I say. I mean what I say." A slight, ugly smile cracks his veneer. "Don't worry. I not asking you to kill her. I want you to find her, that's all."

"Sir, I can't be a part of any killing...murder...you're talking about murder!"

"Yes, you can, Mr Glasson MP, yes, you can. You see, I have information I'm sure will change your mind about killing."

"I don't want to hear any more about this. It's impossible. I can't help you, sorry."

"You can, and you will," threatens Aswar. "You see, like an eye for an eye, you help me remove one problem, and in return, I remove another."

"I...I don't know what you're talking about," stutters a nervous Conrad, feeling he's been called on to repay all the debts racked up over the years.

"I often wondered if it wasn't just me who knew the secret."

"What secret? Sir, I don't understand what you're talking about or asking me to do."

"I'm not asking you to do anything other than to find an illegal entrant into your country, that's all. You have to enforce the law, don't you?"

"Yes, but you said. What was it? You said, in return, you will remove another. What do you mean by that?"

Aswar is enjoying watching sweat bead on Conrad's brow. But the time has come to hit Conrad with some home truths.

"Who is Jude Yimenes?" Aswar asks, checking for any sign of awareness in Conrad's eyes.

"Who?" Conrad asks, trying to shut out his father's lawyer's voice in his head.

"Mirla and Jude Yimenes in Dili, East Timor."

"Mirla? Yes, she works for my father in the Dili office."

"Correct. And Jude Yimenes?"

The conditions of the Will flood Conrad's mind. He shakes his head and gives a slight shrug of his shoulders. "Husband or son, I presume."

"Son is correct," says Aswar, as if he's a judge in a TV quiz show. "The son of Mirla and..." He leans forward to whisper. "And one Professor Marcus Glasson."

Conrad had leaned closer to hear the whisper, then recoils at the words with a shaking head.

"I'm sure in your father's Will he leaves rather a large sum to Mirla and Jude Yimenes. You have seen the Will, have you not?" Conrad is having trouble coming to grips with this news and ignores the question.

"Yes, I'm sure it has come as a shock to you, as it will to your sister."

The thought of how Harper would take such news sent a ripple down Conrad's spine.

"Now, you see, by helping me find and remove one problem, you are helping me remove your problem...and all you have to do is what you should do as a law-abiding member of parliament. Locate my Noi!"

The word slams like a loose cannonball inside Conrad's head. Noi! Noi! The codicil Noi!

Pushing aside the shock of hearing about a secret son of his father brings the text of the codicil to mind. Sure, he can use his power to put the search for Aswar's wife on the high-priority list. With all the security he could muster, it would not take long to find her. He could cover up any further involvement by saying he had a tip-off from an anonymous caller. The authorities would have Aswar's wives on record with photos. It could be over in a matter of days. Yes, he sees a benefit in agreeing. In fact, millions of dollars benefit if it removes one beneficiary. He's about to agree to Aswar's proposal but stops with mouth half open. No! No! The codicil! The bloody codicil states that if this woman, Noi, dies in suspicious circumstances, all the money will go to charities.

He looks at Aswar who's waiting for him to agree. No way will Aswar get rid of his wife any other way than through suspicious circumstances. He wants her dead, and while he will not do it himself, the way she dies will not matter. It will be cold-blooded murder by gun or knife — not by natural causes.

"Why kill her?" Conrad ventures to ask. "I can have her handed over to you. You need not have her killed."

"She knows too much, and, as I no longer have her under my control, I can't risk her talking...and neither can you!"

"What? What do you mean by that?" Conrad asks, feeling oncoming heat.

"We have helped each other over some years, right?" Conrad gives an uncertain nod. "Done things I'm sure you wish kept secret, right?" Conrad does not nod, despite knowing it to be true. "Therefore, it will be best for both of us if she remains silent!"

After a nervous pause, Conrad had no choice but to nod. He wonders if he should tell Aswar about the codicil? Would he understand and not have her brutally murdered? Hardly! But there may be a way, and he needs time to think.

Conrad looks at his watch. "I need to get back to the House. I'll talk to the right people, and I'm sure it will not take long to find her." He stands. "I may see you at the state service, but apart from that, I want to hear nothing of what happens, you understand?"

Aswar also stands and offers his hand. "Of course. And again, my deepest sympathy on your loss."

Conrad does not miss the double meaning.

CHAPTER 29

Conrad has much to think about as he's driven back to Parliament House. Ever fearful of Aswar and well aware of how brutal he can be, whatever he does, there is a need to have a backup plan to protect himself and his inheritance. There's also the unpalatable matter of what to tell his sister. There's no way he can hide knowledge of the secret son of their father, but how much else should she be told. Conrad feels squeezed between two ferocious personalities.

He has only minutes to make one call before the bells ring summoning members to the chamber for question time.

"Harper, hi," he begins, unsure how to continue. "Listen, um, I've just learnt something you should know." He listens to her reminding him of civility and to ask how she was. "Yeah, but I can't tell you over the phone. Can you get to Canberra later today and meet me around six?"

"Sounds intriguing," she replies suspiciously. She knows her brother can overdo the dramatics and often what he has to tell her could be scribbled on a bar coaster and passed around the bar to get to her. "Do I have to come there? Can't you tell me now or send me an email?"

"What I have to tell you affects our inheritance."

There is silence on the other end of the line, and Conrad knows he has her full attention.

"Where will I meet you?" she asks in a more serious tone.

"Someplace open and away from the polly dives. Meet me at the Canberra Centre food court."

"Is everything okay?" she asks with a slight stammer. "It sounds serious."

"It is. I'll meet you there at six. The bells are ringing, bye." There is no time to hear her reply.

As Conrad approaches the lower house chamber, he spots the Minister for Immigration ahead and rushes up to him before they take their seats.

"Gerard," he says, grabbing his arm. "I need to speak to you about an immigration matter. Can we talk in the chamber?"

Gerard Kirkland is a twelve-year veteran of the party. He came up through the ranks as a hard-nosed public servant with the Immigration Department, eventually becoming the Minister. A dedicated and intense operator who harbours a suspicion of everyone. His motto is: they're illegal immigrants until proven otherwise.

"You stole my thunder, Conrad; I want to talk to you also."

"Oh, why?" asks a stunned Conrad.

"Once questions are over, I'll meet you over coffee."

Conrad nods and takes his seat with a stampede of thoughts rampaging around in his head. Why does he want to see me before I see him? Has Aswar been in contact with him? If so, can I risk being linked to what he knows?

Conrad's mind is not on the questions, arguments and banter from the backbenchers until Gerard stands to answer a question from the opposition.

The matter brought up is regarding illegal immigrants. Conrad looks to Gerard, fearing being dragged into a discussion surrounding this girl, Noi. But with overwhelming relief, the debate is focussed on those arriving illegally by boat. Twice the minister is ordered to take his seat while the Speaker decides on points of order. Conrad feels this could drag on for most of question time and prepares himself for when they'll meet after.

***

"Sorry, Conrad," says Gerard as the two sit down in the parliament canteen. "Bloody Greens and their sympathising compassion! No place for it when it comes to immigration. No papers, no visa, no passport, no entry I say."

Conrad takes advantage of the opening. "That's what I want to talk to you about, Gerard. An unknown source passed me information about an illegal."

"Same here," replies Gerard.

"Sorry, what do you mean, same here?" asks Conrad.

"I rarely look at every file of unknowns who come into this country, but one was brought to my attention as it referenced you."

Conrads face tightens. "Me? How come?"

"Oh, don't worry, I'm sure it's nothing to do with you. We have an overenthusiastic junior researcher who's employed to identify a person's origin. Apparently she's good, but that's beside the point. Anyway, she had a case of a girl in a hospital up north in Yeppoon. She's in a coma, no-one can identify her and no-one has come forward asking about a missing person who fits her description. Our overzealous research girl took it upon herself to go there and see the girl in the flesh and heard two men from Indonesia mention your father — oh, sorry about the news, tragic, right?"

"Yes, thanks, um, two men?"

"Oh, I'm sure there's nothing to it, as your father dealt with the Indonesians. But this researcher also heard the men asking if any Asian girl had been to see him before he died."

Conrad's mind is spinning with what Aswar told him. Could this girl in a coma be his wife?

"We checked all the reports surrounding your father's collapse and later death. I'm sure you're aware of the police and ambulance reports. Well, there's nothing to suggest this girl had any connection with him. There was no sign of a second person in the boat your father came to Yeppoon on...not a thing. Nice little spot Yeppoon, have you ever been there?"

"Um, no..." Conrad's voice trails off as he considers the possibility that he's found the girl. Then Gerard's voice becomes audible again. "What? Sorry, what did you say?" Conrad asks returning his focus.

"I was asking what it was you wanted to talk to me about. Are you okay? You look flushed."

"Yes, fine, a bit of hay fever. Um, yes, I wanted to tell you, some-one...someone unknown, you understand...well, they think a young man...um...African...is here without the proper visa." The urge to end this conversation and follow up on what Gerard has revealed to him is overwhelming. "Look, I shouldn't bother you with it; it's just I saw you as we entered the chamber and, well, you know, save me some legwork, I thought I'd just mention it."

"No, no, you did the right thing. African you say? Any idea which part?"

"Um, not sure. Sudan, they think."

"Quite possibly. Any description? Anything we can use?"

"No, my impression is he looks similar to most from there."

"Yes, it can be damn confusing. Was a place mentioned?"

"Sydney, Blacktown area, I think they said."

"That makes it harder. Bloody easy to get lost there. Anyway, I'll pass it on, you never know."

"Yes, well, I must get back," Conrad says, standing. "Oh, and thanks for telling me about my name popping up. I'm sure you're right; my father had close connections with Indonesia, as I do."

Meanwhile, in the bowels of the Immigration department, Kailee is sitting at her desk, unsure if it is to be her last day working there. She has a case to work on while those higher up decide her future. She does not focus on the person of interest in the file, and an email arriving on her phone stimulates her interest elsewhere. As it's nearing the end of the working day, she waits until she's out of the building and walking back to her apartment before reading the reply to the email she sent to Glasson Marine BioMed in Dili.

Dear Miss Banks,

This may sound strange, but in response to your email asking if I know the identity of the man circled in your photo, I ask why you show so much concern at his identity?

Yes, I know who this man is, but other matters surrounding him make it essential that we talk to you in person. I'm sending someone to meet with you. His name is Evelyn Sunday. I see you are in Canberra, and that is where he will be tomorrow if you nominate a place.

Can I trust you to keep this email and any arrangements to yourself? Mr Sunday will explain all.

This a matter of urgency. If you tell anyone else, you could find yourself involved in an international embarrassment.

I hope I can trust you

Mirla Yimenes

Kailee is excited at the chance she may have uncovered something big, but concerned at what this means now she has passed on all she knows to her superior.

But her determination to prove herself wins out. She is about to reply with a place and time, then stops. With no idea what Evelyn Sunday looks like, she'll send a photo of herself so he'll know who to look for. She rushes back to her place to take a snap using her computer camera.

She rejects the first photo and takes another without her glasses, then another smiling. Unhappy with all, she concedes she is a geeky-looking girl and that this matter does not need her ego to get in the way. She attaches the first photo of her wearing glasses to the reply email with a place and time to meet.

CHAPTER 30

C ommuters and shoppers at the end of their working day fill the Canberra Centre with a scene of hustle and bustle. Some are rushing to get home with their purchases, while others are meeting for catch-up drinks. Teenagers are parading around and failing to act adult while others are crowding the food court before home or a movie in the cinema.

Harper Glasson is uncomfortable in such ungodly urban surroundings and asks Conrad, "Why here? Let's go to a bar and have a glass of wine and something decent to eat. The bloody smell of doughnuts and fried food is making me sick."

Conrad has no problem with the place, as he brings his two children here often when they're in Canberra. Even when the House is sitting, he sometimes buys food to take away. That's to argue about another day.

"You know what Canberra is like; eyes, ears, and the whiff of intrigue is everywhere. The place leaks like a sieve...as you well know, being a recipient...but it's reasonably safe to talk here," he offers as a reason.

"So you need to tell me this world-shattering news among cretins. Not much difference to those in government, I'd say."

Conrad ignores her snide remark as he's well used to them. "This girl Noi mentioned in the codicil. I've found her."

Harper stops fiddling with the packet of cigarettes in her pocket and the craving to have one.

"You? How? Where?" she says, leaning across the plastic table now that secrecy has suddenly become important.

119

"I've other news, and please control yourself when I tell you." He knows she'll explode as she often does with bad news.

"Fuck the people," she calls out, making sure they all heard. Then, leaning closer and in a whisper, asks, "What?"

Conrad looks her in the eye. "Our father fathered a son."

Harper stares at him blankly, shakes her head and says, "Yeh, I know I'm sitting opposite the prick."

"A-n-o-t-h-e-r son," Conrad spells it out.

Harper freezes as it sinks in. "You're kidding, right? How come I never found out?"

"We!" Conrad corrects her. "The Will, right? Not the codicil, but the Will. The mention of the Dili office and those employed there and the huge amount he's leaving them?"

Harper's mind is racing. "Mirla and Jude Yimenes, right?" She asks, remembering their names.

Conrad nods.

"Our dirty old bastard father was fucking a chink up north and turned out a bastard son. Is that what you're telling me?"

Conrad nods again.

"How old is this bastard son...shit...bastard half-brother!"

"Around thirty, I think."

"What? The fucking prick kept a bastard son secret for that long! How the fuck did you find out?"

Conrad has given up trying to keep her language under control. "I can't tell you," he mumbled, knowing what's coming.

But Harper remains silent — evil-eyed silent.

After a moment, she asks, "The girl in the codicil, is she another bastard kid?"

"I don't know."

"Shit!" Harper is struggling to control her anger and enable thought. "Suddenly a two-kid family has grown to four. Shit, we'd be lucky to get anything from the dirty bastard's estate."

Pointing a rigid finger at the table, thinking about tapping it, but the thought of what has been dropped or dribbled on it stops her. "We need to do something, Conrad, or all we'll get will be the bloody bare bones!"

Conrad holds up his hands to calm her. The urge to tell her the full story of his meeting with Aswar, and the added threat to any inheritance if Aswar got his way of dealing with the problem, even in this crowded and noisy place, talking about murder is not wise.

"So, where is this bloody girl, Noi, then?" Harper says with menace in her voice.

"Look, you know what the codicil said. Anything happens to her and we lose the lot."

Harper stares into her brother's eyes, and her talent for picking up lies and cover-ups ignites her suspicions. "What is it, Conrad? What are you not telling me?"

He shakes his head. "I can't...not now."

"Shit, you're a weak prick, Conrad. Okay, I can do my own digging. This bastard Jude and his whore mother will be easy. This latest news has just added another chapter."

"Hang on, Harper. I don't want you rushing off half-cocked. Think, for Christ's sake. If we stir things up, they'll take legal action, and it could hold the estate up for years. Look, we have time. The coroner has yet to decide on a cause of death. There may be something in why it's taking so long we can use. We'll sit down then and work something out."

Harper sees reason in what her brother is saying, but her instinct tells her there's more.

"This girl, Noi? You know where she is, right?"

Conrad's silence lets him down. "Look, Immigration is on her case. That's all I can tell you. If she's found to be illegal, then we may have a case against the codicil."

"So she's in Australia then?" says a smug Harper.

Conrad slumps his head at his stupidity. "Leave it, Harper. Give me an ounce of credit. I know the workings of government. I can mould them to get the result I want. Give me that much at least."

Harper knows all too well how her brother moulds. She finds it hard to, but in the end agrees. "Okay, but now I need to get out of here and get that drink."

CHAPTER 31

In the sombre atmosphere of the Dili office, Mirla is bringing Evelyn Sunday up-to-date before he catches the late afternoon flight to Darwin, then on to Canberra. His eagerness to help made it easy for Mirla to ask him to meet this researcher girl.

"She's from the Immigration Department, and I sense there's more to it than Aswar's bodyguard." Then adds with a frown. "It's now more than ever critical that we find Noi and keep her safe."

"Who?" Jude calls out, entering the office. "What girl? What about immigration? If she has anything to do with Noi, I need to know. Shit! The more people looking for her, the greater the chance of Aswar finding out."

"You're right, mate," agrees Evelyn. "That creep has feelers out everywhere."

"Evelyn's seeing her tomorrow," informs Mirla.

"I'm going with you, Ev," insists Jude.

"Jude, I need you here," Mirla says, knowing it was a waste of words.

"Where are you meeting her?"

"Canberra," replies Evelyn, then to Mirla adds, "Best if Jude comes with me, Mirla. I know this guy, Afif, but not much about Noi. Jude could read into what this girl says and pick up clues."

Mirla looks in need of more convincing, but the stubborn faces looking at her are enough.

"You better hurry and pack," concedes Mirla.

***

Most of the books Kailee Banks has read over the years have been textbooks: medical, psychological, and philosophical, with some historical books thrown in. But for a while spy thrillers occupied her imaginative mind.

Sitting, watching and waiting at an outside table of a café in the heart of Canberra, the characters in those novels come alive and surround her. The sun is shining, but wearing sunglasses she considered too clandestine, so in keeping with the photo she'd sent, her everyday glasses are more appropriate.

Punctuality is a big thing with Kailee, and as it approaches one minute to when this man Evelyn Sunday is due to appear, she's pre-judging him. He's not eager enough to arrive early, or he's a disorganised person with little respect for formality.

The waitress interrupts her character assessment to remove the second empty cup of tea and asks if she would like another. Before she answers, a deep, accented voice comes from behind.

"Get me a VB, thanks, luv," comes the throaty order.

In a flash, Evelyn Sunday is sitting opposite a startled Kailee. "You want one? Or maybe...let me see." He looks over the spectacled, geeky girl before him. "Bitters, lime and soda, yes?"

Kailee hates being judged. She does that enough to herself, but judged correctly, proves she's utterly predictable.

"Thought so," Evelyn says with a nod to the waitress to fill the order.

"Make that two VBs, thanks," comes another voice behind the head-spinning Kailee.

She now feels ambushed as Jude sits beside her.

"I'm Evelyn Sunday, he's Jude Yimenes. And you are Kailee Banks, I reckon," says Evelyn, thrusting his large hand across the table. The letters I-R-O-N prominently tattooed on each finger.

The rapid transition from a calm, daydreaming wait in the sun to an occupied table has Kailee struggling to come up to speed. Her gaze turns from Jude to Evelyn's hand, thirsting for attention. The man is a bear ready to crush her delicate hand...instant dislike! The audacity to presume he knows her favourite drink is bitters, lime and soda, and the size of the man is so intimidating.

"He looks ugly, but he won't bite," offers Jude.

She shrinks back in her chair and wearily reaches out to shake Evelyn's hand, expecting never to have use of her fingers again. To her surprise, the grasp was firm yet well controlled to stop her delicate fingers becoming one.

"Hello," she says meekly. Shattered is the aura and glamour of being in a spy novel. What was she thinking? Already she is well out of her depth. How can she deal with a tattooed giant with a shaved head and a stubbled face?

Seeing her discomfort, Evelyn smiles, showing a hint of a gold tooth. "Don't let my good looks scare you, luv. I'm as gentle as a girl when I want to be. That's why they named me Evelyn."

Kailee takes back her survived hand and attempts a smile. "Yes," is all she can say, then angry at herself for saying such a dumb thing.

Next comes a normal hand, and the glamour of a spy novel returns. Tanned and muscular, yet finely boned. Her shyness keeps her eyes lowered as she takes Jude's hand and feels a surge of dark-alley-in-Paris intrigue. She knows what he looks like and likes what she sees so much that she's afraid to cast her eyes over him again. The need to retrieve his hand breaks the spell, and the waitress breaks the impasse with their drinks.

Evelyn ignores the glass and takes a long drink from the stubby, lets out a burp and places the bottle back on the table.

"Bloody law here is hard on a man that never has a cigar out of his mouth. But, for the sake of not embarrassing you, I'll control myself."

A cigar too! Kailee adds to the profile.

"Have a drink and loosen that tongue, Kailee. I promise not to bite."

She does what she's told, and the cold drink eases her tense insides.

"And while you relax, I'll start, okay?"

With the straw still in her mouth, she nods, yet wondering why she's meeting with two and not one as arranged.

"Good. Now, why do you want the name of the man you circled in the photo?"

The reason she is where she is comes back to her. Her work and the driving need to name a mystery girl give her a sense of importance to these now two people.

"He may help me identify someone."

"Someone?" asks Jude, already fishing for the right answer.

"A girl," she says with a slight glance into the handsome face of Jude.

That is the answer he wanted. "And this 'girl', tell me about her and why can't she tell you herself."

"She can't," is all Kailee will say at this point.

"Can't or won't?" Jude asks to keep up the pressure.

"Can't. But that man in the photo is why you're here, isn't it, not the girl?" she asks, eyeing both men.

Evelyn is not a patient man and gets to the point. "Yes, I know who that man is, and now you've mentioned the girl, I think we know who she is."

"You do? Great! I mean how? I mean..." She tries to control her excitement and not be so girlish.

Evelyn stumps the 'N' finger at the table. "I want you to tell us all you know, where the girl is, then go back to your job and forget everything." Subtlety is not his strong point.

Kailee takes another suck of the straw, and a surge of energy washes over her. This is her case. She was the one who put the pieces together in her own time and with her own money, and she is not about to walk away from what she believes could be her only big chance of proving herself. She places her glass down on the table, straightens up, suppresses the quiver in her stomach, and says, "No!"

Evelyn retrieves his cigar from his shirt pocket, and without lighting it, rolls it from one side of his mouth to the other without breaking eye contact with her and waits for a more acceptable answer.

"You have no right to do that. Just walk up and take away the case I've devoted so much to, then tell me to walk away and forget it! No, I won't."

She looks to Jude for understanding, but he remains silent. Then something comes to mind. Jude Yimenes? The email she sent to Dili was to Mirla Yimenes.

Evelyn stops chewing and grins with an intense sparkle from his gold tooth.

"I understand...um...Kailee. I'd say the same thing if I were in your position." Kailee finds that impossible. "I appreciate you want the rewards...I understand that. But are you sure you know what you've got yourself into?"

The thought had crossed her mind. As soon as she found a link between the girl, the professor and his son the politician, she was stepping onto thin ice. But if it means identifying the girl, she's willing to take that risk.

"I can handle whatever, but I need to follow this case through to establish the girl's identity...that's my job!"

"Okay," Jude interrupted. "So, what if I tell you the girl's name, will you walk away then?"

Jude's looks continue to mesmerise Kailee, adding confusion to the issue.

"I need you to promise you'll walk away and forget the whole thing. Will you?" insists Jude.

Kailee is so desperate to know the girl's name and confirm her belief she is East Timorese, she's on the verge of giving in to his request. But, as her mind clears, she believes there's more to this girl than getting involved in some petty political squabble.

The surge of adrenaline is something Kailee has rarely experienced, and she challenges both men. "You want to know where she is, and I want to know her name and where she came from, so I reckon we have, what is it they say, we are in a stalemate, would you agree?"

Evelyn leans back into his chair, rolls the cigar around in his mouth while scratching his stubbled face and giving Jude a questioning look. Jude looks back at Kailee. She feels his eyes examining all of her, and without looking, tries to remember what she's wearing. Whatever, it's not what she would have chosen if she knew who she was to meet.

Jude looks back at Evelyn with an almost hidden nod.

"Seems you have us by the balls there, girly," Evelyn says through gritted teeth.

Kailee hates being called girly like her father always did, and it adds more fuel to the fire building in her belly.

"What will you do with her if you see her?" she asks, thinking she has control of the conversation now.

Evelyn takes the cigar out of his mouth, looks around for an ashtray to tap ash from an unlit cigar, and leaves Jude to answer.

"Save her," he says.

Kailee looks from Evelyn to Jude. "Save her? From what?"

Jude pauses, judging whether she is ready for the answer. "Being killed," he replies.

The words echoed in Kailee's head.

"And," Evelyn adds. "If you get in the way, you're in danger of the same."

Kailee grabs at her drink and slurps a mouthful.

"Are you prepared to put your life on the line for this girl?" Evelyn continues without easing up his colourful explanation of the situation.

"Look, Kailee," Jude breaks in to soften Evelyn's directness. "Save yourself the grief. Tell us where the girl is. I'll reward you for the work you've done, and if, after she's safe, we'll credit you with her safety. I give you my word."

"Killed?" Kailee lets out the word that has not left her head.

"Killed!" confirms Evelyn.

"That man I asked about, is...is he..." Her words trailed off.

Jude can see Evelyn is losing patience. "Look," he says. "We need to come to some agreement before we can say any more. Will you tell us what you know and walk away or not?"

Kailee knows what her answer will be, but something else weighs on her decision...she wants to see more of Jude.

"No, I'll not walk away." And before either can argue, she adds, "I will not tell you where she is until you tell me who this man is and why she would be in danger. And even then," she pauses, wondering if she is about to say the right thing. "Even then I will not tell you where she is, but I will take you to her." Then, as an afterthought, adds, "But only if you pay for the flight."

Jude and Evelyn review their options. Evelyn could threaten her with violence to tell him. Jude could say forget it and walk away, leaving Kailee with the girl still a mystery. Or, they can accept her proposal, go with her to the girl. Once they know where she is and confirm it is Noi, it would be easy to separate the two and take Noi to safety. Kailee would be out of danger, and the case is out of her hands.

"You're a hard negotiator, Kailee Banks," Jude admits. "You win. Let's go."

"Go? Now? Right now?"

"Unless you have something more important to do."

This was so unexpected. "But...but we need to fly there! And my work, I can't just..."

"Sure you can," Jude interrupts. "This is your work, isn't it?" This is all so sudden, but all too important not to take up the opportunity.

"We need to fly to Rockhampton first." She replies, her mind in a spin.

Within fifteen minutes, calls are made, the bill is paid, and they're waving down a taxi to the airport.

CHAPTER 32

ailee sensed the two sitting on each side of her were hiding
K something the moment the plane took off from Canberra.
Both have gone quiet, not that she expected any conversation
regarding what they were planning to do. Especially in a plane
filled with government people and public servants.

Kailee has her glasses off and lowers her head, confident no
one would recognise her — in the unlikely event anyone would.
After a short stopover in Brisbane, the three settle in for the
flight to Rockhampton. The mood of the three has not changed.
Evelyn hates being without a cigar in his mouth. Jude appears
distant with multiple problems on his mind. Kailee is in a state
of mixed emotions: excitement, confusion, and fear.

"So, what is it you actually do?" asks Jude, surprising Kailee.
"You know, in the Immigration Department?"

Kailee feels her pulse quicken that someone so handsome
could be interested in her beyond what she knows of this girl.

"I decide where people come from," she replies coyly.

"Fascinating," says Jude, and as a test, adds, "And where do you
think Evelyn's from?"

His accent left no doubt in Kailee's mind. "The Deep South
United States, possibly Louisiana, as you have the slightest hint
of French in your accent."

Jude looks to Evelyn for his reaction, who responds with a
confirming nod and comment. "Too easy, girly. The accent and
my good looks gave me away, right?"

"And me?" asks Jude.

Kailee hoped he wouldn't ask. Now she must stare into his eyes and try not to betray her thoughts. But he has set the challenge, and after a moment to study his face, she stifles the word 'heaven' and instead offers her opinion.

"You're an interesting mix, I have to say. Portuguese Timor for sure, with something more difficult to pinpoint. English, or even Australian, would be my guess. There is a difference, you know?"

Jude smiles back, but her answer is far too close to his secret, and he wishes he hadn't asked. He takes the inflight magazine from the pocket of the seat in front and flips through it.

Kailee looks around to Evelyn, who has his eyes closed, feigning sleep. She takes the hint and tries to relax until they arrive in Rockhampton.

The jolt of the wheels banging onto the tarmac awakens Kailee. Surprising her that she had actually fallen asleep. The other two are wide awake, and she wonders if they were pretending to be asleep so as not to give anything away.

As soon as the three enter the terminal, Jude asks, "Where to from here?"

"You'll need a hire car," answers Kailee, expecting ramped-up pressure to tell more.

Without hesitation, Jude goes to the car hire desk, leaving Kailee alone as Evelyn also leaves her to walk around the terminal. She watches as he stops at the exit doors, pauses for what seems like a couple of minutes before returning to Kailee's side.

"Is anything wrong?" Kailee asks, sensing he's unease as he rolls his unlit cigar around his mouth.

"Not a thing, girly...not a thing."

Kailee senses that's not the case and looks around the terminal to see what may have spooked him. Passengers who arrived on their plane have left or are about to leave. Apart from some staff manning counters, and with no plane to depart for some time, the place is relatively empty.

"Okay, Kailee," says Jude, startling her. "It's time to tell us where she is."

"Once we're on the road, I'll direct you," she says, not ready to give in yet.

"Let's go," snaps Evelyn, overly eager to get moving.

***

Fauzi and Afif have been keeping an eye on the airport for the past two days under orders from Aswar. Afif has fallen asleep in their car parked in the car park with an uninterrupted view of the terminal entrance. Fauzi nudges him awake and nods towards the terminal. He holds several photos in his hands and flips through them. Fauzi shows Afif a picture of Jude Yimenes for confirmation. He gets a nod back.

"You know the other two?" Fauzi asks.

Afif peers through the windscreen. "The big guy runs a bar in Dili. The girl I don't know." Then, after a second thought. "That girl? I've seen her someplace." He searches his memory. "The hospital in Yeppoon! She kept looking at us."

Without a word, they wait for the hire car carrying Jude, Evelyn and Kailee to pass on its way to the carpark exit. Afif expects Fauzi to follow, but he doesn't.

"Why you not follow?" he asks.

"I know where they're going," he replies, unfazed.

As soon as Jude drives out of the carpark, Evelyn, sitting in the front passenger seat, manoeuvres the side mirror to see a white Hyundai Elantra pull out of a parking spot.

Many things are going through Kailee's mind now that they are on their way to Yeppoon. She's positive that once they know where the girl is, they'll ditch her and take the girl without revealing her name. That they got her a return plane ticket and not for themselves confirmed it.

Then there's Evelyn and whatever keeps him checking the side mirror. She turns to look out the rear window and sees nothing.

Meanwhile, as soon as Fauzi sees Jude turn left into North Street, he breaks the stern look on his face with a half smile and turns right. He'll take an alternative route that crosses the Fitzroy River via another bridge, confident they'll get to Yeppoon first.

CHAPTER 33

The carpark facing the entrance to the small but serviceable regional hospital at Yeppoon is equally compact and serviceable. While Jude drives around searching for an empty parking spot, Evelyn is spinning his head around checking out all the cars that are not empty.

Kailee has led them this far and knows it's now crunch time. She directed them to where the girl is, and they should have no trouble finding her. As per the agreement, she's about to ask for the girl's name, and to at least confirm she's East Timorese, when Evelyn calls for Jude to stop the car.

"What is it?" Jude asks, sensing something's wrong.

"Get out of the car and take Kailee with you. I'll park it."

"What is it, Ev?" asks Jude, looking around the car park.

"Just do it, Jude! Find the girl, and I'll wait in the car. Aswar's heavies were at the airport, and somehow they've beaten us here. Now hurry and be careful."

Kailee is not sure what to do. The smell of danger is foreign to her. She's confused, and Jude has to wrench her out of the car and lead her to the hospital entrance. Through the glass doors, he sees two elderly people seated and a mother and child talking to the woman behind the counter. With no one else in sight, he tightens his grip on Kailee's hand and whispers to her, "Let's not announce our visit or who we're visiting, hey? Do you remember the ward you saw her in?"

Kailee is now convinced more than ever that she's got herself involved in something illegal, or dangerous, or both.

"Kailee?" snaps Jude. "Do you remember?"

Something clicks inside her. She takes a deep breath as an unusual calm surfaces. "No further until you tell me the girl's name and where she came from."

Jude can't believe she's asking right at this moment, but has no time to waste arguing. "If it is who I hope it is, her name is Noi de Jesus. She was born on Atauro Island, to the north of Timor-Leste. There, now do you remember what ward?"

Kailee stays behind Jude, shielded from the lady at the desk as they pass. The receptionist looks from the mother and child and assumes they're visiting a patient and know where to go.

Knowing now who this girl is and from where, Kailee's mind has wandered trying to put it into to some context. Jude snaps her back to the matter at hand. After re-setting her bearings, they arrive at the recovery ward where she first examined Noi. Through the window in the closed door, she's surprised to see it now occupied by a middle-aged man tubed, wired up and asleep.

"She was in there, I'm positive she was," says Kailee, looking up and down the corridor.

Before Jude can stop her, she approaches a nurse coming out of another ward.

"Where is the Jane Doe who was in there a day ago?" she asks.

"Do you know her?" asks the nurse.

Kailee flashes her Department ID. "The Department is still trying to name the girl, but new information has come to light, and we need to see her."

Before the nurse can study Kailee's ID closer, it's placed back in her pocket. "Is nurse Julie on duty? She helped me last time I examined the girl."

"No, it's not her shift," the nurse replies. "If she thought it was okay, I suppose you have the authority. She's awake, but her condition hasn't changed. That's why they've placed her in a confined ward."

"Confined ward? What does that mean?" asks a worried Jude.

"You'll need to speak to the doctor about that. I can try to find him if you care to wait."

"No, that's fine," Jude replies. "It's just a facial feature we need to confirm from a relative who has contacted us. If it compares with the description given, we may have her name. We only need to take a couple of photos."

Kailee is not sure what Jude is on about. There's been no relative come forward, but he seems to know something.

The nurse accepts the story. "Very well, follow me."

As they follow the nurse, Jude looks around for any sign of Aswar's men.

At the closed door to the ward, the nurse stops them from entering. "You must take your photo through the window, I'm sorry. She's in restricted isolation."

"That's fine," Jude accepts. "I can see her from here. My phone camera has a strong zoom."

"Very well. Be quick, as I need to get back to my duties," urges the nurse.

Jude looks through the window in the door and struggles to hide his shock at seeing the extent of her injuries. Her eyes are closed as Jude takes a couple of photos of her face and a close-up of her bare arm on top of the blanket.

"Thanks, that's all I need," he says, grabbing Kailee's arm. "We can see our way out, thanks again."

As soon as the two turn into another corridor, Kailee stops and pulls her arm free from Jude's grip. "What was that all about? There's been no relative come forward or I would have known about it."

"Two things," Jude replies. "I needed to confirm she was Noi and to know where she is. Now we go about getting her out."

"Out! She doesn't appear well enough to move, and they must have put her in isolation for a good reason."

Jude ignores her. "I need to talk to Ev, and there's something else I need to do. Come."

Evelyn has backed into a parking space a row back and in eyesight of the white Hyundai Elantra. He sees Jude and Kailee coming out of the hospital and flashes his headlights.

"Any movement, Ev? What are they doing?" asks Jude as he and Kailee get in the car.

"They're just sitting there waiting."

"Waiting for what?" asks Kailee.

Evelyn turns back to face Kailee. "If they were here asking about the professor and an Asian girl, someone might remember them. They're waiting for us to get her out, then they'll make their move away from the hospital." He turns back to Jude. "Did you see her?"

Jude nods and shows Evelyn the photos he took.

"Shit! If I could spend five minutes with the bastard who did that to her," says Evelyn, cracking his knuckles.

"I'd say that they're long gone," breaks in Kailee. "Even the police aren't that interested; she being just an Asian girl."

Evelyn sees Jude keying in words on his phone. "What are you doing, Jude? You don't need you to call for help."

"Yes, I do, Ev. Something's not right, and I need Mirla to see these photos." He hits the send button and sits back to wait for a reply.

CHAPTER 34

Kailee is looking back at the hospital, concerned that taking the girl away from the care she'll get inside is not a good idea. Meanwhile, Jude stares at his phone as if willing Mirla to reply immediately, while Evelyn has not taken his eyes off the Hyundai.

Inside, Fauzi and Afif are staring back at the three sitting in their car with a puzzling look. They expected the two who entered the hospital to come out with Aswar's wife; but they didn't. Was she released or moved somewhere else? To tell Aswar this is the last thing Fauzi wants to do. Whatever, the others have a better chance of finding where she is, so they'll continue to wait for them to lead the way.

A ping on Jude's phone announces a new message and breaks the tense silence. A look of concern washes over his face as he reads Mirla's reply.

"What is it, Jude?" asks Evelyn, taking his eyes off the Hyundai for a moment and sensing a problem.

"It's not good, Ev. Mirla thinks Noi's skin has taken on a colour and texture similar to one of the test mice not long before it died."

"Died?" Kailee calls out. "Is she going to die?"

"Not if we can do something in time," replies Jude.

"What?" asks Evelyn, looking back at Fauzi and Afif looking back at him.

"We need to get Noi into the sea, and real fast. The serum remains independently active inside Noi and the baby for a period to adjust to being out of the carrier's environment. But the serum's effect is wearing off and needs to absorb familiarity through the host's skin. Meaning in the sea and somewhere around coral."

136

Kailee looks at Jude in total confusion. "What are you talking about? What serum and what's it for if it's putting her life in danger? If that's the case, should we be taking her out of the hospital?"

Jude ignores Kailee. "That's not all, Ev. Mirla says if we can't find another worm soon, then both Noi and the baby will die. Mirla reckons whatever we do, the serum is losing its potency and she needs another dose. Until then, we need to slow the rejection and get her near coral."

"What? What worm?" calls out Kailee.

"I'll fill you in later," Jude advises dismissively. "First, we need to get Noi out of the hospital without being seen."

"What then?" asks Evelyn. "How are we going to get her back to where you found the worm?"

"We're not. Not yet, anyway. Not sure whether Marcus knew this when he chose this place to bring Noi, but we're at the southern end of the Great Barrier Reef."

Kailee is looking at the backs of their heads while building up a mountain of questions.

Jude continues. "There are islands off the coast from here with coral reefs. Going by what Mirla is saying, Marcus would have made sure Noi was near the sea and the coral reefs, so he must have a boat here somewhere."

"I read somewhere he collapsed at the marina," informs Kailee, still confused about what's going on.

"Then let's get Noi and go there. Ev, you're the one with a knack for getting out of sticky situations, what do you suggest we do to get those two off our backs?"

Evelyn takes a moment to size up the situation.

"Okay, here's what we do," he says, rolling his cigar from one side of his mouth to the other and scratching his stubbled head.

***

Fauzi and Afif are sitting back, relaxed and happy to trust their judgement that those in the other car will get Aswar's wife wherever she is. They'll follow them, grab her, deliver her — or bits of her — then binge for a few days.

Suddenly, they both stiffen up in their seats. Striding towards them in his calf-high embossed tan buckskin cowboy boots is the towering, robust figure of Evelyn wearing only boxer shorts emblazoned with replica wanted posters for various Louisiana gunslinging outlaws.

There's a flurry of hands as they reach for their weapons, forgetting that because of airport security, they couldn't risk being caught carrying them. Accepting Evelyn has nowhere to hide a weapon, they relax a little. He is alone, and despite his size, they have proven skills in hand-to-hand combat.

As they ready themselves for a fight, Evelyn walks past the driver's side with only a slight glance in Fauzi's direction. Both turn their heads to watch Evelyn approach a tree growing in a dividing plantation behind their car with his hands a set distance apart. Afif and Fauzi face each other, expecting the other to have an answer. Each replied with a shrug and a shake of their head without noticing the snap of a branch.

By the time they turn their attention back to Evelyn, he has wedged the broken branch between the driver's door and the car it's parked next to. He then steps back to the rear of the car, pops the fuel cover, unscrews the cap and urinates into the fuel tank.

Fauzi cannot open the wedged driver's door, and Afif has not reckoned on how close to the car on the passenger side Fauzi has parked. But Evelyn had.

By the time Afif had half squeezed himself out of the door, Evelyn was facing him. With his modesty adjusted, one punch is all that's needed to send Afif back into the car where Fauzi is still struggling to open the driver's door.

Evelyn casually returns to his now empty car without a glance back and drives out of the carpark.

***

As the near naked Evelyn was attracting Afif and Fauzi's attention, Jude and Kailee exited their car and crept low behind other parked vehicles until reaching the entrance to the hospital. Jude quickly glances back to make sure no one noticed them before entering.

138

Kailee has Evelyn's pants, t-shirt and jacket over her arm as they walk towards the corridor that leads to where they saw Noi. The woman behind the counter is answering a query from an elderly couple with only a quick glance at the two passing. Assuming they're bringing a change of clothes to a patient, she returns her attention to the customer.

Fully aware how fast Evelyn needed to act, they rushed to the isolation ward. When clear of nurses and doctors, they enter.

Noi is drowsy but awake, with a hint of recognition in her eyes as Jude comes to her bedside. He has a finger to his lips, motioning for her to be quiet, then whispers that he's here to save her again.

The heart monitor is the only thing Noi is plugged into. Kailee turns it off and removes the sensors. Clear of all, she and Jude help Noi out of the bed and wrap her in Evelyn's baggy clothes.

Whether intended or by instinct, Kailee grabs the medical chart from the base of the bed as Jude checks all is clear outside the room. As they are about to leave, Noi pulls away from Jude's grasp to retrieve her small spoon from under the pillow.

With Jude and Kailee on each side of Noi to support her, they quickly make their way to the emergency department. When all is clear, they make it to the outside and hide behind a parked ambulance to wait for Evelyn.

Their wait is short as he pulls up at the end of the driveway.

Jude carries Noi to the car and places her in the back seat with Kailee. As soon as he's in the front passenger seat, Evelyn slams his size fourteen cowboy boot down on the accelerator.

When they turn onto the road that feeds the hospital, Jude turns back to see the Hyundai leaving the carpark and giving chase. He glances back at Evelyn, who looks unfazed as he steers toward a four-exit roundabout.

Evelyn judges the traffic and squeezes into a line of cars, resulting in screeching tyres and protesting horns. At the third exit, he drives off toward the coast, looking in his rearview mirror with a smile and a roll of the cigar at seeing the Hyundai splutter and stall on the roundabout, causing a salvo of car horns and increasing gridlock.

Evelyn figures it won't be long before the two henchmen dump their car and get a taxi. They've seen him drive towards the Yeppoon coast, and they'll assume they're taking Noi away by sea.

Kailee is becoming worried that Noi keeps drifting off and her breathing is shallow. Her medical training, while limited, is enough to hold grave fears for her. To get an idea of the strange state she's in, Kailee looks over the commandeered medical chart.

"Jude," she calls out. "Noi is not looking good. I've looked over the medical chart, and even though I only managed two years at medical school, my feeling is the hospital did not know what they were treating."

Jude looks back to see Noi struggling to stay awake and her complexion an eerie colour.

"Get your phone and photograph the hospital report. We'll send it to Mirla once we got on the boat."

It takes another ten minutes to arrive at the marina entrance. When asked, Noi, through her drowsiness, could not remember much about the boat, except that it was old, red, and not very big.

Jude tells the three to stay in the car while he checks if Marcus' boat is still moored and where.

Informed that it is, Jude tells the girl at the desk that he's returning the boat to its owner. To convince her of his relationship to Marcus Glasson, who signed for the boat's mooring, he hands her his business card showing he is a director of Glasson BioMarine. After payment is made for the time moored, arrangement made for the hire car to be returned, the keys are in Jude's hand.

Evelyn has his pants and shirt back on by the time Jude motions for them to park the car and bring Noi. Keeping her identity hidden by Evelyn's large jacket with the collar up, they hurry along the jetty until reaching the boat.

Kailee helps Noi on board, then steps back from the boat.

"Well, I guess this is goodbye then," she suggests, accepting the case solved. "You have her now. I know who she is. So we don't need each other anymore."

Jude jumps back onto the landing and takes her hand. "We need you. You're coming with us."

"But I can't! I mean..." she half protests.

"Look, I'll lay it on the line. If I can't search for another worm, Noi will die. But first she needs stabilising, and I need your help. If we could take her back to Dili, we would, but she needs time in the sea right now. You said you have some medical knowledge, so I need you to stay with her."

Kailee feels her mundane life is about to change, if it hasn't already. Not having to say goodbye to Jude overwhelms her, and without warning, she kisses him on the mouth.

Jude pushes her back while looking over her shoulder.

"I'm sorry," Kailee says out of embarrassment. "I didn't mean to do..."

Before she can finish, Jude has her back on the boat while releasing mooring ropes and calling out to Evelyn to hurry and start the engines.

Fauzi and Afif have emerged from the Marina office scanning the rows of jetties and boats. Afif sees Jude and sets off after him, reaching the old coast guard vessel as it moves from its berth. With an athletic leap, he lands onto its deck.

Kailee grabs Noi and moves her away from the struggle. Evelyn is busy steering through the maze of boats and jetties and unable to help. But looking back and sees Afif getting the better of Jude. With no other choice, he grabs Kailee and thrusts her into the captain's chair. "You take it from here. Just head to the opening and the sea," he orders.

Kailee has never been on a boat before, let alone steer one, but now is not the time to argue as Evelyn has already left her to help Jude.

Afif sees him coming and gives a karate kick to the face. Evelyn's cigar takes the force and spreads over his stubble. Wrong! Nobody does that to his Perdomo Slow-Aged Lot 826 Glorioso Maduro cigar and gets away with it. His large right hand swings up from below and grabs Afif's crotch while his left hand goes for the throat. There's a gurgle from Afif as the firm grip muffles the cry of pain as Evelyn's powerful, IRON branded vice-like hand squeezes Afif's testicles.

As the pain neutralises Afif's strength, Evelyn picks him up by the throat and crotch and tosses him overboard. Jude has regained his feet and rushes to Kailee just in time to grab the wheel and steer the boat away from the rocky breakwater wall and towards the distant islands.

Fauzi watches from the jetty as the boat rounds the breakwater and goes out of view. Afif is still in pain and struggling to swim back towards him. He goes to help Afif out of the water but spots something lying on the jetty. In all the rush and confusion, Kailee had dropped the hospital chart. Fauzi takes a confused look over it while ignoring his partner's call for help. Unable to understand the medical jargon, he folds it up and takes out his phone.

Fauzi is well aware he's in for a severe outburst from his boss for letting his wife slip away. He distances the phone from his ear, allowing the Indonesian expletives to carry across the marina. At the first chance to get in a word, he tells Aswar where he believes his wife is being taken. They know what their boat looks like, and the islands they are heading towards are small enough so finding them again should be easy.

There's no comment from Aswar. The message in his silence is clear: they'd better!

CHAPTER 35

C onrad drops his keys onto the entrance sideboard, having re-turned to his Canberra apartment. Before he can take his jacket off, his mobile phone buzzes. The caller's ID is unknown. Usually, he'll not answer, preferring to wait for whoever rang to leave a voicemail message. But with so much going on at the moment, he takes the call.

"Hello?" he dubiously answers.

The raspy breathing identifies the caller immediately. "Your new half-brother has once again taken my wife — in your own country — and I want to know what you are going to do about it?" Aswar says without introductions. "They left Yeppoon marina in a boat, and need I remind you that what I know about you and your dealings here and elsewhere, so does my wife."

Conrad sits to take the weight off his weakened knees. Not only has his father died, leaving troublesome issues, but he's now being pressured to clean up the mess because Aswar's wife — this girl, Noi — knows about his questionable dealings. This is nothing short of blackmail, he reasons with growing frustration.

He needs a moment to think.

"I'm waiting for your answer," comes the impatient, threatening voice from his phone.

"I need time to think," Conrad snaps back, realising too late that it's not the tone to take with this man.

But how does he reply?

Sure, he has access to government agencies who'd have no trouble locating them, but they would undoubtedly uncover his links and dealings with the likes of Aswar and others.

"Anyone else with them?" Conrad asks, hoping it's just two.

"A Dilli bar owner and a girl my men believe works with your immigration department."

That is not what he wanted to hear. A Dili bar owner may not be a problem, but any thought of calling on a government agency for help is pointless as one is already involved!

The answer becomes clear and unavoidable.

"Will I use this number to call you back?" asks Conrad, his mind racing.

"You have twenty-four hours to find her before I make a formal call to your government for help."

His phone went silent, leaving Conrad shaken. A formal government request from Aswar does not bear thinking about.

He takes off his jacket and pours a stiff whisky. His nerves need calming, not just because of Aswar's threat, but because he's about to call his sister.

***

Harper is in her top-floor Sydney apartment on the north side of the harbour. If she were at all interested, she could see her brother's apartment block on the south side.

But Conrad was least on her mind. She has just filed a story that exposes the gambling habits of a large charity organisation's CEO and raises the question of how he covers his sizable losses.

Harper never pretends to offer any answers. Her method is to start a rumour that will ultimately lead to an outcome that others will determine. A process that hurts those not involved the most. It's what trashy tabloid readers want, and Harper has made a good living out of other's pain.

Each time she files one of these stories she rewards herself with a small treat...two lines of coke up her nostrils.

The moment she wipes the residue from her nose and licks her fingers, her phone rings. She answers the call with a sniff.

As soon as she hears her brother's voice, she's tempted to hang up on him for interrupting her moment of pleasure.

"Harper, I need your help...it's important!" stops her.

"Look, Conrad, I'm with someone. It'll have to wait," she says, prepared to hang up on him.

"Bullshit, Harper! Clear your nose and listen." Conrad is well aware of her lonely celebrations. "We have a problem that needs a quick solution."

Harper shakes her head to clear it. It half works, but the other half is swimming in grotesque images.

"Harper, are you listening?" snaps Conrad.

"Yeah, yeah, so what is this big problem among the other big problems?"

"This Noi, they've found her..."

"Great," breaks in Harper. "So now there's no problem."

"No, wait...we don't have her...yet. That's why I need your help."

"Shit, Conrad, make some bloody sense. We either do, or we don't!"

"We don't...but our new half-brother does!"

Harper slumps back into her chair, "Come again?"

"Our father's bastard son found her, and they're on a boat that left from Yeppoon. We need to get her before someone else does."

"Conrad, I have no fucking idea what you're talking about!"

She hears Conrad give a heavy huff over the phone before answering.

"While this Jude Yimenes — our half-brother — has her, she's safe. But someone wants her killed."

As the murky images in her mind wash aside, she asks, "Who?"

Conrad hesitates a moment, knowing his answer will most likely result in another frenzied outburst.

"The girl's husband!"

There's no response.

"Harper, did you hear what I said?"

It takes a moment for her to reply. "Shit! You're telling me we could share our inheritance with someone else's wife? What the fuck has our bastard of a father been up to?"

"Let's not get into that at the moment. The immediate problem is he wants her dead."

There's another moment of silence as Harper tries to keep track of what's crowding her mind. Then, in a calm voice, she says, "Then, shouldn't that solve one problem?"

"No!" snaps Conrad. "You don't get it. This guy doesn't care how it's done. Most likely the more brutal it is, the better, but remember what the codicil states: 'death or harm in suspicious circumstances' and we get nothing. We must find her before they do. I'm sure you have contacts and ways of getting things done."

"Why me? Look, if I had my way, I'd let him kill the bitch and worry about the codicil later. Who is this guy, this husband, anyway?"

"Harper, you really don't want to know. Will you help or not?"

"Why can't you tell me? You seem to be pals with this guy."

"I can't...there's someone in the government involved."

"Sorry, say again?" comes the confused response.

"Seems a girl from Immigration is with them."

"What the fuck! How the...no, never mind, I get it now. You don't want her to see you. It all gets back to the party, and you can't be part of any scandal that affects the party, right?"

"Will you help or not?" Conrad asks, ignoring her accurate summation.

"I need to meet this guy. I'm sure I can come up with a better solution than your feeble attempt. Who is he?"

Conrad is uneasy about his decision to get the two together, but his sister is far more forceful and could convince Aswar to let the girl live.

"He is Djan Muhammad Aswar, the head of a covert security unit in the Indonesian Government," he tells her, expecting this information will frighten her off.

Instead, she replies, "Sounds like he's just my sort of man. Arrange a meeting."

146

CHAPTER 36

$\mathbf{T}$he Great Barrier Reef is one of nature's wonders that extends for 2,300 kilometres down the Queensland coast. The coral that forms the reef is undergoing a battle for survival from industrial pollution and the changing climate. Lying at the reef's southern end are the Keppel group of islands, where another battle for survival is taking place.

Despite clear weather and a relatively calm Coral Sea, the ageing vessel carrying Jude, Evelyn, Kailee and Noi is taking longer than the usual thirty-minute fast cat ferry to Great Keppel Island.

Jude continues to look back towards the mainland, expecting Aswar's men to commandeer a speedboat and give chase. They're not, but he is sure that will definitely change.

Evelyn, meanwhile, needs to ease up on the knots to save the remaining fuel in the tank.

Kailee is also worried. With no food to offer the weakened Noi, and water from only one small bottle, she cradles Noi to keep her comfortable.

After forty-eight agonisingly slow minutes, Jude calls out to Evelyn. "Head to that small island on the left. We need to get Noi into the sea and best not go to the main island."

Evelyn nods, chewing on a fresh cigar. "Those guys are resourceful, and it won't be long before they're on our tail."

"Yeah, I know," replies Jude. "I'm hoping they'll go straight ahead to the main island, so look for a cove or some place we can't be seen as they pass."

Suddenly an ABBA song catches the wind to the bemused surprise of Jude and Evelyn and to Kailee's embarrassment.

"Um...a message has come through on my phone."

"Is it from Mirla? What does she say about the hospital chart?" asks Jude.

"She confirms what I said, that the hospital did not know what they were dealing with. But she stresses you need to get Noi back to the lab in Dili as soon as you can, and, um, that the water around coral is only a stopgap and not a cure. She finishes by asking if there's anything she can do to help get her back."

Jude thinks for a moment, then turns to Evelyn. "Any ideas, Ev? I'm pretty sure there's a landing strip on Great Keppel."

Evelyn takes the cigar out of his mouth and spits out a loose bit of tobacco. "There's a guy I knew in INTERFET who started up an air charter business somewhere in Queensland. Not sure what he calls the business, but tell Mirla to look up Turtles Air Charter. Knowing Charlie Turtles, his ego will have to show up in the name. Then tell Mirla if she gets hold of him, to say Sunday's Turtle Roast needs help to get off Great Keppel Island and it's urgent."

Kailee and Jude look at Evelyn for an explanation.

Evelyn gives a shrug. "How else will he believe Mirla? Only Charley will know who it's from."

Leaving that story for another time, Jude watches Kailee send the message, then looks towards the approaching small island. After checking they're not yet being followed, he says to Evelyn, "Go around the far side of the island and we'll look for a place to anchor."

"Gotcha, captain," replies Evelyn, his mind wandering back to the 1999 INTERFET peacekeeping days in East Timor with Charlie.

***

"Yes, Mister Minister, you have good news, I trust?" comes the answer to Conrad's call to Aswar.

Conrad takes a deep swallow. "I don't have your wife...but," he adds before getting a spray, "I have someone who could get her."

"And who might that be?" asks Aswar, sounding less than convinced.

"My sister," he replies taking another nervous swallow.

"Ah, your dear sister, Harper Glasson. What an intriguing suggestion."

Conrad is waiting for more, but there's only silence.

"She wants to meet you," he says, hoping to reignite the conversation.

"She often amazes me with her ability to dig for dirt. I would be most interested in what she has on me. While it's not the solution I was expecting from you, it is a tempting offer."

"Yes, I'm sure you'll find her thoughts on our mutual problem more in line with yours."

"Most interesting! She lives in Sydney, yes? I was planning to leave Sydney for Jakarta tomorrow morning. How fast can you arrange a meeting?"

"She is ready to meet you anytime. I'm sure you would prefer to nominate a place."

"Would her apartment be out of the question?"

Conrad senses an ulterior motive in his tone, and while he is far from being a protector of his sister, the thought of Aswar groping her is repulsive.

"Yes, she would prefer somewhere more public. I'm sure you understand."

There's a laugh over the phone. "Is it you or your sister who does not trust me?"

"Neither; she believes her apartment could be bugged."

"Ah, yes, I can see that would be a possibility, having made many enemies. Then may I suggest we meet at the casino. My last night in Sydney and I need some excitement."

"An ideal place. It's her second home. Say seven o'clock in the Black Bar?"

"I look forward to it. But, Mister Minister, do not for one moment underestimate the urgency in getting my wife."

Conrad knows a threat when he hears one.

CHAPTER 37

~·~·~·~

The small, uninhabited Middle Island lies a kilometre west of the larger Great Keppel Island, where a smattering of eco-friendly resorts attract holidaymakers and day-trippers.

Evelyn steers the boat to the island's north side, where a rocky outcrop descending into the clear water of the Coral Sea hides a small cove unseen from the regular sea route.

"We need to get Noi into the water now," says Jude, noticing Noi's worsening condition. "You can swim, can't you, Kailee?"

Kailee looks shocked. "Swim? You want me to get in the sea as well?"

"I want Evelyn to stay on board and wait for Mirla to call. He may need to talk to his mate with the air charter. I spotted coral below, so best if the two of us are with Noi."

Kailee is flushed with embarrassment. There's no beach in landlocked Canberra, and the man-made lake is seldom open for swimming because of water quality and algae. Despite that, she rarely exposes her body to the sun, let alone anyone else. But swim she can from her school days.

Jude is becoming impatient. "Come on, Kailee, Noi is not looking good. Take what she's wearing off so she can get the full benefit of the sea," he says with his t-shirt already off and his pants being undone.

Seeing his trim and well-defined bronzed body is too much for Kailee, and she can't see herself stripping off in front of him or everyone else. If she wore a bra, it might not be as confronting, but she gave up wearing a bra as her petite breasts needed no support.

"Now!" snaps Jude, showing his impatience.

A groan from Noi overrides any embarrassment Kailee is feeling, and she strips Noi of Evelyn's jacket and hospital gown. Evelyn has turned his back on them, and Jude is still taking his trousers and socks off so the quicker she can strip and get Noi and herself in the water the better.

Jude is first over the side and into the warm tropical water. With a grip on the side rail of the boat with one hand, he offers his other to help Noi over the side.

Kailee supports Noi until she's in the hands of Jude and eased into the water. Now, with no one to hide behind, it meant a quick and rather clumsy jump over the side and into the water.

The three rest a moment for Noi to get used to being in the familiar environment. The effect is encouraging, as she becomes alert and finds strength returning to her legs. Helped by Jude and Kailee on each side of her, they dog paddle to where coral lies under deeper water.

"Noi? Can you hear me?" Jude asks after deciding they have gone far enough.

She looks at him with a slight nod of the head.

"I need you to do a little dive with Kailee and me. Not deep, just a little closer to the coral, then back up, okay?"

"I'm not sure I can dive," Kailee says.

"Sure you can," snaps Jude, concentrating on Noi.

Before Kailee can utter a word, Jude and Noi take a deep breath and dive, forcing Kailee to do the same.

The water is only eight metres deep, and the bottom comes up fast. Jude stops Kailee before she reaches the coral and shakes his head and cocks his thumb as a sign to surface. As soon as the three are on the surface, Jude checks on Noi. She smiles with an improved complexion. He then looks at Kailee.

"Don't touch the coral," he says, trying not to sound too harsh. "Okay, another dive for a second or two longer."

Noi and Kailee both nod, and the three arch their backs for another dive.

Kailee suggests Noi needs a rest after two more dives.

"Okay," he agrees. "Four or more dives every half hour. You up for that, Noi?"

"I feel stronger with each dive. I can go another," she replies. "It's good to be back in the sea."

"No, let's take it slow," advises Jude, with Kailee's approval. They swim back to the boat where Evelyn helps Noi and Kailee on board while averting his eyes as much as practical. Kailee gets Noi comfortable, then stands as Jude climbs onto the deck. She cannot resist another glimpse of his wet and muscled body. But when she raises her eyes to his, Jude is looking over her. Her deep longing to be wanted delays any attempt to cover herself.

Jude likes what he sees. Gone are the glasses, the geeky clothes, and the straightened hair. This is not the same girl. Her hair is wet and bedraggled; her eyes are as naked as her perfectly proportioned body.

Their mutual appreciation is timely interrupted by ABBA announcing a new message.

"Mirla's hunted down Charley. He wants me to ring him to work out details," advises Evelyn.

After several minutes talking with Charley, Evelyn fills in the others. "He can't get here until tomorrow morning sometime. He's checked the specs of the runway on Keppel Island and his planes are too big to land there, so it'll be by chopper. Mirla told him we need to get a sick girl back to Dili, so he's flying a jet into Rockhampton then picking up a chopper there. He does Medevac charters, so there'll be medical equipment on board the jet if required."

"Well, thank you, Charley, that's great," acknowledges Jude, then looks up to the sky. "We have about another hour before it's dark, so when you feel up to it, Noi, best we try for more dives."

***

To get to Great Keppel Island at short notice and late in the day was a matter of walking the jetties to find someone willing to take one soaked but both rather rough-looking men. When money is offered well over the regular fee, Fauzi found a taker.

The skipper of the boat happily takes the money but has his concerns. Neither looked nor dressed like tourists. They have no luggage if staying on the island overnight, and when asked why such urgency, he's silenced by a threatening glare that has him wondering if he's made the right decision.

Thirty minutes later, they approach the main island, with Fauzi and Afif looking around for any sign of the boat carrying Aswar's wife.

"What are you looking for?" asks the skipper.

"Just keep going around the island," comes Fauzi's blunt reply.

"Look, I need to get this boat back to the marina before dark. The deal was to get you here and not do a tour."

Afif is about to threaten him, but Fauzi, not wanting to draw attention to them if it ends up in a fight, shakes his head to stop.

"You can come back to the marina with me if you can't find what you're looking for. Otherwise, I'll drop you off on the island."

"Where's the jetty?" asks Fauzi. "The boat I'm looking for could be there?"

"There's no jetty," informs the skipper. "The beach ahead is where everyone gets off."

Fauzi does a 360-degree scan of what's around them. "That island over there, I want to go around it?" he says, pointing.

"Look, sorry mate, but I won't have time to go around Middle Island, drop you both off at Keppel and get back to the mainland before dark. You can get on one of the boat tours in the morning or even hire a couple of jet skis and look around at your leisure."

Fauzi considers his options and nods his head towards the beach landing site.

CHAPTER 38

The Italian Renaissance-inspired Black Bar is dark and lavish. A hint as to why it's Harper's favourite. She has arrived early and is sitting in the darkest corner. While eager to discuss the matter-at-hand, she is not that keen to be seen with Djan Muhammad Aswar.

She'd spent the afternoon delving into his background, and despite being repulsed at this man's appearance, Harper formed a sick admiration at his ability to survive after all the bloodshed he'd caused over many years.

Less clear in her research was the matter-at-hand — his third wife. The only photo she found of this so-called Noi was in an Indonesian regional newspaper. There was no caption, so her being the only young, attractive girl among the government's entourage was speculation. Being in the background together with the coarse screen of newsprint made it almost impossible to get a clear picture of what she looks like. Though it made no difference to Harper. The purpose of this meeting is to get rid of her.

Harper has made a very successful career of plotting her interviews to get what she wants while not representing the facts, but this may be her toughest. While several 'scoops' resulted in someone's death, it was by suicide. This time it'll be murder. She must make sure nothing she says or does will link her to it.

Despite the darkened corner, the bulk of Aswar still casts a shadow as he arrives at her table. Harper looks up and succeeds in hiding her shock. Of all the photos she has seen of him, it proves that the camera can lie. Over her career, she has mixed with the roughest of characters, but this man is far beyond rough.

Never one to stand and greet her appointment, Harper only nods at the empty seat assigned to him so his back is to the room.

"I ordered a bottle of Ruinart Blanc de Blanc Champagne," she says, watching Aswar's expression change at being spoken to first. "I assumed you would be paying." It was not a question.

Aswar smiles, accepting that he and Harper will get along fine.

"I don't drink that shit. Order me a single malt Scotch and make sure it's no younger than eighteen years," comes his retaliatory reply.

It does not offend Harper. In fact, she is looking forward to matching wits with someone other than wimpish, corrupt politicians and corporate crooks. She snaps her fingers at a nearby waitress to order Aswar's Scotch.

Aswar takes his eyes off the behind of the waitress as she walks away and returns his attention to Harper.

"Let's not waste introductory small talk," he says, plucking an irritating hair from his veined, bulbous nose. "We both know much about each other, I'm sure."

Harper can only give a secretive smile as she places the glass of champagne to her lips.

"Your brother speaks most highly of you," Aswar says with a hint of mirth. "So high, in fact, that he needs you to do what he cannot."

Harper keeps her stoic poker face, having conditioned herself to resist any form of flattery, whether it be fact or fiction.

Aswar continues. "Of course, neither of you carries a high regard for your deceased father."

"Neither do you if your claim he stole your wife is true," Harper says, not in defence of her father, but to throw some doubt back at Aswar.

He smiles. "Yes, it comes down to a matter of trust. I'd have preferred meeting you at your apartment, but was it you or Conrad who lacked trust in me?"

Harper can only offer a strained smile as the hairs on her back quiver with repulsion.

"Such a pity," Aswar says, raising the newly delivered glass of Scotch to his lips while glancing back at the retreating waitress. "The three of us could have cemented everlasting memories."

"And while you are at the bottom of someone else, we would not get to the bottom of what we're here to talk about now, would we?"

Aswar salutes her steely mind with another sip. It is now time to get down to business.

"We each have a problem that needs removing. I have a simple solution, but my gut feeling is that it's not that simple for you and Conrad. Care to enlighten me on why?"

Harper uses the time to refill her glass, accepting that Conrad has not told Aswar of the threats in the codicil. And nor will she reveal such details.

"It may come out during our final arrangement. Until then, may I ask what you expect of me? You are head of a security unit that can surely offer more than I can?"

Aswar leans back in his chair and studies Harper for a moment. He's not used to being challenged, but this challenge is enjoyable.

"I'm sure you now know of your father's secret life in Dili, but we both need to know why he smuggled my wife all this way to Queensland instead of returning her to her birthplace, Atauro Island."

"And where you cannot set foot on East Timor soil," Harper interrupts.

Aswar gives an accepting grin. "So, you know I have a price on my head there?"

Harper sees no point in agreeing.

Aswar smiles at her knowing silence. "It's only a matter of time, you know, before I have her back."

"Dead or alive?" asks Harper.

"Yes," is the direct response. "Now, your brother's nervous at the thought of her delivered dead. I've wondered about that. He wants nothing to do with her death. That I accept, but I believe there are other reasons."

He waits for Harper to interrupt, but she remains silent for a teasing moment.

"What do I get if I get your wife back to you alive?" she asks.

Aswar smiles at his accomplishment. "I have first-hand knowledge of your government's questionable dealings over the Timor Sea oil and gas deal. I can give you the names of those behind the bugging of the Timor-Leste government. Is that enough?"

Harper is almost salivating at the headlines with her byline attached. But to trust this man would be foolish. Once he has his wife — dead or alive — he'll have what he wants, and his promises will be worthless. This would mean the end of any inheritance, and for what? A couple of breaking news scoops in the media. That is not enough.

"You were in Balibo when the five Australian journalists were murdered, weren't you?"

Aswar's ruddy face pales, giving Harper the courage to add more. "You're also involved in the people-smuggling business and the sex trade of minors. Am I correct? No need to answer...I have enough proof. All I need is that when you have your wife back, you keep her alive for at least eight months. We both keep our end of the bargain, and we both benefit."

Aswar studies Harper intently for a moment. Anyone else with so much information on him would be found in an alley with their throat cut.

His greatest fear is to become the centre of an international trial circus. Even if he evaded sentencing, it would mean the end to his cushy job in the Indonesian government and losing the control he has over those he uses in his dirty dealings.

It's new for Aswar to be on the receiving end of blackmail. With vast experience of doing the same to others, he accepts Harper is no fool and that what she has compiled on him will be available to others should something happen to her.

He accepts the situation and indulges for a moment in the possibility of them working together in the future.

Returning his thoughts to the current situation, he sees Harper's investigative ability as a far better way of getting things done here in her own country than he could, despite his shadowy network — a network that includes her brother.

"Your father has developed many medical marvels. Even knighted for his endeavours," he says to the surprise of Harper at his change of subject. "To bring these medical benefits to the people requires experimenting and testing. On rodents at first, but testing on humans is the ultimate criterion." He pauses for effect before delivering his punchline. "Is he using my wife as a...how you say...guinea pig?"

This is something Harper had never thought of. But the suggestion has ignited her journalistic juices. Could it be true? Are the conditions in the codicil because of this? Harper needs to come back quickly with an answer so as not to give Aswar reason to dig deeper.

"That's ridiculous," she says, with a shake of her head. "If there's any credibility in what you say, then my father would need to monitor her under strict conditions in his lab in Dili, not bring her to Australia."

"Great Keppel Island, in fact," he adds. "I have two of my men closing in on the four as we speak."

"Four?" Harper questions. "Who else apart from your wife and my half-brother?"

"A bar owner from Dili who is proving to be a thorn in the side and girl from your immigration department. Why she's involved is a mystery. But if she gets in the way, that's her fucking problem."

Harper has the germ of an idea. If his wife is being used as part of an experiment, it raises the prospect of keeping her alive whether or not she is?

"You realise if your wife is part of some medical discovery and something should happen to her, you're killing off millions in royalties."

Harper watches as her words sink in, and she can almost hear in his mind the cha-chink of incoming money.

Aswar's greed ponders the thought that she may be right. He's well aware of Professor Marcus Glasson's success rate and the vast millions in royalties his discoveries continue to make.

He's about to agree to preserve his wife's life when it hits him. His men have orders to kill her if they can't bring her to him alive.

"I need to make a call," he says, taking out his phone.

Harper watches Aswar's impatience and anger intensify as he struggles to get a mobile connection to his men. He slams his phone down and turns on Harper in order to pass blame.

"Your country has the worst telecommunications!"

Harper chances a smile as she takes out her own phone.

"Who are you calling?" he asks.

"The airport. If you can somehow stop your men killing your wife, then we have what we both want. If not, I'm going to Dili to get what I want."

158

CHAPTER 39

~~~~~

A fif and Fauzi had used the remaining daylight to check out the few scattered resorts for any sign of Aswar's wife or her abductors. Their search proved unsuccessful, and it would be useless looking any further in the dark. All they can do is stay out of sight and wait until morning.

Fauzi's mobile phone gives a feeble buzz. If it had not been turned to vibrate, the incoming call would go unnoticed over the music from the resort festivities a short way up the beach. But the uncharged battery has only enough energy to show the caller's ID before it dies.

"Who was it?" asks Afif.

"The boss," replies Fauzi, giving the phone a shake in an attempt at squeezing out more juice. "I reckon he wants to know if we have her yet. He'll have to wait till I can charge up the phone and get back to him. If he tries to call you, he'll be talking to the fish, seeing you lost your phone back at the marina."

"Nothing to tell him anyway," replies a despondent Afif.

They both stare out into the dark sea. Each in their own thoughts of where they would rather be.

The reggae vibes of Bob Marley mixed with laughter drifting down from the resort are getting Afif edgy. Being a regular club-goer in Jakarta, it's where he would rather be than getting sand up his arse sitting on a lonely stretch of beach in the dark and away from all the action.

After some consideration that what he is about to say could be dangerous if it got back to 'the boss', Afif takes the chance of passing on his thoughts to his senior partner.

"Why do we always get the shit jobs?" he says, tossing a pebble into the water.

After getting no reply, he looks at Fauzi, who is unmoved and fixed on the expanse of water ahead.

"Don't get me wrong. I mean the pay ain't bad, and we have our moments. But this chasing after the boss's wife is not only becoming a pain in the arse but sand up there as well. We'll be sitting here all night, and what, expect her to just walk up to us?"

"You better not let the boss hear you talk like that or you'll get more than sand up your arse," replies Fauzi, continuing to stare out into the darkness with his own thoughts.

"Yeah, but what do you think?" asks Afif, getting a little agitated. "What are we gunna do when we get her? She'll put up a fight, that's for sure, and there're the others as well."

Fauzi remains quiet. He lowers his eyes and runs his fingers through the sand.

Afif continues. "You know what he said. If we can't bring her back alive, deliver her dead hands. How is he to know she died despite all our attempts to keep her alive? I mean, he'll end up killing her, anyway!"

Fauzi picks up another pebble from the sand and tosses into the water. After a period of sombre silence, he looks to his younger partner with something else on his mind, then shakes his head to dismiss what he wants to say and instead utters, "We better get ourselves a couple of sharp knives then."

***

Noi slept more than the other three during the night. The water of the Coral Sea has returned some strength, and the greenish tinge to her skin has lessened.

Kailee, Jude and Evelyn took turns in watching over her between grabbing what little sleep they could. While pleased there's some improvement in her condition, concern remains if she'll last the long trip back to Dili without proper medical care.

The sun breaching the horizon is a welcome sight. The red hue it cast over the sky and mirrored upon the water presented a picture-perfect image of a less than perfect situation the four are about to face.

"Time to get over to the main island and wait for our lift," suggests Evelyn, as he lights up a fresh cigar.

"I think Noi should have another dose of coral to give her the strength to last the journey," says a worried Kailee.

Jude looks at Evelyn. "What do you reckon, Ez? We have time?"

"Guess we have to make time. Just be as quick as you can, hey. Not sure when Charlie will turn up, and those two goons could be anywhere."

Two quick dives were all they could manage before Evelyn waved them back.

When all are back on board, he starts the engine with a worried look at the fuel gauge. "We're just about out of fuel," he says, tapping the gauge. "Best we can hope for is the top of the main island. If it's still ticking over, I'll beach on the opposite side to the resorts and as close to the airstrip so there's less bush to get through."

"Okay, do what you can," agrees Jude, then turns to Kailee. "Do you have enough charge on your phone, Kailee? Mirla may have given your number to Charlie and not Ev's."

Kailee checks her phone and replies with a confirming nod.

"We'll hear and see the chopper coming anyway," Evelyn adds, as he eases the boat away from the sheltered cove. "We then head in the direction it lands,"

***

On the main island, the resort staff are just starting their daily routine while the guests continue to sleep off the late-night party. It'll be some time before anyone notices missing items from the kitchen.

Fauzi claimed a large, pointed chef's knife while Afif opted for a meat cleaver. With each wrapped in a tea towel, it was now time for the two to go hunting.

The resort's water activity shack is being opened by a young, blonde-haired, tanned attendant as Fauzi approaches with an eye on a jet ski.

"We hire ski," he says bluntly.

"You staying at the resort?" the attendant asks with some suspicion because of their lack of beach or resort wear.

Fauzi takes out his bulging wallet and hands him five-hundred dollars. "Is that a good enough answer?"

The attendant looks around to make sure no-one is in sight and pockets the offer.

"I'll check out that small island over there while you stay around here," Fauzi tells Afif. "If they're not there, I'll circle this island until I see their boat. If you see them first, let nothing stop you doing what we agreed on."

With his pants rolled up and his shoes hanging around his neck by their laces, Fauzi heads off, leaving Afif holding the concealed knives.

***

To the north, Evelyn steered the boat to the nearest point of the main island, expecting the engine to gasp for fuel at any minute. It does! He gives the fuel gauge a robust tap, but the gauge remains on empty! While the engine is spluttering, the boat still has some motion. Evelyn swings the wheel to head straight for the nearest beach.

With the last gasp of fuel vapour, Evelyn allows the boat to be driven by an onshore wave. "Hang on, guys," he calls out as the hull scrapes the bottom until digging deep into the sand a few metres from shore.

Evelyn is first off the boat, then taking Noi onto his back, wades to the shore with Jude and Kailee following.

Immediately they face their first hurdle. The thin stretch of sand that's left after severe erosion is covered with washed-up debris that needs to be stepped over. Then there is a metre-high steep bank held together by a thick line of bushes and trees that needs to be climbed.

Evelyn's size, with the added weight of Noi on his back, only crumbles the fragile bank with nothing solid to get a foothold.

Jude grabs a tree root that the erosion has revealed and pulls himself up. He reaches out a hand to help Noi while holding onto a tree branch with the other to stop being pulled back down as the sand continues to crumble under his feet.

Kailee is next to be helped up, and then Evelyn. All now have a solid curtain of thick foliage to tackle. Since they had nothing to cut their way through the dense growth, Evelyn and Jude had no choice but their bare hands.

It takes several minutes of breaking tree limbs and crunching dead wood underfoot to get through the coastal barrier. To their minor relief, the way ahead is not as dense, but still presents a challenge.

Half an hour goes by and only about twenty meters travelled. Kailee calls out to stop. Despite Kailee's help, the effort is taking its toll on Noi.

"I don't know how far we have to go, but if it continues like this, Noi needs water to drink. She's getting very weak."

Evelyn looks at Jude for an answer, but there is none. They had used up the small amount of water on the boat. The ground is bone dry, so no puddles remain from the rain long past.

"Well, we can't just stop. We need to keep moving and hope we come across some water. If not, we'll have to get to one of the resorts," is Jude's only solution.

"I'll carry Noi," says Evelyn, then adds, "Jude? Any idea how far it is to the airstrip?"

"It has to be near the main resort somewhere, so my guess is one, maybe two kilometres. We need to head south and stay not too far from the beach in case we need to get Noi to one of the resorts for help."

Evelyn nods and looks around for Kailee to follow, but she is nowhere to be seen.

"Jude, where's Kailee?" He asks, to Jude's surprise.

"I'm here," comes the reply as Kailee steps from behind a thick bush, holding a bunch of yellow berries. "It's not much, but these Wombat Berries just may have enough moisture for Noi to continue."

"You never cease to amaze me, girly," says Evelyn.

"Likewise," Jude adds, making Kailee blush.

She feeds Noi with what little moist flesh there is on each berry, keeping some in case no more can be found.

She is still on Evelyn's back as he tilts his head one way and then the other, as if listening for something.

"What is it?" asks Jude.

"Shush," replies Evelyn, straining his ears until hearing the distant sound of a chopper.

"There, I see it," calls out Kailee, pointing to a break in the tree canopy.

All but Noi look up and watch the chopper pass overhead until the trees block it from sight, but not out of hearing.

***

Fauzi could not hear the chopper over the whine of the jet ski until he slowed to coast around a rocky outcrop of the small island. Hoping to find a boat tucked behind rocks, he sees only rippling surf onto the empty beach. The idling jet ski allows the sound of the chopper to reach his ears. He follows its path, then spins the jet ski around to head at full speed back to the resort.

Afif lacks awareness and assumes the chopper is bringing more tourists to the island. He watches it go overhead, then turns back to scan the beach. It's not long before Fauzi rides the jet ski onto the sand to join him.

"They're using the chopper to get her away," he says, urging Afif to follow him in the direction the helicopter is descending.

Charlie Turtles has piloted his chopper to the island's airstrip expecting to see his waiting passengers. But the strip is empty and overgrown. He pulls back on the collective joystick to gain elevation and does a broad sweep over the area. He spots two figures running along the beach towards the airstrip. Neither big enough to be his old mate, Evelyn, so he flies deeper into the island, and more by luck than ability, he spots three figures coming in and out of view among the thick forest. One figure he thinks he recognises, but for the added weight being carried. He hovers above the three, and when Evelyn looks up and waves, he sees he has someone on his back. Unable to land, he turns the chopper around and flies slowly to the airstrip so they can follow in his direction.

Fauzi has stopped Afif and looks to where the chopper hovered for a moment. "They must be somewhere below the chopper. I reckon it's leading them to where it'll land. We'll cut them off, grab the wife and force the pilot to take us to the mainland."

Evelyn's bulk is helping to clear a path through the dense undergrowth while Noi fends off low branches. As the pace picks up, Jude has hold of Kailee's hand to stop her tripping over the dropped branches, twigs, and weed clumps on the forest floor.

As soon as Charlie is certain he has shown the way, he lands on the airstrip with its rotors almost silently idling. The crackle and crunch of dried leaves and twigs underfoot now heard.

"There's someone up ahead, Ev," Jude says under his breath.

They all stop and listen.

"Yeah, I reckon those two are trying to cut us off before we get to the chopper. You take Noi and keep going. I'll stall them," orders Evelyn, lowering Noi off his back.

Jude and Kailee sandwich Noi between them, with one arm each around Noi's waist. She places an arm over each of their shoulders to help as much as she can.

Evelyn stops them after only a few metres and looks back to where they came from. "There's also someone behind us. I think they've separated," he whispers. "You head towards the sound of the rotors. I'll do an arc and surprise the one ahead so you can get to the chopper."

"What then?" asks Kailee. "We can't just leave you?"

Jude stays silent, leaving Evelyn to answer.

"You will if you have to. The priority is to get Noi on her way to Dili. I'll follow later."

Kailee is about to protest, but Jude is already moving off.

Evelyn watches them merge into the thick shrubbery before spinning his head around to pinpoint other movements. The loudest sound of breaking twigs and disturbed foliage is ahead and to his right. Behind, whoever it is, has a softer tread. He heads off to the right.

The density of the trees and the tangle of roots and fallen branches make progress of three abreast slow and difficult. Kailee is the first to trip, bringing Noi and Jude down with her. Jude is quick on his feet and helps Noi up. Kailee attempts to stand, but the trip has twisted her ankle, and the pain has her slump back down.

"You go on," she says with a grimace and a wave of her hand. "I'll only slow you down."

"We can't leave her," insists Noi, finding her voice.

165

"Yes, you can," comes the deep voice of Fauzi as he breaks through the trees and grabs Kailee with the chef's knife at her throat.

Evelyn appears behind Fauzi, ready to grab his hand holding the knife, when Afif surprises him from the side with a swing of his cleaver. Evelyn ducks just in time as the cleaver slices off a branch.

"Cool it, man, or I'll cut her throat," Fauzi calls out.

Evelyn sees the fear in Kailee's eyes and drops his hands. Afif sees his chance to retaliate for all the pain this big man has inflicted on him and raises the cleaver again.

Evelyn is the only one to wonder about the sound of others coming up behind them. Had they recruited help? The answer is immediate.

Breaking through the bushes are two of the island's feral goats, charging at a rate such that a collision is unavoidable. The first one, an angry brown with straggly black hair, crashes into the side of Afif. One of its long, twisted horns piercing the pit of his raised arm holding the cleaver. The second goat is a long-haired white whose horn barely misses Evelyn's stomach.

In a move that hints at a past stint as a rodeo steer wrestler, Evelyn grabs both horns and twists the goat's head, forcing it to crash to the ground, collecting Fauzi on the way. The impact forces the knife at Kailee's throat to drop before he and Kailee stumble on top of the goat wrestling to stand up.

Jude grabs Kailee and pulls her clear of the kicking goat as one of its cloven hooves connects with Fauzi's chest, leaving him breathless and in pain.

Evelyn looks back at Afif standing upright in shock with blood pouring from a gaping hole almost severing his arm.

The brown goat that inflicted the injury is surveying the scene with a challenging look in its pinkish eyes. Its companion, in its effort to stand, again digs a hoof into Fauzi's chest, adding to whatever damage has already been done.

Evelyn has his eyes focussed on the brown goat's eyes, like staring off a bull at a rodeo. Jude and Noi remain still while shock has frozen Kailee.

The two goats snort their displeasure, then loudly bleat in unison. Their call answered as trampling through the bushes got louder and closer. Jude and Evelyn look at each other, questioning whether to be chased down if they run, or chance not being trampled where they stand.

The decision comes from above.

The trees suddenly creak and bend. Leaves and dust fill the swirling air, and the shrill noise of the hovering helicopter above silences any sound of oncoming goats. The brown and white goats lose interest in the humans as their long hair whips them in the downdraft. They run back into the bush to join others of their herd in retreating.

Jude is holding Noi close and calls out to Evelyn over the noise of the rotors. "We need to get Noi out of here; she's not looking too good."

Evelyn scoops up the stunned Kailee into his arms, and all four follow the elevating chopper as it leads the way to the airstrip.

Fauzi closes his eyes from the dust and struggles against the pain of possibly broken ribs and loss of wind to get to his knees. Beside him, Afif has collapsed and is losing a lot of blood.

Their chase is over.

Charlie has landed his helicopter on the grassy airstrip and waits at the edge of the treeline for his passengers. As soon as they appear, he helps the traumatised Kailee on board, then Noi and Jude. With a nod and a wink for Evelyn to join him at the controls, he hands him a fresh cigar.

As the helicopter lifts and does a wide sweep over the bush, Evelyn looks down to where the bush has flattened by the downdraft and spots the figures of Fauzi and Afif.

"Better make a call to the resort that there's been a goat attack on two of their guests," he suggests.

Charlie waits until they are over the water and heading towards the mainland before radioing in.

CHAPTER 40

Harper has never set foot on Timor-Leste soil. She came close a few years back, when, as a cadet reporter, her paper wanted her to cover the signing of the controversial Timor Sea Treaty. She made excuses not to go by feigning illness. The actual reason: she didn't want to run into her estranged father, who was living there.

There was no chance of that happening this time, but running into his mistress-cum-de facto partner is a certainty.

She had rung Conrad before leaving Sydney to ask if he was interested in following her to Dili. He declined. Was it not wanting to meet their father's secret family, or is there something politically sensitive that's stopping him? Both, no doubt, but Harper has long felt her brother always keeps hidden something beyond the obvious.

Whatever the reason, she's happy he rejected her invitation. She always operated better on her own.

As soon as she steps out of the hot and humid airport and into the hotter and even more humid open-air, she questions why her father gave up the luxury of Sydney to live here. She couldn't wait to get to her air-conditioned hotel room to plan for the next day.

If she had arrived an hour earlier, she might have noticed a Challenger 300 nine-seater jet taxiing to an apron beside the main passenger terminal.

Because of the serious condition of the patient on board, and how well-known Jude and his father's business were to airport administration, entry formalities were rushed through.

Jude has had his 4WD parked at the airport since flying to Canberra to meet Kailee, and it was not the hospital he took Noi to, but the office of Glasson BioMarine where Mirla Yimenes anxiously waited.

At the rear of the single-story building, and beyond the secured lab, was a small clinic set up to study the effects on volunteers offering themselves to test new and developing drugs. Sir Marcus Glasson was one. In fact, he refused to allow any volunteer to be a test subject until he first submitted himself to the drug to be sure it was safe for others. He did this, of course, after a precise program of non-human testing.

To protect the privacy of those volunteering, a thin, rocky, potholed laneway allowed for a nondescript, partly obscured back entrance. That is where Jude's 4WD pulls up.

Mirla found it hard to suppress her shock the moment she laid eyes on Noi. Her skin had returned to the green, slimy texture with a network of erratically pumping veins visible just beneath the surface. Her mouth gapes for breath like a fish out of water, and her eyes are wide open and full of tears and fear.

If that wasn't confounding enough, something else had Mirla intrigued.

"Jude? Didn't you say she had head injuries from an assault?" she asks.

"That's what we first saw, but the injuries began to fade after we got her into the seawater."

"Well, there's little sign of them now. No swelling or bruising, just minor cuts and scratches that have almost healed."

"Why is she slimy green?" comes a soft voice from the back of the room.

Mirla spins around. In her intense interest in Noi, she hadn't noticed Kailee.

"Sorry, Mirla," offers Jude, answering the question on his mother's face. "This is Kailee. She's with Aussie Immigration and the one who sent you the email that led to us finding Noi."

Mirla turns to Evelyn for confirmation. He nods and gives Kailee a wink.

"Well, I have much to thank you for, young lady," says Mirla. "But I must ask two things of you. Did you know what you were getting yourself into? And would you go with Evelyn? I'm sure he will find you a room in his place next door. I have a lot to do here. We'll talk later."

Kailee is about to answer the first question, but Mirla has turned her attention to Jude. "First thing in the morning, Jude, I need you to set out and find me another worm. I need not tell you how urgent it is."

"Come, Girly, you need a rest and I need a beer and a new cigar," Evelyn says, steering Kailee to the rear exit. He stops and turns back to Jude. "I'm coming with you in the morning, Jude."

Kailee looks back at Jude who replies with a smile and a nod. Then, remembering, she hands over the small wooden spoon she had kept safe since the hospital. "I think Noi would like to hold on to this."

There's a murmur from Noi as her hand reaches out for the spoon, then clasps it to her stressed heart.

As Evelyn leads Kailee to the rear entrance of his Sunday Roast Bar, she pulls him up and, in a stern tone, says, "Did it cross your mind I could also do with a beer? And don't call me Girly!"

***

The cosmopolitan cocktail almost made up for the lack of decent champagne on offer at the first-floor open-air bar of the Esplanada Hotel. It was not Harper's preferred choice of accommodation, but the hotel was only a short distance from the Glasson Lab.

The ceiling fans are offering some respite from the sultry evening air as she cowers in the furthest corner from the other residents enjoying the tropical atmosphere.

Across the road, the sound of water lapping at the shore is relaxing between bouts of laughter and dated songs broadcast for the benefit of the tourists. Harper studies those seated at a sufficient distance away. She has never been a tourist. What they wear and how they wear what they wear is how she will need to look in the morning. Nothing she had packed was at all suitable.

She will not have time to find a shop that's open in the morning, so what she had packed would need dismantling, crumpling, and rid of all high-fashion appearance. The one must-have item of clothing missing is a t-shirt.

One girl in a group of young travellers attracted Harper by her overall image. She was younger than Harper. Her hair dark and messy in contrast to Harper's severely combed-back black-dyed hair. She had little or no makeup, and her clothes, or what little she wore, were loose and grungy. Her khaki-grey t-shirt looked as if she had slept in it for days. On the front is a charcoal-like sketch of a broken heart with the words 'NO HARD FEELINGS' scribbled below. The denim shorts she wears are overly torn, stressed, frayed, and barely cover her crotch. It will be a challenge, but Harper chose her to model herself after.

A moment later the girl is up out of her chair. Harper is afraid she's leaving too soon as she has more detail to examine and copy. Instead, she heads towards the toilets. Harper downs the last of her cocktail and follows.

Harper learnt years ago that money can buy almost anything, and before long she was walking out of the toilet wearing the girl's broken-heart t-shirt. A moment later the girl exits the toilet and dances back to her friends wearing a $760 Stella McCartney black crepe top and waving a fistful of dollars.

CHAPTER 41

Harper got little sleep during the night. It was not because of the limited effect the air-con had on the humidity, but the hours spent dismantling her icy, austere image of many years. Usually after washing her shoulder-length jet-black hair, she would blow-dry it straight, comb it severely back, then secure it with a circular blood-red hair clip with a diagonal pin as per the DO NOT symbol. This time she let it dry un-coaxed, unkempt, un-clipped and natural.

Her luggage contained only one pair of pants — a Donna Karan white, loose-fitting cotton pair she had attacked with the blade taken from her underarm razor and cut the legs off just below the crotch. She encourages some fraying and rubs some mid-tone face powder into the fabric to kill the whiteness. The only item of clothing that required no such destructive attention was a pair of Saint Laurent off-white sneakers. Though some dirtying up won't go astray.

Harper checks herself in the wall mirror and finds the result not only intriguing but unrecognisable as her old self. The lack of her signature bright red lipstick, severe black eyeliner and mascara, or any other makeup, was challenging to accept. But if she can hardly recognise herself, neither will her father's mistress if she's seen a photo of her. Which is unlikely, as her father would not have had any pictures of her taken over the past twenty years.

Harper has always been protective of her image. While other journalists had headshots to go with their by-line, Harper refused. In fact, she would threaten brutal reprisal if anyone pointed a camera in her direction.

The mistress, Mirla Yimenes, though, she will recognise after her research uncovered some photos of her. Only a few, as she appears to shun attention unlike her jet-setter son, Jude. At twenty-five years her junior, she now felt closer to his age, such was her transformation. If he were not on an island off the coast of Queensland, it would be most interesting to get his reaction.

She turns sideways to the mirror and runs one hand down the front of her t-shirt and pleased with herself that her braless breasts still have enough firmness to stretch the cotton that covers them. Her legs, though pale, have kept their shape, and she wonders why she had never exposed them more often.

She takes out a khaki nylon lightweight fold-up shopping bag she always carries in her Manu Atelier tote, unravels it and puts in her purse-cum-wallet, phone and notepad. Hangs it casually over her shoulder, then with one last check in the mirror, heads to the beach opposite the hotel.

The sun is rising on the other side of the island, but the wispy clouds are picking up its pink and orange glow as Harper makes her way along the beach, passing stalls and smoking fires. The smell of food cooking reminded her she had not eaten since the meagre rations on the plane. Yet, despite her new grunge image, eating hawker food is beneath her.

A little further on she stops and sits down on the low stone wall separating the beach from the road and takes out her notepad. She writes something down, but it's only a guise to cover her observation of the single-storey building across the road. There was no sign, but she knew the address of Glasson BioMarine and her GPS marked the spot.

She is hoping Mirla will eventually come out and they'll accidentally bump into each other. This she preferred as opposed to knocking on the door and having to introduce herself.

She is expecting a long wait, but movement across the road changes that. A man of considerable size exits the bar next to the Glasson office and walks into their carport attached. She does not consider him as the bar-owner Aswar mentioned, as he's away with Jude. But that quickly and surprisingly changes when he comes back out, followed by her new half-brother.

Harper needs to rethink her plan. If those two shook off Aswar's men and made it back here, so must the girl Noi — that's if she is still alive.

Harper watches the two men get into a 4WD parked in the carport and reverse out. She waits to see which direction they head, then looks around for a passing taxi. Luck is with her, and she waves for one to stop. The driver is a young man who has trouble keeping his eyes on the road and off her bare legs. Even when he is looking ahead, it's through spiderweb cracks in the windscreen caused by kicked-up stones.

"I want to go where that car ahead goes," she orders, determined not to fall into the trap of saying: 'follow that car'.

Harper's concentration on the car ahead and the need to come up with a new plan are loudly interrupted when the driver turns up his bass-heavy techno music. She looks at him as he looks back at her with a cheeky smile. Shit, is he making a pass at me? Finding it hard to believe, but it reinforces that all the effort in changing her appearance was worth it.

The 4WD pulls up at a dive shop. Harper orders the gum-chewing taxi driver to stop and waits to see who gets out of the 4WD. It's Jude.

"You wait, understand?" she instructs the driver. He nods with a broad, toothy smile, then peers over the steering wheel to further study her legs and more as she walks towards the shop.

Evelyn is waiting in the 4WD and also gives her a head to toe examination until she enters the front door.

Jude is having a joke with his mate behind the counter as the hiss of air tanks being filled comes from a back room. The stop attendant turns to Harper and asks if he can be of help.

Jude takes a quick glance before suggesting he'll go help with his tanks.

"Are you a diver?" Harper directs at Jude who stops and turns back.

"Sorry, are you talking to me?" he questions.

"The best around," interrupts the attendant.

"Then you're the one I'm after," says Harper, taking a step closer to Jude. "I'm Tory Harper."

The error, known only to her, caught her by surprise. She had meant to say Harris, and now it is too late to change. "I'm doing a story on diving around the Banda Islands, and I'm wondering if you have the time for an interview?"

174

Jude immediately sizes her up, noting that she has never dived in her life.

"Sorry, lady, but I don't have the time. Excuse me," he says, disappearing into the back room.

"I have the time," chirped the attendant. "Know the islands like the back of my hand, I do."

Harper turns to him, and with a wry smile, says, "Maybe another time."

Before she can leave the shop, the broad figure of Evelyn, who has come to help Jude gather the tanks, blocks her.

There's a pause as Harper sizes him up, remembering what Aswar said: a thorn in the side. Evelyn steps aside to allow her to pass, gives her another look over, then a wink back at the shopkeeper.

Back in the taxi, she asks the driver where the divers moor their boats. He points down the road. "We go there?" he asks.

"No, take me back to where you picked me up."

Her heart rate is up during the drive back. The impromptu plan didn't quite work out, and she's annoyed at the stupid mistake. She must remember her name is Tory Harper from now on. She has come face to face with her new half-brother. If he has any knowledge of the names of his father's legitimate children, the mistake could blow her cover.

CHAPTER 42

Harper's mind is on Jude, the surprise at seeing him back in Dili, and the slip-up with her name, and she is unaware the taxis has stopped in front of the Sunday Roast Bar and not on the beach side of the road.

In a rush to cross over and blend back in among the food stalls on the beach, she pushes the car door to close it, but it gives out a metallic grind and froze. The driver sits waiting and watching her without offering to help. Harper gives him one of her famous dagger stares and puts all her weight behind the door, forcing it to slam shut with a loud bang. The effort has her step back unbalanced and into a figure coming out of the bar. The collision caused her shopping bag to slide off her shoulder and fall to the ground.

"Sorry, let me help," comes the voice from behind.

The taxi speeds off, kicking up a mouthful of dust that adds to Harper's confusion as she looks around to face Kailee.

Harper does not know what Kailee looks like, but she can recognise a Canberra public servant when she sees one.

Kailee smiles and helps retrieve the dropped bag

"Thanks," is a word Harper rarely says as she watches Kailee walk to the Glasson office entrance and knock on the door.

Not wanting to appear interested, Harper makes out she's dusting herself off and checking her bag's contents. The sound of the door latch being unlocked is too tempting not to look up.

Mirla opens the door just slightly. Seeing Kailee, she opens it wider for her to enter, at the same time locking eyes on Harper.

For a moment Harper suspects she's recognised her true identity, but after a polite smile, Mirla turns, follows Kailee inside, and closes the door.

Harper tries not to appear too anxious, crossing the road to the beach. Once there, she takes off her sneakers and walks to the water's edge. The water is cool and calming. For a moment she tries to think of the last time she waded along a beach. If it was with her father, it and any other occasion has long been erased from her memory.

Her mind focusses back on the past hour. She has come face-to-face with her father's secret life and the people possibly harbouring Aswar's wife inside the Glasson Lab.

A sense of being out of place on this tropical, war-torn island comes over her. The years of comfort and luxury, while exposing corruption in high places, have been her life. Here, she feels vulnerable. In the last hour, those that were only a name have become faces and uncomfortably personal.

***

Inside the Glasson BioMarine office, Kailee is looking at the photos on the walls and asks Mirla, "How is Noi doing?"

She looks back after getting no answer.

"Who was that?" Mirla asks, staring at the closed door and appearing distracted.

"Who? The woman outside, you mean?"

Mirla nods as she turns to Kailee.

"No idea. She dropped her bag getting out of a taxi, and I helped pick it up. Why? Is something wrong?"

"No, not at all," replies Mirla. "I suspect everybody. Especially with Noi here, and to answer your question, she's stable for the moment, but I have grave concerns that if Jude does not find what we're after, she and the baby may not make it."

"Why is this happening to her?" asks Kailee. "I mean, I studied medicine for two years and have seen nothing like the way she looks."

"What has Jude told you?" asks a worried Mirla.

"Not much. They both — Jude and Evelyn, I mean — kept me in the dark, mostly. "

Mirla studies Kailee for a moment. "Do you want a coffee?"

"Yes, that'll be great, thanks."

As Mirla busies herself making coffee, Kailee tours the outer office. There's not a lot to look at apart from framed underwater photographs of strange sea creatures.

"These photos are wonderful. Who took them?" She asks as Mirla places a coffee pot and cups on the desk.

"Jude and Marcus."

Kailee notices Mirla's downcast eyes.

"Oh, I'm sorry. I should have offered my condolences earlier."

"No need, and thank you," Mirla says, pouring the coffee.

"Mirla, I don't mean to pry, and I'm sure it's none of my business — well, I guess it is now — but how come all this is happening?"

Mirla takes a sip of her coffee as she considers how to answer. After putting her cup down, she gives Kailee an intense, searching examination.

"First, tell me about yourself," she says, leaning back into her chair. "What I gather is that you didn't have to get involved. You are, what, a junior research assistant with the Australian Immigration Department? If you had concerns about what you discovered, you could have passed it on to one of your superiors?"

"I did," replies Kailee, showing a tinge of the anger she felt back in her department. "But, you know, an Asian girl with no ID gets labelled as someone who works in the sex trade and her case goes to the bottom of the queue. I knew from the start this was a false assumption and had to help her."

Mirla continues to study Kailee until deciding it was time to tell her all.

"What do you know about Noi? What did you come up with in your search to find her identity?" She asks, searching for any sign of dishonesty.

"Apart from her being assaulted, the apparent connection to your husband, and that others are after her, nothing."

"Partner," corrects Mirla. "We never married."

Kailee remains silent, unsure how to respond to that.

"Have you ever heard of a man called Djan Muhammad Aswar?"

Kailee shakes her head. "Should I have?"

"He is Noi's husband and the most brutal man you would not want to meet."

"Is he one of the men in the photo I sent you?"

"Compared to Aswar, they're angels, but very dangerous just the same. They're two of his...what should I say...bodyguards, henchmen, yes men? I'm sure you get the picture."

"They attacked us on Great Keppel Island!" adds Kailee. "Talk to Evelyn; he'll tell you about the goats and what happened."

"Yes, Jude filled me in and said how much help you have been."

Kailee allows herself an internal smile before asking, "So the baby is Aswar's? That's why he wants his wife back?"

Mirla gives Kailee a strange smirk of a smile. "Not quite."

Kailee shakes her head. "I don't understand."

After a moment to consider if she should include Kailee into her trust, she answers, "I believe it is time for you to return to Canberra. We appreciate your help, but we can handle things from here."

Kailee feels offended at being dismissed again, just as she had been by her superior.

"Look, if I've come across something secret, an experiment of some sort, you can trust me not to say anything. And anyway, if it weren't for me, you'd never have found Noi!"

It's not usual for Mirla to have her decisions questioned — especially with a hint of blackmail. She gives Kailee a long, penetrating look before gathering up the coffee cups.

Kailee feels she may have gone too far and she'll be on the next plane back to Canberra.

"I need to check on Noi," says Mirla after placing the cups in a sink. "I could do with your help."

CHAPTER 43

K ailee helps Mirla wash then wrap Noi in a towel saturated with water from the holding tanks of other deep-sea creatures. For the time being, Noi appears calm and her skin stable. However, it is uncertain how long this will last if another worm cannot be found to replenish the serum.

With nothing more to do, and Mirla not showing any interest in talking, Kailee prepares to leave. "I guess if there's nothing more I can help you with, I need to work out how to get back to Canberra," she says with a touch of sadness.

"You have a good feel for patients," Mirla says, stopping Kailee from leaving. "The way you turned Noi over and swabbed her back is not the first time you've done that, yes?"

Kailee smiles with a slight shrug of her shoulders. "Thanks, um, no, I nursed my mother for some time before she died."

Mirla offers no sympathy, having hardened to death over the years.

"Your father? Is he still alive?"

"No!" The blunt answer reveals far more than one word.

Mirla studies Kailee for a moment, then with a nod invites her to sit back down.

"Are you aware of what we do here?" she asks

"I did some research into your business. It's impressive, what with your discoveries and all."

"And in your research did you find we developed an undetectable euthanasia drug?"

Kailee is not sure where this conversation is going, but confirms, "Yes, and it created quite some controversy."

"Where do you stand on euthanasia, Kailee? Would your mother have considered it?"

"I can't answer that," says Kailee as she looks to the floor.

"Yes, it's the ones who are not facing death that find it hard to answer. They don't have the fear of dying but the fear of guilty thoughts."

Kailee remains silent.

"Yes, Noi is an experiment," says Mirla, deciding to allow Kailee into her confidence.

Kailee looks up with confused expectation.

"Marcus and Jude came across a very rare deep-sea creature. We found it could protect against or repel any ailment or infection that would threaten other creatures, including humans. Over several years we found only a few, and our testing was...how should I put it...curtailed by the lack of ample specimens."

Mirla pauses, for what she is about to add may not go down well.

"We tested on mice and animals with some success, but the depleting serum and failure to find more worms pressured Marcus to test for side effects on himself. But he was a man, and what we discovered was that the full effect of this serum worked best on unborn babies. When the baby is born, it will be immune to all known diseases. The jelly in its umbilical cord has enough doses of the serum to pass onto four other pregnant women who will bear more immune babies." She looks at Kailee for a sign that she understands what she's saying.

"What you're telling me," offers Kailee, "is that over several generations, all babies will be immune?"

"Globally!" adds Mirla.

Kailee looks at Noi wrapped in a seawater-saturated towel. "Did you know this would happen?"

"No," replies Mirla with a mix of regret and anger. "Once he found out she was pregnant, Marcus took it upon himself to give the serum to Noi, telling no one. You see, he knew he was dying and time was running out to achieve any success. Marcus saw this as a parting gift to Noi, who has been through so much torment. She would become the Eve to a new generation."

Kailee is at a loss for words while Mirla reflects on what could have been had Marcus not died.

"I don't want to die," says Noi, having stirred and heard all they'd said. "If I have to, then my baby must live."

Kailee watches as Mirla gently strokes Noi's forehead until her eyes close and she drifts back into her private slumber.

"Is there anything I can do? I feel so helpless," Kailee says, unsure of anything anymore.

"Until Jude finds another worm, we are all helpless," Mirla confesses. "But I'd like you to stay. That is, if you want to."

CHAPTER 44

T he constant vigilance of Noi, and the need to keep her covered with towels saturated with the depleting supply of tank water, made for a long, worrying day. The sharing of past personal experiences between Kailee and Mirla helped pass the time and brought the two closer together. Despite being tired, Kailee offers to stay, but Mirla insists she go back to her room in Evelyn's place and try to get some sleep.

Kailee knew sleep would not come easily with so much new information swimming around in her head. Instead, she needed a drink at the bar to relax her.

As soon as she entered the Sunday Roast Bar, Kailee had a clearer understanding of where she was and what she had got herself involved in.

Despite the bar being half full with patrons, the larger-than-life presence of Evelyn was missing, and she thinks of him and Jude searching for the desperately needed, but elusive, worm.

The rush to get to bed and sleep on arrival the night just past meant this is the first time she has to look around Evelyn's bar. The dim lighting adds further mystery as she takes in the array of memorabilia hanging on the walls. Posters celebrating the country's independence, photos of times when Evelyn was with the peace-keeping force, and other moments in his varied past. A feeling of belonging washes over her.

She turns towards the bar for the promised drink.

Evelyn had introduced Kailee to his barman Carlo the night before, and he had silently watched her from the moment she had entered.

"Sit here at the bar, Miss Kailee, and I'll get you a drink."

"Thanks, Carlo. I'll have a..." She stops herself ordering her usual bitters, lime and soda with a wry smile as memory of Evelyn's judgement of her bites. "A glass of dry white wine, please."

Carlo nods with a smile and says, "As you are a guest of my esteemed bar owner, you shall have top shelf."

The wine is smooth, dry and oaky, but Kailee's mind is wandering again, and before she realises it, her glass is empty.

The sound of someone coming into the bar through the plastic strip fly barrier turns Carlo's head. He straightens up and brushes a strand of loose hair from his face, and steps to the end of the bar as Harper Glasson pulls out a bar stool.

"Hi, my name is Carlo. What can I get you?"

Harper looks behind him at the display of bottles. A strong desire for a tall glass of French champagne would not go down well, considering her new grunge image. She is about to opt for a locally brewed beer when she sees Kailee has an empty glass in front of her.

"Can I buy you one? Just a small thank you for helping me this morning."

Kailee had her mind on other things, and it didn't quite register who had just entered.

"Oh, no thanks, it isn't necessary."

"Well, then, can I buy you one, anyway? I hate drinking alone."

Kailee hates drinking with strangers and even more talking to strangers. Before she can refuse, Harper gives Carlo the nod, then slides onto a bar stool beside Kailee.

"I'm Tory Harris," she says, forgetting the error on meeting Jude. "Are you Australian?"

As uncomfortable as she feels, Kailee could do with a fresh conversation after the long and detailed revelations between her and Mirla.

"Um, yes, Canberra, actually."

"Oh, really, a public servant? Sorry, I tend to assume the only jobs there are government jobs."

"That's okay, most people do, and yes, I'm one of them...well, was."

"So, are you holidaying here in Dili...um, sorry, what's your name?"

"Kailee...Kailee Banks. Well, I guess so." As soon as she said it, Kailee regretted it came out like that. "And you? Are you travelling around the area?"

"Actually, I'm trying to write an article on diving around the islands."

"Trying? Is there a problem?" asks Kailee, quick to pick up the doubt.

"Oh, not really. It's just when I approach anyone for an interview they're too busy to talk."

Carlo is busy drying some glasses and listening to the conversation while enjoying having two attractive females to serve. "You should talk to Jude. He knows more than anyone about diving around the islands," he offers.

"Well, thank you," says Harper, surprised at how fast Jude has crept into the mix. "Where can I find this Jude...?"

"Yimenes," Carlo pronounced. "Next door," he adds, nodding to his right.

Harper feels this is going better than she had hoped and turns to Kailee. "You went in there after helping me with my dropped bag. Do you know him? Could you introduce me?"

Kailee is not comfortable with where this is going. There are too many secrets, and the biggest is lying ill next door.

"I don't know him that well. All I can tell you is that he's away at the moment."

"Oh, do you know when he'll be back?"

"No, sorry, I'm not privy to his movements." Kailee is beginning to take offence at this woman's forcefulness.

"Was that his mother who opened the door for you? Could she help me?"

Kailee has to stop this intrusion. "Look, it's not a good time to visit her. She has just lost her husband and needs time to grieve."

Harper senses she is pushing things too fast. In her typical hard-hitting journalistic style, she would go in harder, but here it could backfire, so she'll leave more questions for another time.

"I'm sorry. Yes, I agree it would be insensitive of me to intrude. Guess I'll check out some other bars and hope to find someone to interview."

Kailee sees no point in commenting and stays silent in the hope she leaves.

"Are you staying here long?" Harper asks, downing the last of her wine. "Maybe we can meet again sometime?"

"Oh, I don't think I'll be here for much longer, thanks anyway," replies Kailee, eager to be alone again.

"Well, nice meeting you, Kailee," she says, placing ten dollars on the bar before leaving.

Carlo has finished wiping tables after the last of the patrons had left, and joins Kailee back at the bar.

"You haven't touched the drink she bought you; can I get you something else?" asks Carlo, hoping at least someone will stay to keep him company on a quiet night.

Kailee looked down at the glass of wine and could not decide if it was the taste of the wine or the uneasy vibe she got from Tory Harris. Her nerves were on edge before she entered; now, they needed something stronger to settle them back down.

"What can you do with vodka?"

"Ah, señorita! You have asked the correct question. I will make you my very own speciality."

Kailee gives a slight smile and leans on the bar as Carlo prepares his concoction.

Her eyes wander from the busy Carlo, across the display of bottles and glasses and some collectible bar signs, until settling on a framed photo. She leans forward and peers over her glasses to get a better look at the two figures posing for the camera.

"Who is that with Evelyn?" she asks Carlo.

Carlo looks up from pouring out a measure of vodka, sees what she is looking at and replies, "That's the professor. So sad, they were great friends."

"May I have a closer look?" asks Kailee. She has not really had a close look at what the professor looked like apart from newspaper clippings and the rare low-res images on Google.

Carlo takes down the photo and hands it to Kailee.

Kailee wipes some dust off the glass in the frame and peers into the two faces staring back at her. She smiles at the face Evelyn is pulling, confirming his gentle nature wrapped within his consider-able bulk. The professor is more serious and looks uneasy being photographed. She studies his features closer. So this is the man who has developed so many good things, yet has left a poor girl fighting for her and her baby's life next door. She registers for future use the features of a brilliant yet obsessive mind. The eyes, the furrowed brow, the shape of his lips, and the squarish shape of his face all add to her mental identikit library.

The feeling she gets when successfully identifying those in the never-ending files that once passed across her desk ripples through her veins. She looks towards the front entrance to the bar and visualises who she has just talked with. Her natural look and lack of any makeup made it easy. She studies the photo closer and, trusting her ability, feels confident they're related.

Carlo has delivered his masterpiece to Kailee and steps back to watch her reaction. Kailee's mind is spinning. She takes up the cocktail glass and throws the contents down in one gulp.

"Can you make me another one, please?" Oblivious to what the drink tasted like or what the effects will be.

CHAPTER 45

C onrad is in his office early, checking over charts and papers to prepare for a meeting with a mining consortium later in the morning when his secretary buzzes.

"Sir, the Minister for Immigration is here and would like to see you if you're free," comes her efficient voice through the speaker.

"Yes, um, send him in," replies Conrad, placing the papers back into their folder before rising from his chair to welcome his visitor.

"Gerard, a pleasant surprise! Any luck with the tip-off I gave you?" says Conrad, offering his hand.

"Came to a dead end there, I'm afraid. No, we have a slight issue in the department, and well, nothing to do with you, I'm sure, but best I give you a heads-up."

"Anything serious?" Conrad asks, feeling the minister has brought a chill into the office with him.

"Probably nothing, but one of our research girls has gone missing. She hasn't been to work for three days, and no one can get in touch with her. Someone went around to her place in case she was ill, but she was not there, and others in the apartment block hadn't seen her. Which is not unusual, it seems, as she's not a very visible type."

"Sorry to hear. I hope she turns up soon, but why are you telling me?" asks a hesitant Conrad.

"Yes, well, it's just that if she doesn't show up soon, we'll need to call in the Feds. As I mentioned to you the other day, a case she was working on had an entry mentioning you and your father's name. Nothing to do with you, I'm sure, but now you know in case the Feds come around to talk to you."

Conrad needs to pull himself together and not give away his deep concern that the Federal Police could get involved. "What was the case again?"

"Oh, an Asian girl with no identification in hospital with injuries consistent with a sexual assault. Probably she's an illegal worker in the sex trade. As I think I told you, our girl took it upon herself to see her. Totally uncalled for, but anyway, as I said, nothing for you to worry about."

"Yeah, thanks, Gerard. Let me know if she shows up. What's her name, by the way?"

"Kailee Banks. Sorry to bother you."

It takes a minute or two before Conrad can take his eyes off the closed door to his office. The mention of the Federal Police getting involved could add another unwanted layer to what is becoming an increasing mess. He spins around, goes back to his desk, grabs his mobile and calls Harper.

It takes a minute before Harper answers. "What do you want, Conrad? I'm busy here," she snaps.

"Yeah, well, things could get busy here too," replies Conrad, with no attempt to hide his frustration. "That girl from Immigration is on the missing list, and it's likely the Feds will be called in, and it's odds on they'll want to talk to me. This is getting out of hand, Harper."

"Shit, slow down, Conrad. She's here in Dili and I've talked to her, so don't go getting your knickers in a knot."

"You talked to her! Does she know who you are?"

"I'm not that fucking stupid; of course she doesn't. Look, I know where Aswar's wife is as well, but I have a sense there's something else going on with her. I need to find out more, so keep the Feds sniffing around down there and not up here. If you can send them off in a different direction, that'll give me the time I need." \

Conrad's worst fear is having the Feds sniffing around him any time, but if they see through his lies, they'll be digging for more.

"Okay, Harper, but let me know if they stick their noses in up there." Then a thought crosses his mind. "This girl from Immigration is a researcher; how come she doesn't know who you are?"

"Unlike you, Mister Minister, I keep a low profile," she replies with a snicker in her voice. "And if you saw me now, even you wouldn't recognise me. Bye!"

***

Aswar steps back from viewing the monitor in his unofficial surveillance bunker two blocks away from the official Indonesian Government department in Jakarta. He gives the computer operator a nod to continue listening in on Harper's phone. The call from her brother is enough for Aswar to take some urgent action.

If the Australian Federal Police get involved, then he needs to get his wife before they trace her to Dili.

With his two henchmen, Afif and Fauzi, in a Yeppoon hospital, Aswar has lost patience with those he pays heaps to get things done.

If it weren't for the long-standing price on his head if he set foot on Timor-Leste, he'd go there and get things sorted himself.

The only choice he has left is to use Harper Glasson.

CHAPTER 46

Kailee woke to three unresolved issues. One is the mix of an unseasoned drinker with Carlo's special vodka concoction, leaving her with a head-spinning hangover. Second is this person, Tory Harris. Her pushy manner in pressing to see Jude and Mirla left Kailee with an uneasy feeling. The third is the photo of Evelyn and the Professor and her obsessive identity-cracking mindset?

Kailee needs to talk to Mirla about the second issue and for more information about the third. The first issue requires a strong black coffee.

Her room is at the back of the Sunday Roast Bar, with access to the rear laneway and the obscure entrance to the lab next door. Mirla suggested she use this entrance instead of the front, which pleased Kailee as she did not want to run into that Tory person again.

Mirla opens the door to Kailee's knocking, then steps aside for her to enter.

"How is Noi?" asks Kailee, looking towards the bed where she lies.

"Asleep for now," replies a tired-looking Mirla. "She had a restless night until a sedative calmed her down."

"Is there anything I can do?"

Mirla thinks for a moment. "I could do with a rest myself if you don't mind sitting by her."

"Not at all," Kailee replies, wondering if she should wait until Mirla has rested before telling her about the night at the bar.

Mirla notices Kailee's worried expression and asks, "Is there something wrong?"

"It's okay. It can wait till you're rested."

Mirla is not one to wait when answered in that way. "Tell me, Kailee. So much is happening. I won't be able to rest until you tell me."

"Well," Kailee hesitates, wondering how to phrase the question. "Do you mind if I ask you about the professor — I mean his past?"

Mirla looks at Kailee to judge her motive for wanting to know.

"It's none of my business, I know, but something I came across last night...I mean, it may be nothing, but..."

Mirla raises her hand. "Tell me," she insists.

"Remember that woman who dropped her bag getting out of the taxi yesterday morning?"

Mirla nods. "Yes, go on."

"Well, she came into the bar last night and bought me a drink. I don't drink in bars normally, mind you."

Mirla is not interested in her habits and makes it known with a look to get to the point.

"Yes, well, we talked — she mostly — then she left."

"Talked about what?" Mirla asks with interest.

"She said she was writing an article on diving and wanted to talk to Jude. Maybe I shouldn't have said anything, but I told her he was not around. Then she wanted to talk to you."

"Me?" asks a surprised Mirla. "About diving?"

"I'm not sure, but I don't think so. Anyway, I told her you were grieving and not to bother you."

The look on Mirla's face tightens. "Is that all? Did you say anything else?"

"No, of course not," she says, sensing Mirla meant anything to do with the experiment. "She just left. In a huff, if you ask me. Anyway, I had noticed a photo on the wall behind the bar of two men and asked to have a closer look. One man was Evelyn, and Carlo, the barman, said the other was the Professor."

"And?" urges Mirla.

"Look, it may be my overreaching interest in facial features, but this woman — Tory Harris is her name — could she be related to the Professor?"

Mirla has gone quiet. Her eyes roam around the room as her mind scans over the many years spent with Marcus.

Kailee senses she may have intruded into her private realm. Before she can apologise, Mirla turns to her with a determined look.

"Marcus has two children from a failed marriage. I've never met them, nor has Marcus talked about them. Until you mentioned it, they've never entered my mind."

"I'm sorry if I've brought up something painful. I could be wrong, but I am good at what I do," Kailee attempts a justified apology.

Mirla walks to Noi's bedside. After a moment, she turns back to Kailee. "With his death and all that has happened since, why would they not show their faces? Marcus is a very wealthy man."

"So, if I'm right, this Tory Harris could be his daughter?"

"If you're right, she's not Tory Harris, but Harper Glasson."

For a moment, they both need to register this new, possible, but most likely, revelation.

Kailee is the first to speak. "I know of the son, Conrad Glasson. He's a minister in my government, and I mentioned him in my report on Noi."

"Have you met him?" asks Mirla, showing interest.

"Oh, no, they never come down to where I work. We have a superior who informs the relevant minister of anything that may interest them. I mean, I know what he looks like and all, but we've never crossed paths."

"You say you mentioned him in your report on Noi, why?" asks Mirla, taking her seat.

"Those two men I emailed you the photo of were asking about the Professor when I went to see Noi at Yeppoon. I didn't know her name then or of any connection, but I made a note of it that ended up in my report that ended up in the system for the Immigration Minister to see."

"Who most likely mentioned it to Conrad Glasson, I imagine," adds Mirla.

"Possibly," agrees Kailee. "But why would Harper Glasson be here?"

"Did she say anything else at the bar?"

"Oh, just what I told you. That she was a journalist here to research diving in the Banda Sea and wanted to know the best person to talk to. It was Carlo who suggested Jude."

"Did she know I was Jude's mother?"

193

"I mentioned it. But I told her not to bother you, so she left."

Mirla takes on a battle-hardened expression that had lain dormant since the bloody struggle for her country's independence.

"If I did something wrong, Mirla, please forgive me," Kailee says, reacting to her steely expression.

Mirla shakes her head. "No, Kailee, you did nothing wrong. In fact, you have raised questions that need answering." She looks back at Noi. "I need to do something in the outer office. Would you keep an eye on Noi, please?"

CHAPTER 47

~∙∼∙∼∙~

The smoke from sizzling fish over hot coals, the constant urging to buy from hawkers, and the abundant flies attracted to her sweet, pale skin, are testing Harper's endurance as she stakes out the Glasson Office across the busy road.

She is waiting in hope for Kailee to leave the bar and enter the office for her to follow, unaware she is already inside, having entered by the rear entrance.

As she is about to lose her cool with one insistent food vendor, a motorbike rider passes. The same rider has passed several times, and each time slows at the Glasson address. Harper judges the rider to be male and non-local compared to other motorcyclists and scooter riders passing. Missing is the local's calm, unhurried manner and the colour of their casual clothes. Instead, this rider is helmeted, dressed in threatening black, and despite not seeing a face, has a determined attitude.

Harper watches the rider once again turn into a laneway between two buildings to the left of Sunday Roast Bar then reappear from a laneway between two buildings to the right of the Glasson Lab. Harper figures a laneway must run behind the Bar and Lab, and therefore both have rear entrances.

She waits for the rider to pass again, but this time the bike stops a mere eight metres from Harper and parks among bikes and scooters lining the beach side of the road.

She cowers down, and to appear to show no interest in the rider, buys the offering from the incessant vendor. Veiled by the smoke from the many barbecues, she backs up to the water's edge while keeping a watchful eye on the rider. Unwittingly, she takes a bite of the smoky, charcoal-flavoured fish portion, then instantly spits it out in disgust. The remaining piece is donated to the birds fighting over the morsel spat out. She wipes the residue from her mouth and brushes away a couple of flies before returning her attention to the road. The bike remains parked on its side stand, but the rider has gone.

Harper frantically looks around the beach area, but it's across the road she spots the dark, helmeted figure disappearing behind the carport of the Glasson Office. If whoever he is has anything to do with Aswar, then why hasn't he told me?

***

Fauzi removes his helmet to squeeze through the thin space that separates the carport from Evelyn's bar. At the back of the building, he crouches down behind a clump of scraggly bushes to take in the surroundings and to study the entrance, calculated to be the rear of the Glasson building.

Since Great Keppel Island, he's mind has been on one thing, and one thing only — revenge!

Afif died at the Yeppoon hospital from the severe injury inflicted by the wild goat and the subsequent loss of blood.

His built-up rage at the loss of Afif unveils his relationship with Afif was more than co-employees of Aswar. He long held an intimate attraction to Afif with his boyish-looks, his honed physique, his immature innocence and his pleasure of the kill. But it was one-sided, and the brutality of their profession did not allow for any display of affection. Afif's attraction to the opposite sex left Fauzi in constant frustration. Now, any hope of convincing Afif otherwise has gone.

And he knows who to blame.

He will ignore any further orders from Aswar. He will be the sole judge of how to handle the removal of his wife. It will be slow and painful, and anyone who gets in his way will get the same.

In his painful struggle to get to his dying partner during the mayhem with the goats, wind, dust and the noise of the chopper's rotors, he heard someone say Aswar's wife was in danger of dying if she didn't get back to Dili. He prays she hasn't died, for that is his mission.

196

With strapped-up ribs, he wasted no time in slipping away from Yeppoon and making his way to Dili using the fake Timor-Leste passport he always carries, knowing if Aswar ever turned against him, as has happened to others on his payroll, he was safe in Dili where Aswar would never come. Then, once he has avenged the death of his partner, he'll disappear into the mountains under a new identity where no one can find him.

***

Mirla has gone to the front office to find the contact details of Marcus' solicitor in Sydney. She dials the number of Schultz and Anders Lawyers, waits for the receptionist to answer, then asks to speak to Dignam Schultz. Told he is busy, Mirla refuses to call back later and tells the receptionist it is crucial she talks to Mr Schultz and that she will wait as long as it takes.

"Who will I say is calling?"

"Mirla Yimenes. I wish to talk to him about the death of Professor Marcus Glasson."

"I'll see if I can interrupt Mr Schultz." The line goes on hold with some soothing music. But Mirla is not in the mood for soothing.

The line goes off hold quicker than Mirla expected. "I'm putting you through now," informs the receptionist.

"Miss Yimenes, please accept my condolences and my apology for not calling you myself," says Dignam Schultz.

"Thank you, Mr Schultz," replies Mirla. "I hope you have a moment to talk?"

"Of course. Are you calling from Dili?"

"Yes," replies Mirla.

"Then let me call you back and save you the cost."

"No, it's fine. I wish to ask you about Marcus and what he has left with you."

"Much, I'm afraid. I'm sure you are aware of the complicated set-up of Glasson BioMarine?"

"Yes, but it's more about his Will if he has lodged one with you."

"He has, and it is what I intended to talk to you about. I'm afraid they forced me to do something I should not have."

"Oh! Has it anything to do with his two children from his late marriage?"

She senses his unease in answering.

"You must understand, Miss Yimenes, they both can be very forceful, but I assure you the instructions in the Will are to be carried out as Professor Glasson wished."

"Are you telling me they have seen the Will?"

"I'm... I'm afraid so. But let me explain."

"Please!" snaps Mirla.

***

Because of the need for a sterile, controlled atmosphere in the lab room, the self-sealing sliding door from the outer office also blocks out noise. This also applies to the door leading to the rear clinic, making the research laboratory a soundproof buffer between the office and the clinic.

The sound of a karate yell and crashing kick from Fauzi to break open the rear clinic door carries no further than inside the clinic and a short distance down the laneway.

The shock and surprise shown on the faces of Kailee and Noi are, to a lesser degree, reflected on the face of Fauzi. He had not expected his quarry to be at arm's length so soon and so easily.

For an instant, there is a stillness as the three size up the situation.

Kailee is the first to move by putting herself between Fauzi and Noi, who pushes herself back on her bed. The second movement is the swinging fist of Fauzi as it catches the side of Kailee's face, sending her glasses flying across the room and her into the wall beside the bed.

Stunned, but driven by the look in Fauzi's eyes as he turns to Noi, Kailee uses the wall as a support to put all her energy into a kick to Fauzi's crotch. It connects, but to her surprise, it does not have the desired result. The grin on Fauzi's face shows pain will be no deterrent to what he has planned for Noi. With another swipe to Kailee's head, he sends her careening across the room and into the examination table, a small filing cabinet, and a side trolley carrying a variety of dressing and medical items. All crash to the floor, spilling their contents and those of a lidded instrument sterilisation tray.

Noi's screaming for Mirla's help follows the crashing sounds. She well knows that her husband's bodyguard has orders to kill her, and in doing so, be the death of her unborn baby.

Fauzi needs to silence her screaming, but a quick death is not in his vengeful plan. He places his hand over Noi's mouth, smothering her screams, but he needs two hands for his torture.

Beside the slumped figure of Kailee is a roll of bandages that he reaches for to use as a gag. A movement to his side catches his eye, and instead of grabbing the bandage roll, he grabs Kailee's hand holding a pair of sharp scissors veering towards him.

Fauzi snatches the scissors from her hand, and not wanting further interruptions, raises the scissors with his eyes on the target of Kailee's heart. Kailee's eyes widened as the image of her killer is etched in her mind.

Before he can strike, a crushing blow to the back of his head causes blood to splatter the area. With all the energy she could muster, Noi pushed the heavy monitor she's wired to off its stand and onto Fauzi's head.

Despite blood flowing from a deep gash, Fauzi needs to finish Kailee before working on Noi. He makes another lunge with the scissors towards Kailee's heart. Noi lunges from her bed onto Fauzi's back, making him miss his mark, but the scissors dig deep into Kailee's side.

In a desperate and painful reaction, Kailee tries to wrestle Fauzi away from her, but he manages another heavy blow to her head that knocks her unconscious.

He pushes the weakened Noi off him and props her up against the wall to render his slow revenge.

***

Mirla is still talking to Dignam Schultz when a continuous shrill beeping comes from her computer. To keep a constant vigil on Noi's condition, the heart monitor transmits its data and any changes to the patient's condition to all computers throughout the building.

The call to Schultz is immediately cut short, and Mirla rushes back to the rear clinic to check on Noi.

Fauzi has Noi pressed against the wall with one hand around her neck and the other holding a scalpel that spilt from the sterilising tray. Options of where to start are all open to him as he looks her over. Is it the eyes first or a slow slicing? No, he wants her to see what he's doing to her, so slicing comes first. The scalpel slides down the front of her hospital gown, cutting it open to reveal her green-tinged body.

Unsure of what he's looking at, he wipes a trickle of blood from his eyes. The pause is enough time for Mirla to come through the lab door, surprising both.

Mirla is quick to judge the urgency of the situation. The skills she gained during her time in the resistance movement have not diminished over the years, and without hesitation, she thrusts the side of one hand under Fauzi's chin, crushing his windpipe. The shock and inability to breathe allowed Mirla another attack. This one is final.

Taking advantage of Fauzi's accelerated heart rate and, unknown to her, his cracked ribs, Mirla drives the point of her elbow into his chest at the third rib area, causing his heart rhythm to falter...then stop.

As his lifeless body sinks to the floor, the scalpel in his hand cuts into Noi's stomach. Mirla is quick to grab the scalpel before it cuts too deep and tosses it aside.

Noi is numb and shaking with fear. She looks down at the blood coming from the cut to her stomach and faints. Mirla eases her back onto the bed. The amount of blood smear that came from the wound to Fauzi's head has Mirla checking for any other external injuries. Satisfied there is nothing more than the scalpel cut, she turns to get some dressing and sees Kailee lying among the upturned table, surgical equipment and monitor with scissors protruding from her side.

While Mirla's primary concern is for Noi and the baby, her medical judgement is to treat the more severely injured Kailee first. She unwraps a sterile gauze pad lying among the spilt items, then eases out the scissors. The wound is deep, but not too serious. She tapes the gauze pad over the wound to stem the bleeding as a temporary measure, for she needs to tend Noi's wound and close the broken door to block the view from the outside.

Mirla has another gauze pad ready to cover the cut to Noi's stomach, but it's beginning to heal itself. With some relief that the effect of the serum is still working, she tapes the pad over the wound anyway to aid the healing. She returns the monitor to its stand and reconnects it to Noi, waits for it to be operational, then checks the readings. An increase in the heartbeat is to be expected, but not enough to worry about for the moment.

The door proved to be harder to close than expected, as the force used by Fauzi to burst in bent the hinges, freezing the door at an open angle. Despite her efforts, the door would not budge.

Mirla looks around for a solution. The only answer she can come up with is to unscrew the hinges. A screwdriver is not something usually found among scalpels and other surgical equipment, but there is a toolbox in the outer office.

Finding the toolbox took some time because someone had moved it from its usual spot.

Back in the clinic she unscrews the hinges, pushes the door back into its frame, then wedges a chair under the door handle to keep it closed.

With the clinic closed from the outside view, she returns to treat Kailee's wound. As she does so, she fears that Aswar sending Fauzi proves he knows where she is and will stop at nothing to try again.

From now on, she must keep Noi in her sights.

CHAPTER 48

Harper Glasson watched Fauzi squeeze through the tight gap beside the Glasson premises until he's out of sight. Not wanting to follow into a confined space without knowing where it leads, she takes the first lane to the left, assuming it leads to a laneway servicing the rear of the buildings.

As she turns into the rear laneway, she hears a yell and a door crashing open. After judging where it came from, she steps back into a garbage and bottle bin recess at the rear of the Sunday Roast Bar to hide. The sounds of a struggle, crashing furniture, and muffled screams reach her, then after several minutes, all becomes still and silent.

Harper keeps low in her hiding spot, expecting whoever she followed to come out, plus anyone from neighbouring buildings attracted by the noise. But all remained quiet.

She furtively creeps to the open and broken rear door of the Glasson Clinic. With her back to the wall, she takes a quick glance into the room. On the floor lay two bodies and one on a bed. The bike rider no longer has his helmet on and looks dead with blood covering the back of his head. The girl on the floor seems to be still breathing but unconscious, as is the girl on the bed. She turns her head away and presses her back hard against the outer wall. Her heart thumping at the unexpected sight. She takes another glance back into the room.

Harper's experience in finding incriminating evidence in unexpected places shuts out the sight of bodies and blood, and she concentrates on the files and folders scattered over the floor. The only clue to what she's looking for is something with Noi's name on it. And unbelievably, there it is, just inside the open door. A green clip-locked polypropylene case file embossed with the letters GBM and labelled Case No. AP80GBM/17. It could have been any of the many case files scattered around, but for the word 'Noi' hand-written in thick black letters.

The sound of someone approaching from within the building stops her from looking for other files. She grabs the Noi file and rushes to hide in the cramped space between two buildings further down the lane.

After several minutes she hears the scraping of a door being pushed into a closed position. She waits a few more minutes, then, feeling it safe to do so, leaves her hiding space, walks as casually as she can down the laneway to the first side street, then quickens her pace back to her hotel.

***

Mirla stirred Noi and Kailee and moved them into the lab away from the body and mess in the clinic and sedated them back to sleep, then returned to the clinic to survey the scene.

She has a dead body on the floor, a mess to clean up, and the knowledge it will not be the last attempt at getting Noi.

With Jude and Evelyn away, she grieves Marcus' loss deeper than ever before. But her inner strength knows now is not the time to let her feelings flow. The immediate dangers are real, and there will be far too many years for that.

She dismisses any thought of calling the police. Aswar's contacts and reach are not to be underestimated and could include the local establishment.

She moves Fauzi's body into the cool room until she can make other arrangements. She rights the upturned furniture; the mess scattered over the floor sorted out, and blood smears and splatter cleaned up.

Then the realisation hits her. Noi's case file is missing.

Mirla goes through all the papers and other files again to be sure, but she had a sinking feeling it was a waste of time.

The file contained all the test data on the worm, findings, notes, and formulas. All had been entered into the computers, so nothing was lost. But the fear that Aswar could now know his wife is pregnant — possibly with his child — and the centre of an experiment.

The question remains: who took it? Did the attacker have an accomplice who waited outside while the other did the dirty work? Mirla goes to the door, removes the chair from under the handle and lets the door lean back enough to see into the back laneway. There's no file lying on the ground or anyone to be seen.

She secures the door back in place as a sense of vulnerability comes over her and the need to talk to Jude.

It takes some anxious minutes before she contacts the dive boat.

"Hi, it's..." Evelyn answers before being cut short.

"Evelyn," Mirla cries out, recognising his raspy voice. "Is Jude there? I need to talk to him. It's urgent!"

"Mirla, what is it? Jude's diving."

"Get him up. I need to talk to both of you. One of Aswar's men broke into the clinic in an attempt at getting Noi and..."

"What? Slow down, Mirla. Have they got her? Anyone hurt?"

"No, Noi is okay, but he stabbed Kailee, though not too serious."

"What about the guy?"

"I need you to get Jude before I go any further."

"He's due up any minute. Still no luck, I'm afraid to say."

"That's what I want to talk to you both about. Call me back when he's onboard."

"Hang on, Mirla, he's coming up now," Evelyn says, leaning over the port side and spotting rising bubbles.

Evelyn puts Mirla on hold as he helps Jude on board and removes his tanks and gear.

"What is it?" asks a breathless Jude. "Ev said something about a break-in."

"One of Aswar's men broke in trying to get Noi. Kailee and Noi put up a struggle, and now he's dead."

"Dead? Are they all right?"

"Yes, they're both okay, but that's not the worst of it. He must have had someone with him who took the data file on AP80 with the latest tests on Noi and that she's pregnant."

"Shit!" exclaims Jude. "Now Aswar will know everything. What do you reckon he'll do now?"

"An even greater effort to get Noi, I presume."

"Have you called the police?"

"No, we can't get them involved. Who knows what will happen if what we're doing and the importance of Noi and her baby get into their leaking system."

"Yeah, I guess so, but Aswar won't stop, will he?" suggests Jude.

Mirla sees no point in answering the obvious and changes the subject. "Have you had any luck yet?" she asks.

"Not until now. Just came up from a dive and I'm sure I got a glimpse of one, but my air was low. I'll mark the location and try again tomorrow. How's Noi doing?"

"Stable, but the remaining water from the sample tanks is running low, and that's all that's keeping her that way. If you can't get the worm by tomorrow afternoon, I need you to come back with a tank full of the surrounding water."

"I'll make sure I get the water if not the worm, then head back. I think we're being watched out here."

"Watched? By whom?" asks a worried Mirla. "It can't be Aswar so soon, can it?"

"It's unmarked and keeping its distance, but my gut's telling me Chinese."

There's no immediate response from Mirla, being well aware of the increased relationship between Indonesia and China, but there are more pressing priorities to worry about.

Mirla continues. "Jude, there's something else I need to tell you. I talked with Marcus' lawyer, and his two estranged children have seen his Will. He told me what was in it and that there is a codicil attached stating if Noi were to die of suspicious circumstances, whatever part of his estate Marcus was to leave to the two would go to charity. Seems he didn't trust them at all, and now, Kailee believes the daughter may be in Dili."

Jude needs a moment to digest this before answering. "Have you seen her? I mean, what would she be doing in Dili? You don't think she's connected with Aswar, do you?"

"It's a possibility we can't ignore," Mirla replies.

"Look, Mirla. Best we get back there quick. I'll do one more dive today before it gets dark, and if I can't get the worm, we'll bring back a tank of water. We should be back late tomorrow."

"Don't overdo the dive, Jude. I need you more than the worm."

"I'll be fine. It's you I'm worried about."

"After what has happened here, I can handle myself. There's a lot to figure out when you and Evelyn get back here, so come back soon...and safely!"

"Will do, over and out."

CHAPTER 49

~·~·~

H arper has had a bottle of Shiraz delivered to her hotel room. The file marked Case No. AP80GBM/17 lay open on the bed, and it soon became apparent that taking in all the technical detail would require considerable time to absorb.

Two and a half hours later, the wine bottle sits empty on the bedside table. Harper places the file down with a notepad carrying pages of scribbled findings, thoughts, and possibilities. Her mind is a rollercoaster of mixed emotions. One was unexpected — a growing respect for her late father.

This discovery, if it works, could change the world forever, she perceives. If what she gathers from the data is correct, such respect brings out her natural attribute...greed!

Everything mentioned in the Will and the codicil has now taken on a very different meaning. It's now vitally important that no harm comes to Noi — not, at least, till the baby is born. That may not be so easy because of Aswar's stubborn determination. She needs to speak to Conrad.

Parliament has risen for three weeks, meaning he'll be back in his Sydney apartment with his family. She checks the time there, takes out her other phone with a local SIM card inserted and calls Conrad.

"Hello?" Conrad answers, unsure of who is calling.

"Conrad, it's me..." is all she can say before being interrupted by her angry brother.

"Harper? What the bloody hell is going on?" he says, with the sound of screaming children in the background. "Hold on, I need to go into another room."

Harper wonders why he's so angry until he comes back on the line.

"I've had Aswar breathing fire down the bloody phone," he whispers. "You were supposed to help him. Now one of his men died in Yeppoon and the other is missing!"

"If it's who I think it is, he's not missing anymore...he's dead!"

"Missing or dead, it doesn't matter. He's been trying to get in touch with you, but you seem to be suddenly unreachable. Listen, Harper, Aswar is not one to mess with. He's bloody dangerous at the best of times...and this is not one of those times."

"Are you finished?" asks Harper, over his heavy breathing.

"What I've discovered, you will not believe, but I can't tell you over the phone. Can you come to Dili tomorrow?"

"Dili?" he says with a touch of fear in his voice. "No, I can't. Why don't you come back to Sydney?"

When the hairs on the back of her neck bristle, experience tells her that something is being kept from her.

"What is it, Conrad? What's stopping you from coming here?"

"When Parliament isn't sitting, it's the only time I get with the kids," Conrad replies.

"Crap, Conrad. When did you ever have time for your kids? You're just like our old man," she snaps. "You got me into helping this Aswar guy. Least you can do is do your bit."

"Why can't you tell me now? Why do I have to come all the way to Dili? And anyway, I won't even think about it unless you give me a good reason."

"Is more money than you ever dreamed of a good enough reason?" comes the blunt reply.

Harper can hear a woman and kids calling out for their father in the background.

"Look, I have to go. Can we talk about this later?"

"Shit, you're a weak under the thumb prick. Just tell me one thing. How up with patent law are you?"

"Patent law? Why? I mean, yeah, I've handled a few cases in the past, but what's that got to do with the immediate problem you're in Dili for?"

"If you could see what I have in my hand, lots and a hell of a lot more."

A moment passes before Conrad comes back on the line.

"How about I meet you in Darwin tomorrow instead?"

Harper has to think for a moment. While it's essential to keep an eye on the lab and the goings-on there, if the police get involved, it may be wise to be somewhere else for a day or two.

"There's a flight from Dili that arrives in Darwin at around ten am. I'll wait in the Qantas lounge till you arrive."

CHAPTER 50

~·~·~

Was it cheekiness or a deliberate act to continue with her grungy undercover guise of a sloppy t-shirt, frayed denim pants showing a lot of bare leg? Both, as Harper is always up for a challenge.

One challenge is getting into the Qantas lounge at Darwin Airport. Despite having a Qantas Gold Card allowing free entry, she wonders if their dress code will stop her. Another challenge is whether she can fool Conrad.

Getting into the exclusive lounge after arriving in Darwin was not a problem. In fact, she thought she was better dressed than some men. At first, she felt uncomfortable — always being one to sneer at those who do not even attempt to look their best in these exclusive lounges — but the looks she's getting from both men and women give her an uncommon thrill. Her regular designer clothes and hard exterior never attract such a response, and she contemplates whether she should reassess her image.

The arrivals board shows the flight from Sydney has landed, and Harper settles back in wonder. Ten minutes later, she watches Conrad enter the lounge, look around several times before returning to the girl at the desk. He's asking if I'm here, so it must be working. Told his sister is waiting, brings on another confusing scan of the room.

Harper is enjoying the moment. Even when his eyes land on her, and the lingering look is not an attempt at seeing through her disguise, but a moment of attraction. While it's enjoyable to watch, there's much to discuss, and the pantomime must cease.

"Conrad!" she calls out as he walks past.

He stops. Her harsh, waspish voice exposes Harper's true identity.

"Harper? What the bloody hell?"

"You like?" she teases.

"You look bloody stupid," he says as an excuse.

"What, you're worried about someone seeing you with a tarty, unidentified girl? That will hit the Sunday papers. Now get me another drink. We have a lot to talk about."

"The need to come all this way better be worth it," Conrad threatens as he settles down with two drinks.

"I'll be interested to know if you think it is," she challenged as she slides the case file onto the small table dividing the two lounge chairs. She has placed the contents of the file inside a new, plain binder to hide the number and Noi's name. As Conrad goes to open it, Harper stops him by keeping her hand firmly on the file.

"Let's get one thing straight before you see what's inside. I don't trust you, so if there's anything in there that you or the government has the slightest involvement or connection with, I want you to tell me — same with Aswar. If there's something else you two have brewing apart from getting his wife back, now is the time. And, Conrad..." she pauses for effect. "You know damn well I can see through your lies, and if I find out you're telling me porkies, I can end your career quicker than you can piss."

Conrad needs no more convincing as Harper slides her hand from the folder.

She settles back in her chair to watch her brother read through all the scientific jargon, notes, and timetable charts.

Over an hour and two more drinks later, Conrad closes the folder and looks up with the same expression in his eyes she had.

"Shit, you got to admire the bastard," he confesses.

"My thoughts precisely. Now, how do we make all that he's done ours?"

Conrad looks down at the file again while forming his words. "I've been wondering how we can contest his Will. Now this shines a new light on it."

"Go on," prompts an interested Harper.

"Well, to put it bluntly, the bastard literally kidnapped this girl to use in his experiment, right?"

"Go on," Harper says, leaning closer across the table.

211

"The last time I looked, kidnapping is a criminal offence. If the purpose was to use her, it also adds, with intent."

"With intent to what?"

"With the intention of experimenting on her. The intent to profit from it, and the intent to deprive the natural father of his child. With your skills and imagination, I'm sure we can come up with more."

Harper leans back in her chair, oddly impressed with her brother, but not enough to show it.

"That would also be the end of Glasson BioMarine because of illegal practices," she adds.

"Yes, it would. Which means..."

"Which means we could make a move to take over the business, and now, having this file, apply for a patent. We then continue to develop his groundbreaking discovery legally."

A relaxed smugness allows the two to drink to all the possibilities flowing into their minds.

Harper stiffens up. "Aswar! What are we to do about him? When I spoke to him in Sydney, he twigged that something like this could be happening. It was a guess, but it stirred the possibility of money in it being the owner of the test subject — his wife!"

"But he wants her..." he looks around the room before whispering. "D.E.A.D."

"That was then. This is now," she says, pointing to the file.

"Do you think he knows anything about what's happening to his wife...or even if she's pregnant?" asks Conrad, trying to work through the Aswar problem.

"I don't know for sure, but reckon not! Someone broke into the lab. I'm not sure if it was to get Noi or the file or both. When I looked, that girl from Immigration was on the floor with a wound to her side..."

"What?" breaks in Conrad. "The girl from Immigration is...? Shit!"

"I think she was still breathing," Harper says to Conrad's relief, then continues. "A girl I reckon is Noi, is on a bed with blood on her but also breathing. Then this guy, who I'm sure is one of Aswar's men, is on the floor with his head bashed in, and definitely not breathing. I don't know who he fought with, but the place was a mess with furniture and stuff thrown about. That's when I saw the file on the floor."

"How did you know it had anything to do with Noi?"

"It had her name handwritten on the front with the case number. Thought it best not to be walking around with that showing, so I put all the files into this plain folder. Anyway, going by the latest entries, there seems to be some genuine worry she may die if another worm thingy can't be found. If Aswar finds out she's pregnant, and how important her baby is, I don't think he'd risk her death by taking her away from the care she needs."

"Possibility," agrees Conrad. "But what do we do about him now that we know? He won't stop trying to get her back, that's for sure. Especially if he presumes she's pregnant with a boy."

Harper settles back in her chair. "Get me another drink. I have the germ of an idea I need to work through."

With two more drinks on the table, Conrad watches with interest as Harper's eyes dart around the room while her devious mind hatches a plan.

After several minutes, she picks up her drink and takes a long swallow, then places the glass down with a deliberate air.

"We tell him!" she announces.

Conrad was not expecting that and questions her reasoning.

"Why? He could claim ownership of everything as it's his wife carrying the answer to royalty riches."

"Look, all we tell him is that she's pregnant — not with a girl but with his son. That'll be enough to want his wife back alive. We don't have to say anything about what's in the file or this experiment. We say that she is ill, and if he tries another attempt at grabbing her, without the care she's getting, she and his son and heir will die. This Jude has gone diving, and I'm sure I now know what he's diving for. There is something in the file that could be coordinates where they've been searching. We tell Aswar, who then kidnaps Jude in exchange for his wife."

Conrad has taken all she says in, but then an unconvinced look washes over his face.

"Fine! Aswar gets his wife back, and if they find a worm and the girl survives to give birth to this money-making baby — where does that leave us?"

"We use Mirla to sort that out," says Harper rather smugly.

"Mirla? How?"

"Have you ever bothered to find out who this woman — this mistress — of our old man is?" Harper continues knowing he hadn't. "She fought with Fretilin during the occupation of East Timor, and, from what I gather, ruthlessly. The hatred she harbours for the militia that killed so many of her people remains strong, and guess who was one of the most brutal militia killers — Djan Muhammad Aswar. She will do anything to get her revenge."

"But Aswar surrounds himself with an army of criminals. How's she going to combat that?" asks Conrad, unconvinced with her plan.

"The reason Aswar can never set foot on East Timor soil is that he has a price on his head and would be sentenced to death for war crimes if caught there. If it works, this could be the closest he'll get to East Timor, and I'm sure Mirla could muster up her own army with the offer of Aswar's head."

Conrad leans back and crosses his arms. "That's a lot of assumptions, and still leaves the question...how it benefits us?"

"If we can take Aswar out of the equation, then we still have the law on our side to contest the Will and take over the company. Mirla and her son are charged with kidnapping, etcetera, and we continue with our dear father's plan. I'm sure there's enough information in the files to pass on to another research lab to continue their work."

Conrad contorts his mouth into a smile. Then, as fast as it came, it faded.

"What is it, Conrad?" asks his sister suspiciously.

"What? Nothing," he replies, then attempts to cover up his telltale expression. "I'm thinking that it all depends on it going the way you plan. What if it doesn't?"

Harper hates being doubted and gives her brother a sneering look.

"I mean, you know, what if Aswar ignores us and does it his way?"

"Well, it's up to you to convince him. After all, you two seem to have some relationship going."

"He works for my equivalent minister in the Indonesian government, that's all," says Conrad, quick to defend himself.

Harper has read enough in his shaky explanation to know he's hiding something but chooses not to pursue the matter; instead, keep the status quo that both remain suspicious of each other.

CHAPTER 51

Harper intended to stay in Darwin overnight. Conrad didn't. But with no flight back to Sydney by the time they'd finished scheming and plotting, he would have to endure his sister's company until the first flight in the morning. At least that's what he thought.

Harper has other ideas. Her new appearance has brought with it a rare naughtiness, and she was intent on exploiting it.

"I'm staying at the airport hotel so I can catch the first flight in the morning. Where are you staying?" he asks, expecting her to pick a ritzy city hotel.

She could stay in a five-star city hotel, but airport hotels have a certain appeal. Most who stay are business people and often alone and up for a chat to pass the time. This she knows from experience when digging for dirt on people to feed her gutter press.

"Same," she replies. "But, Conrad, I don't want to be around you. Why don't you stay in your room and sort things out with Aswar before having long cosy chats with the wifey and kids?"

He ignores her snide remark. It suited him to talk to Aswar alone, anyway. "Will I see you in the morning?" he asks, rising from his chair. "You'll want a report on what Aswar has to say, I'm sure."

"Breakfast in the dining room at seven," is her blunt reply. "And just be careful what you say to him."

Harper watches her brother leave, then makes her way to the airport shops to buy clothes — clothes she never dreamt of buying. Her new image, and the fact that even her own brother failed to recognise her, has opened up a fresh avenue of dirt-digging and exploitation.

Conrad, though, is more than happy to stay under the radar when not involved in government matters. Particularly when threats to life and kidnapping are concerned.

After checking into the airport hotel, and with his room key in hand, he stands at the elevator waiting for its descent to the ground floor. The doors slide open, and he waits for a male passenger to alight. The man pauses and turns back to Conrad.

"Minister Glasson?" he asks, then, sure he is, adds, "What a surprise."

Conrad's mind is on what to say to Aswar, and he struggles to remember the man.

"I sat in meeting you attend couple of days ago," the man adds.

"Ah, yes," Conrad replies, now struggling to come up with a name.

"Mr Chong Liu Yang. I there for DongYan Rare Earth Company," he says, offering an outstretched hand.

"Yes, of course, Mr Chong, I remember you," replies Conrad, accepting his handshake.

"It is fortunate that I meet you, Minister. My company is very interested in your thoughts on the report presented to you at the meeting. Do you have time to discuss?"

This unexpected addition to his thought-load has rattled Conrad, but diplomacy when dealing with the Chinese is important. "Yes, absolutely," he agrees. "If you allow me to go to my room, freshen up and make a phone call, I'll meet you at the bar in thirty minutes."

Mr Chong nods his acceptance while backing away to allow Conrad into the elevator.

Conrad has bought himself thirty minutes to get his head around the meeting and the report that, with relief, he has read. Conrad wonders if this is a timely and fortunate coincidence? With the file data on Noi and the serum fresh in his mind, any further knowledge he can squeeze out of Mr Chong could be handy in his talk with Aswar.

Conrad sees no point in calling Aswar before meeting Mr Chong. He uses the time to think and settle down with a miniature whisky from atop the bar fridge.

Meanwhile, Harper has finished her shopping and is eager to get to her hotel room and change into her new clothes. As soon as she enters one of the two elevators, the neighbouring elevator opens, allowing Conrad to step out.

With her purchased attire laid out on the bed, Harper stands back, shaking her head and wonders why anyone would buy such cheap, awful clothes. But this adds to her new persona, cheap and awful, and ready for some uncharacteristic cheeky fun. She heads off to the shower.

***

Conrad enters the lounge and sees Mr Chong sitting at the bar. He hates talking to anyone at the bar, let alone someone dealing with the government. He lost trust in bar staff a long time ago when one of them tipped off the media about something overheard that caused Conrad a great deal of embarrassment. So much for anonymous sources and underhand retainers.

"Minister Conrad, what can I get for you?" welcomes Mr Chong, with a slight rise from the bar stool. "

"A beer will be fine, thanks," replies Conrad, then adds. "Shall we sit at a table?"

Conrad leads the way with drinks in hand to a table in a distant corner. After settling down and saluting each other with a clink of glasses, Conrad starts the conversation, hoping to get it over and done with as quickly as possible.

"What brings you to Darwin, Mr Chong?"

"In transit," he replies. "I fly to Dili in morning."

"Dili?" repeats a surprised Conrad. "You have business with the government there?"

"Yes and no." He shakes his head while waving a dismissive hand. "That sound evasive, I know, but it has a connection to matters discussed at meeting."

"It was my understanding that the Timorese government is not involved," replies Conrad, slightly uncomfortable.

"They are not, Mr Conrad. My meeting with the government is a courtesy visit, nothing more. In fact, my reason for going to Dili is to make sure they know nothing of our plans."

"You suspect they know?" asks Conrad.

"Not sure, but possible."

Conrad thinks about this for a moment, looks around the room, then leans across the table to talk quieter. "Does it matter? I mean, once the project is operational, it would be hard to hide. And anyway, it's in Indonesian waters, and they have no claim."

"That is true, Mr Conrad, but we have long studied the controversial and protracted negotiations over the Timor Sea Treaty and wish not to fall into the same trap."

Conrad leans back in his chair. Surprised Mr Chong has brought up any mention of the Treaty.

"Mr Conrad, I wish you no disrespect. We both know of the unsavoury actions all governments call on from time to time, and your bugging of the Timor-Leste government is no exception."

Conrad has taken exception and could counter with knowledge of some questionable Chinese actions. But with negotiations surrounding this new project still underway, he errs on the side of diplomacy.

"Yes, well, let us not get into a tit-for-tat discussion. My immediate interest is in this current project and whether there has been any further progress made since the meeting."

"That depends on what I come across in Dili, Mr Conrad. Until then, nothing has changed." He pauses before continuing. "What is the purpose of your visit to Darwin, if I may ask?"

Conrad feels under pressure and, maybe, suspicion.

"I'm visiting a relative who is undergoing a transformation," he replies, surprised at the truth in it.

"I see," replies Mr Chong. "I wasn't aware you had a relative living here in Darwin."

"Oh no, not living here, holidaying from overseas. It was the only chance to meet. Now, the report you wanted to discuss," says Conrad, eager to change the subject and end this meeting quickly without appearing un-diplomatic.

Over the following fifteen minutes, nothing of significance came out of their discussion that would interest Aswar nor change anything in the report.

With drinks empty, Conrad makes an excuse to retire back to his room.

"If you'll excuse me, Mr Chong, I would like to talk to my children before they go to bed. It was a pleasure to see you again, and I look forward to our next meeting. I'll order you another drink on my way out."

They shake hands and bow to each other.

***

Harper had entered the bar moments earlier, and seeing Conrad, found a table hidden from his view.

She does not know the man he is talking to, which stirs her interest. He has the aura of ministerial power, Chinese, and is reasonably presentable.

She watches Conrad leave and waits for the elevator to close behind him before approaching the bar. The barman is about to deliver the drink Conrad ordered to Mr Chong.

"Is that for the gentleman over there?" she asks with a turn of her head. "He's a friend. Pour me a glass of your best Shiraz and I'll take them."

CHAPTER 52

"May I join you?" stops Mr Chong Liu Yang keying in a note on his phone. He looks up, and a broad smile spreads across his face. He stands up, bows, and offers the opposite chair for his 'good luck' visitor to sit.

"My name is Tory, and this is your drink," says Harper, placing the drinks down on the table before sitting.

"My name Dan'l," he offers, then lowers himself back down into his chair. "You are most attractive."

Harper beams with a slight flush, never having had that said to her before. She answers with eyes down, thinking to herself that this will be easier than she imagined.

"Why, thank you, Dan'l. What a lovely name."

"Same as Dan'l Craig. You like James Bond?"

"Oh, yes, I see a resemblance. Are you an actor?" Harper is wondering how overly sweet she can go.

It's having an impact as Ching Liu Yang is struggling to conjure up a fake past.

"No, but I manage actors," he says before realising the consequences if Tory turns out to be an actor.

"So you're an agent, then?" She asks, testing his lie.

"You actor?" he asks, hoping she's not.

"Oh, no...well, I mean it depends on what you call acting? They have known me to...um...perform."

Dan'l's face reddens. His 'good luck' visitor may even be luckier as Harper raises her glass. They touch glasses, then both take a deep swallow.

Harper wants to get to the truth before Dan'l gets too drunk. There is a point where the tongue loosens before the too drunk kicks in and he'll want to karaoke.

"What brings you to Darwin, Dan'l? Casting a film, maybe?" she teases.

"No, I in transit. I fly to Dili in morning."

Harper needs to consider what this means before replying. As she's booked on the only morning flight to Dili, there's the problem of being on the same flight, then in the same place at the same time. The way he is almost drooling over her, he'll never leave her alone. If she can get out of him what's going on with Conrad this evening, she could take a later flight.

"And why you in Darwin..." he looks down at Harper's hands. "...Miss Tory? Performing, maybe?"

Harper gives him a cheeky smile.

"I would like to know you more. Would you dine with me tonight?" he asks.

Harper is not sure about dining in the hotel, as Conrad might be there. They could go to the city, but she has an alternative.

"I would like that, but could we have room service in your room where it'll be much more comfortable."

Again, Dan'l's eyes light up.

"That is, if you're not sharing the room with your friend."

Dan'l shakes his head, confused. "No friend," he says.

"Oh, as I walked in, you were with someone."

"Oh, he no friend."

"One of your clients, then?" she presses.

"Not a client. We talk possible business."

"He didn't seem like an actor, more like a politician."

Dan'l gives a slight titter while averting his eyes.

"So he is a Polly then," she pressed further. "Not into politics, but they all seem to have that same boring look. Unlike people like you who are in the arts — far more interesting."

Dan'l straightens up and appears to push out his chest. A dead giveaway, proving what Harper pictured him to be from the moment she first saw him...a boring Polly.

"Why don't I get us another drink before we go to your room," she suggests, moving to stage two of loosening his tongue.

CHAPTER 53

The weather over the Banda Sea had worsened by morning. For Jude, not to dive was out of the question. Despite pressure to return to Dili with water from around the volcanic vents, without a worm, is against his nature. He sensed he was close to getting a worm, but just how much time he could allow himself before giving up could be out of his hands.

The spot where he believed he spotted a worm is deeper than he liked, and the change in the weather, the surges and diminished visibility required careful consideration.

The other matter to consider was air!

While they had a compressor on board to refill tanks, it was not capable of refilling the one Nitrox mix tank saved for deeper dives, such as the one Jude is now facing.

Evelyn's cigar is getting a rigorous chew as he watches Jude stare into the ocean darkened by heavy cloud cover.

He is well aware Jude is psyching himself up to dive for as long as the Nitrox air will last or he finds a worm — whatever comes first.

Jude looks from the ocean to the sky, and his experience tells him the weather window of opportunity is near.

***

In Darwin, the weather is fine, and there's early activity as guests are checking out and waiting for the shuttle to take them and their luggage to the airport, only walking distance away.

Harper is also checking out. But not before a quick breakfast with her brother.

Mr Chong, or Dan'l, proved a worse drinker than she expected, or was he trying to impress? He passed out well before midnight, and Harper took it upon herself to re-arrange his travel plans. Finding his plane ticket, she arranged with the airline to have Mr Chong Liu Yang on a later flight because of illness. She gave instructions to the hotel reception not to disturb Mr Chong until mid-morning and to inform him of his change of flight.

This will give Harper the day in Dili without looking over her shoulder in case he was around. First, she has enough time before her flight to test Conrad's reaction to what she has learnt.

Conrad is almost finished his breakfast after giving up waiting for his sister.

"Had a rough night?" he asks as she joins him at his table. "I thought you'd checked out."

"Get fucked, Conrad," she snaps back, taking exception to his judgement of her appearance. "I gave up my sleep for research, what did you do? Did you call your mate?"

"Aswar is not my mate, I keep telling you. And yes, I called him, and he's still pissed off that he can't get in touch with you or you to him."

"Do I look like I give a shit! What did you tell him?"

"What we agreed on."

"And...?"

"That was it...he hung up."

"He hung up? What, saying nothing?"

"Not a word. It was as if what I told him was all he wanted to know, and that was it."

This troubles Harper. Did Conrad go beyond what they agreed to say to him? What she learnt from Dan'l proved her brother may not be the dumb, stupid prick she always believed him to be. Or he is stupider beyond imagination, and everything will go haywire.

"Conrad, I'll ask you once, and I want none of your bullshit evasive political crap answers. What's going on with this Chinese mining deal?"

Conrad almost chokes on the last piece of toast as his face drains of colour.

Harper continues without waiting for him to recover. "If this deal has the slightest impact on our contesting the Will and the takeover of this serum research, I want to know."

Conrad wipes his mouth and dabs at the beads of sweat sprouting on his upper lip.

"What? How? Who told you about..." he stops himself from saying any more.

Harper smiles. "I spent a fascinating evening with your Mr Chong. Or, Dan'l, as he likes to be called."

Conrad wonders if she is talking about a different person?

Harper keeps the pressure on. "Look, I saw you talking to him, and when you left, I took over the conversation. Did you know he can't handle his booze well? Anyway, once in bed, he wouldn't stop talking until he passed out."

"What? You and him in bed? Harper, how could you?" he asks, shaking his head.

"Don't you look down at me from your pillar of virtue, Conrad. You may not fuck around, but you sure fuck with corruption."

Conrad stiffens up, ready to defend himself, but eases back, accepting her skill at getting information out of people.

"Look, there's nothing settled," he tries to explain. "It's still under negotiation."

"Details?" snaps Harper, as cutting as she can. "I want details and hurry, as I have a plane to catch."

***

When Harper turns her other phone on after landing at Dili, she's surprised there were two unanswered calls. Conrad was the only one who knew her number, but the caller was not him. If it's Aswar, Conrad must have given him the number. She is about to turn the phone off when it rings. She answers and waits until Aswar finishes his outburst.

"I found her for you, didn't I?" she cut in. "And the plan to get her back!"

"At the expense of one of my men," he yells into the phone.

224

"You hire idiots, and that's what happens!" Harper will not stand for any more abuse. "I will not get involved in any more of your goons' fuck-ups. You have a way of getting your wife and unborn baby back, so you don't need me anymore."

Aswar has gone quiet except for his rampant breathing.

Harper waits for him to control his rage, but after a longer than expected silence, Harper twigs. Conrad did not tell him about the baby.

Aswar ends the call, and Harper needs to think.

Not telling Aswar about his baby means only one thing. Conrad does not care if he kills Noi. He sees the deal with the mining company as a longer-lasting and more lucrative outcome than the inheritance and serum royalties.

Then it strikes her.

Mining the Banda Sea will mean the demise of the serum-giving worms!

CHAPTER 54

Harper Glasson's afternoon is ticking over slowly. Since arriving back in her Dili hotel room, she can't get the sweep of conflicting emotions out of her head.

Babies and motherhood had never entered her world. In fact, her world closed the door on such things. She had no friends who had families. She never even socialised with her brother and his family — his children — her own blood relatives.

So why is she now having such thoughts?

She reckoned it was far too early for Kailee to have a drink at the Sunday Roast, if indeed at all, considering her injury, or the fact she may no longer be alive! Or, there was also the possibility she had already gone back to Canberra to get as far away as she could from a crime scene and a dead body. But just in case, she mingles among the smoke, hawkers and frolicking children on the beach opposite.

Meanwhile, inside the Glasson BioMarine lab, Mirla finishes changing the dressing on Kailee's wound. Satisfied it's healing well and Kailee is in no pain, she asks her if she's well enough to stay with Noi while she takes a brief nap. Kailee insists on it.

It was well over forty-eight hours since Mirla had slept. The broken rear door needed boarding up, and a body needed wrapping and stored away. All without seeking help for fear of questions being asked. But most of her awake time she spent looking over Noi and Kailee while coming to grips with killing someone. A vow she made never to do again since fighting for East Timor's independence ended.

In the secure, sealed lab, Kailee swabs Noi's stomach with the depleting worm water, careful not to waste any. Noi's wound has closed up without stitches; such is her serum-induced ability to heal.

As they sit together, they relive the break-in and killing of Fauzi. It's created a bond between the two and allows Noi to open up about her nightmarish years under the control of Aswar.

The more she talks about it, the less painful becomes the degrading abuse that had been her constant companion. Her body relaxes, expelling the stress, and for the first time, Noi feels pregnant.

"Kailee?" she asks, reaching out for her hand. "Promise me I will live to see and hold my baby."

Kailee knows it's an impossible promise to make, but with a reassuring smile and a firm grip on her hand, she hopes that will suffice.

"I wanted to get rid of it...his baby...even kill myself as soon as I realised I could be pregnant, but Professor Glasson convinced me otherwise. I so wish his death is just another nightmare that will pass, but it won't."

"Mirla will carry on where the Professor left off, you know that, don't you?" reaffirms Kailee.

"And all because you found me," she admits. "When the professor died, I was so lost and alone in a strange place; I didn't know what to do."

"Well, it's all over now," says Kailee, wishing she hadn't, knowing it's far from over. "Now, enough talk. You should rest."

For the next two hours, Kailee had tried to put herself in Noi's position but failed. While her life had its problems, nothing could come close to the stories Noi had just told her.

When Mirla woke and took over care of Noi, she suggests Kailee go back to her room to rest and give her wound time to heal. Kailee agrees, and with the back door boarded up, the front door is the only way out.

Kailee has no intention of going straight to her room. The events of the last few days needed something stronger than sleep to dull her senses. Carlo was just the man to help.

"Hello Kailee, I haven't seen you for two days," he says as she steps up to the bar. "What can I get you? My special again, or something different? I have many specials."

227

"Surprise me," replies Kailee. "I'm up for anything."

Harper was pleased to see Kailee was alive and mobile as she watched her leave the Glasson building. The long wait had put her through a period of indecision. Whether or not to face her. Her final decision goes against all that her life had been built around, and with trepidation, she follows Kailee into the Sunday Roast Bar.

"May I join you in the surprise?"

Kailee does not look around, but into the mirror behind the bar, already aware who it is by the raspy tone of her voice.

If Kailee's mind wasn't already crowded with surprises, another surprise just arrived.

Unsure how to react since learning who this fake Tory Harris really is, Kailee decides to listen to what she has to say.

"Why not," she says, nodding to Carlo to double the order and turns to face Harper. "Not sure what you'll be getting, though."

Harper smiles as she eases herself onto the neighbouring bar stool.

There's a collision of words to start a conversation followed by silence. A moment passes as each challenge the other to continue.

Carlo breaks the impasse. "Do either of you ladies have any allergies?" he asks, pausing over his cocktail shaker.

Together, Kailee and Harper see the pointed relevance in the question, as each holds damaging secrets about the other. There's a knowing smile between the two before Kailee replies. "I'm sure we're willing to take a risk."

Without hesitation, Kailee's expression stiffens, and she says to Harper, "I know who you really are!"

Harper smiles at having underestimated Kailee's talent for revealing true identities.

"May I still have my drink?" she asks

"What are you doing here? Or should I ask, why are you still here?"

"I like someone who comes straight to the point," says Harper as Carlo slides their drinks across the bar. She picks her glass up with a respectful nod to the creation. "Shall we drink to no beating about the bush?"

Kailee accepts the challenge.

The first sip takes their breath away, and they salute Carlo with a silent nod.

"If you tell me why you believe I'm here, I'll tell you my thoughts on why you're here?" challenges Harper.

Kailee needs a moment to consider it. Harper Glasson is a ruthless journalist with a way around words to get the responses she's after. Whereas Kailee is the silent type, where words do not come easily. But this is her new life. Nothing more could break the shackles of her mundane past than the last few days of an epic, fictional, intriguing thriller — despite there being nothing fictional about it at all.

Kailee waits for Carlo to leave the bar to collect glasses before taking up the challenge.

"You're here to protect your inheritance."

Harper waits for more.

"Is that all?" She says with a shrug.

"And I believe to build on it," Kailee adds.

This leaves Harper wondering how much more she knows — or how little. She reins in her ruthless interrogation approach in case she lets something slip out that Kailee is unaware of. Instead, she goes straight to her reading of Kailee.

"For a start," Harper begins. "I'm not sure you actually intended to be here. I reckon you got caught up in something you started, then got swept along by others. Others who have you now involved in kidnapping and murder."

Kailee can't hide her shocked expression. How does she know about the killing? Was she there? Did she witness what happened? Was she part of the plan to break into the clinic? Is she working for Noi's husband?

"What are you talking about? What murder?" she asks, testing how much she knows and her involvement.

Harper regrets mentioning murder.

Kailee sees a weakness and steps in with, "You were there? Maybe not inside, but..." Another possibility crossed her mind, remembering Mirla mentioning the missing file. "Or was it something special you were after?"

Harper sees no point in prolonging her confession, as it was bound to come out anyway.

"You mean the file on this girl, Noi? Yes!"

It surprises Kailee that her confession came so quickly, and says, "Then you know how important her baby is."

Harper looks down at her drink, then around the room as Carlo comes back to the bar. "Let's move to a table so we can talk openly?"

Kailee agrees, and they pick up their glasses.

Before Kailee settles into her seat, Harper lets loose with her change of heart.

"Look! Initially, I wanted this girl out of the way. My father has bequeathed so much to her and this secret family of his, leaving my brother and me with mere crumbs. I never knew who this Aswar fellow was, but my brother did. He got me involved in helping get his wife back. I thought that would be the answer to everything, no matter what he did with her. And yes, I didn't want to think about the process, him being such a repulsive man."

She takes a drink to moisten her parched throat while Kailee waits for her to continue.

"Then I read that report on Noi and the baby. First, I thought it was all pure fantasy. A wishful dream of an eccentric scientist. But the reality is my father is — was — neither a wishful dreamer nor an eccentric. He is a highly acclaimed and successful biologist who has given so much to medicine. And, yes, before you read my mind, I thought of ways to pressure my father's mistress into cutting us a slice of the action."

"You mean, blackmail her?" interrupts Kailee.

Harper smiles at her directness.

"If you like. But I had to talk to my brother — he being an ex-lawyer. We had a plan, and it was legal. Then only last night I found out my brother was doing something behind my back and, well, something — something I never thought I had — surfaced."

She waits, expecting Kailee to ask what, but Kailee remains unmoved until straightening up in her chair and says, "You stopped thinking about yourself. Just for a moment, but enough to allow thoughts for the baby to enter your cold heart."

Harper accepts it to be harsh, but true.

Kailee continues. "So what? What do you want from me? Just to hear your confession, to ease your conscience?"

Harper has allowed no one to speak to her like that. In the past, she would have slapped whoever across the face and walked out on them. That's still a possibility if Kailee doesn't walk out on her first.

But Kailee has entered a part of her conscience she never for one moment recognised.

"I want you to tell Mirla something," Harper says, pushing her glass aside to lean closer. "I'm sure she'd never want to talk to me, so tell her if she doesn't find another worm soon, there may never be another chance."

Kailee shakes her head. "What do you mean...never?"

"Never! The location marked in the file is destined to be mined for minerals!"

Harper slides a ten-dollar note across the table. "Buy yourself another drink. I'm heading back to Sydney in the morning, so I doubt we'll ever see each other again."

Kailee finds no good reason to stop her and watches as she walks out without a look back.

The urge to go to Mirla and tell her is strong, but Kailee decides she can do nothing until morning and everyone needs a rest. She gets up with the ten-dollar note in her hand. Her appetite for another drink has faded, and it would be wrong to keep the money. It'll go into Carlo's tip jar.

As she passes the chair Harper sat in, she stopped. Lying on the seat is case file No. AP80GBM/17.

CHAPTER 55

K ailee is awake early and eager to tell Mirla about her talk with Harper. As soon as she enters the Glasson building and sees Noi, her heart sinks.

"Oh, Mirla, Noi looks the worst I've seen her," remarks a concerned Kailee.

Noi's skin has taken on a translucency, revealing dark, throbbing veins below the verdant-tinted surface. Her eyes are closed but unable to stop a tear tinged with red to escape and roll down her cheek.

Mirla wipes away the tear then continues dabbing sweat from Noi's forehead. "She had a bad night. I think all this stress is overloading all her other problems. She seemed relaxed when you left, but it's during the night that her demons return."

Noi had allowed Kailee into her world of demons and torment, and what she is to tell Mirla will only add more. She places a hand on Mirla's arm to encourage her to step away from Noi.

"Mirla, I have something important to tell you, but not..." she whispers with a nod toward Noi.

Mirla sees the worried look on Kailee's face and takes the hint. One more wipe of Noi's brow and she follows Kailee into the office.

"What is it?" asks Mirla, sensing whatever it is, is not good.

"I talked to Harper last night. She came into the bar after me. She's the one who took the file."

Mirla is unsure how to react. Be it Harper or someone else, it really didn't matter now Noi was deteriorating.

"She met up with her brother in Darwin the day before yesterday, and they discussed the project and ways to get their hands on more than what they would inherit from the professor's estate."

"I expected that, but that's not high on my list of worries at the moment."

"Yes, I understand. But something else came out of their talk. There are plans to mine the area where Jude found the worm."

Mirla looks up. Her expression flushed with disbelief.

"Seems her brother, therefore the Australian Government, is involved in negotiations with the Chinese through some sort of consortium. And Mirla, I also suspect it involves Aswar and the Indonesian Government."

Mirla shakes her head. "They can't do that! Surely, if they read the file, they would see that what we can achieve far outweighs any profit from mining. There is still so much we can learn and so many undiscovered creatures living down there that could deliver enormous benefits to humanity."

"I agree, Mirla, and so does Harper with her change of heart. That's why she told me and left me the file."

She hands Mirla the file, who takes it and checks that everything is there.

"If they discussed this file, then all involved in this mindless destruction will know the public will be on our side if it got out. They can't afford that publicity and will hurry their efforts to mine. Do you think she made copies of the file?" asks Mirla, her mind shifting between two thoughts.

"For some unknown reason, I don't think so. And what I can read into her brother's actions, the contents are not important, just royalties from what they dig up," replies Kailee.

"Do you trust her?" challenges Mirla.

"Never! But with this, I think so."

***

The weather over the Banda Sea has eased, but the time wasted has increased the pressure on Jude. The calls from Mirla over the previous day had not helped. Now she's calling again.

Gone is the worry and panic in Mirla's voice, calmly wishing him good luck with the day's dive.

Mirla decided not to tell Jude about the plan to mine. If she did, he would ignore safety over desperation to find a worm.

While the conditions to dive had become acceptable, Jude and Evelyn agreed that visibility at such a depth was still questionable. But the urgent need to get at least a tank of water back to Noi left only one option. Dive and hope for the best.

Jude's first dive will be with a regular tank to check visibility. If it's clear enough to dive deeper, he'll change to the Nitrox mix.

It is, and Evelyn has the Nitrox tank ready for him.

Jude's priority is to collect as much water from around the live volcanic vents. If he spots a worm, then that becomes the top priority.

With a collapsed, empty bladder making it easier to dive with, he'll then use a hand pump to suck in water until full. He'll need several trips to collect a sufficient amount of water to keep Noi comfortable. A light and atmosphere-controlled tank will store water in to keep it at its natural temperature and sealed.

Jude looks to Evelyn that all is in order. Evelyn nods back, and Jude falls backward into the deep water.

It takes Jude several minutes to descend to the closest vents at forty-one metres. Jude is used to this depth without the Nitrox mix. The water is still murky, but without delay, he pumps a bladder full of water from the mouth of one of the active vents. He feels the heat from the water and must get it to the surface and into the controlled tanks as fast as he can. The first yank on the attached rope is a signal to Evelyn that he's heading to the surface. Jude looks into the clear plastic bladder, hoping he sucked in a worm. No such luck! A second yank on the rope signals Evelyn to pull the full bladder to the surface and throw in an empty one. The hand pump attached to the empty bladder will help it sink, but not fast enough. He grabs it and heads back down to a deeper vent.

Evelyn also takes a hopeful look inside the full bladder before releasing the valve and emptying its contents into the holding tank. To prevent the water coming into contact with outside air, the collection tank has a floating seal that rises with the added water. The temperature of the added water must match the reading Jude has taken from inside one of the hydrothermal vents. Heating elements in the holding tank adjust to ensure the temperature remains constant.

By mid-afternoon, the tank is almost full, but still no worm.

Jude and Evelyn must decide whether to take the water collected back to Dili while there is still some hours of daylight left, or will Jude go deeper with the Nitrox tank and search for a worm until he has only enough air left to decompress and surface?

Allowing a maximum of one hour's search time, Jude puts on the Nitrox tank and returns to the deeper water.

CHAPTER 56

～.～.～

Jude finds the submarine volcano vents and fissures mesmerising beyond forty metres. The variety of species living at this depth can interfere with one's concentration. But concentrate he must if he is to find the one evasive creature he's after.

In the deep, darkened water, the line tied to the water-collecting bladder is the only contact Jude has with the surface and a troubled Evelyn.

A light plane has circled overhead several times, and now a fourteen-foot cruiser has appeared coasting a short distance away. Evelyn has always relied on the feeling in his ample gut and takes a worrying draw on his cigar. He looks at his watch. Jude has been down only fifteen minutes and unless he finds a worm, won't surface for maybe another hour.

A flash of reflected sunlight from the loitering boat catches his eye. Someone is looking at him through binoculars.

To appear unconcerned, he readies another bladder. While doing so, he uses it to shield his hand reaching for a nearby flare gun. A speargun, used to defend against sharks or to catch a meal, is in an adjacent cabinet. To fetch and prime it to fire will be difficult to hide from prying eyes, but that was a risk he needed to take.

The moment he removes the speargun, the boat speeds up toward him. The need to figure out who or how many are onboard is distracting him from loading the gun, and he fumbles.

It only takes seconds for the cruiser to close the gap, and Evelyn makes out four on board: the skipper and three other mean-looking men.

Casting aside the gun, he kept hold of the spear just as the cruiser broadsides the dive boat, knocking Evelyn off balance. Two of the men jump aboard, armed and ready to restrain the big man, but they underestimate his strength. An elbow into the ribcage of one has him double over. The other is not fast enough to aim his assault rifle or deflect the spear from piercing his rifle hand. Evelyn grabs at the dropped gun, but a shot from the invading boat catches him in his right shoulder.

Now, with only one good arm, Evelyn makes another attempt at getting to the rifle. The shooter is quicker, jumping aboard and striking Evelyn on the head with the butt of his gun. A second blow renders him unconscious and bleeding heavily.

***

At a depth of fifty-one metres, Jude is oblivious to what is happening above. He's concentrating on a cluster of volcanic tubes that are spewing out more heated discharge than any of the others he has come across. He places the collapsed bladder over one tube to collect the more intense, mineral-laden water. As soon as he starts suction-pumping water into the bag, up pops a worm! Despite being the object of his search, it came as a shock. His controlled breathing lapses for a moment, and he fumbles trying to get the worm into the bag. To stop the worm retreating into its tube, he speeds up his pumping. As the bladder fills, he looks through the transparent plastic at the prized captive looking back at him.

The need to get it into the holding tank quickly tempers his elation. He tugs on the rope for Evelyn to haul up the bladder. There's no response. He tugs again, but still no response. Angry and confused, he heads to the surface.

Needing to decompress while ascending from such a depth frustrates Jude. As he approached the pause depth, the shadow of a second boat above sent a ripple of concern inside his wetsuit. A rush to the surface could bring on the bends, and with the nearest decompression chamber hours away, Jude needs to be patient.

A mix of seawater and blood spills over the deck of the dive boat. The one hit in the ribcage has recovered while his companion needed to pull the barbed spear all the way through his hand to get it out. He looks with seething anger at Evelyn, now semi-conscious and trying to raise himself up. Without hesitation, he plants a heavy steel-capped boot into his injured side.

The skipper of their boat in the meantime has been watching bubbles rising. He orders his men to be ready to grab the diver with a grappling hook when he surfaces.

As the four men wait, staring over the side for the first sign of Jude, Evelyn recovers enough to crawl towards the collection bladder. One man turns at the sound of movement, but not fast enough to stop Evelyn raising the flare gun and fire. Concussion affects his aim, and the flare just misses the skipper on the other boat.

Evelyn stops another kick to his head by grabbing the booted foot and twisting it until he hears the crack of an ankle bone breaking. He then makes a lunge for the one with the bleeding hand, but the shooter is too quick and fires another shot into Evelyn, then steps aside to allow him to fall overboard.

The sight of Evelyn descending through blood-slicked water above puts a stop to Jude's decompression pause. The need to save Evelyn is more important. Even more critical than the worm. He drops the bag containing the precious cargo and rushes to his sinking friend.

It's an effort for Jude to share his air while getting the unresponsive Evelyn to the surface. The moment he does, the grappling hook pushes Evelyn back under.

Jude takes a chance on assuming they only want him. He rips off his mask and yells. "If he dies, you won't see me again."

CHAPTER 57

Mirla has been waiting for Jude to call, and when the satellite phone shows his ID, she answers before he can say a word. "Jude, have you had any luck yet?"

"He hasn't...but I have!"

Mirla almost dropped the phone on recognising the gravelly voice. She had not heard that voice for many years, but it and the images of those he murdered are seared in her memory.

"I have something of yours, and you have something of mine I want back," says a smug Aswar.

"Well, come and get it then," replies Mirla.

Aswar laughs. "You know I can't do that. Bring my wife to where you know your boy is diving and make it quick."

"I want to talk to my son first."

Aswar hands the phone to Jude.

"I'm all right, but Ev's not good. They've shot him and..."

Aswar snatches back the phone.

"It should take you only four hours to get here. If you involve anyone else, then you'll need to go to the bottom of the sea to find your son and his friend."

The call ends.

"What is it?" asks Kailee, seeing the pain on Mirla's face.

"Aswar has Jude and Evelyn!"

Kailee shakes her head. "What does that mean?"

"He'll release them when he gets Noi back."

Kailee looks back to where Noi is resting in the lab. "But you can't do that. You can't send her back to that animal. And what about the baby and its potential?"

"If I have to hand her over to get my son back, I will," Mirla bluntly replies.

"But Mirla..." Kailee protests, but accepts it to be useless as Mirla heads towards the door.

"I need to get to the dive site, and there's no time to waste. Evelyn's been shot, and I need to talk to Carlo next door."

"What can I do?" asks a frenzied Kailee. "I mean Evelyn will be all right, won't he?"

"Get Noi ready for a boat ride," Mirla snaps, avoiding the question.

As soon as Carlo sees Mirla walk into the bar, he senses a problem.

"Hi, Mirla, what's up?"

"Carlo, Evelyn's injured and I need to use his boat to get to the dive site."

Carlo puts down the glass he's drying and prepares to leave the bar. "I'll take you," he offers.

"No, Carlo, I need you to do something else...something more important."

"What? I'll do anything you ask."

"Come with me to Atauro where I'll drop you off at Beloi. I'll tell you what to do on the way. We must hurry."

Kailee is trying to calm a raging Noi when Mirla returns with Carlo.

"What's going on?" asks Mirla.

"What do you expect?" replies an angry Kailee. "We're giving her back to that evil bastard."

Mirla has no time for this. She walks over to Noi and slaps her hard across the face, to the shock of Kailee and Carlo.

"I'm not prepared to lose my son or Evelyn over your hyster ics. Now pull yourself together and do what you're told."

Kailee can't believe what she has witnessed. Then Mirla turns to her.

"We're going in Evelyn's boat, and I need you to come with us. I can't drive the boat and look after Noi on my own. Carlo is only coming with us to Atauro."

"After what I just saw, I'm not letting Noi out of my sight!" insists Kailee.

"Good, now go with Carlo to the boat. It's anchored just off the beach across the road. I'll follow, but I need to pack a medical kit first."

By the time Kailee and Carlo wade to the boat carrying Noi, Mirla emerges from the lab with a bag over her shoulder. Once onboard, Carlo kicks the powerful twin outboard eight-footer into action.

The weekly ferry to the island takes two hours. A water taxi about an hour. Carlo will make it in thirty minutes. From there it's estimated to take another two hours at least to get to the dive site when it'll be early evening and fading light.

As soon as they reach Beloi, on the eastern side of Atauro Island, Carlo jumps over the side of the boat and gives Mirla a reassuring nod of understanding before wading to the shore.

Mirla looks back at Kailee sitting behind her with an arm around Noi. No words can ease the pain of the inevitable as she turns the boat to face the open sea.

***

Aswar has returned to his cruiser that had stayed back a distance until all was under control on Jude's dive boat. He sees no point in waiting on the dive boat for Mirla and his wife to arrive while there's food, drink and comfort available.

Jude is doing all he can to stem his friend's bleeding. Evelyn is showing his true grit by insisting on a new cigar to chew on despite the grimaces of pain. The boat's first aid kit is helping, but he needs to get to a hospital. Jude's pleas to keep him captive in exchange for someone to take Evelyn to the nearest island fell on deaf ears.

"Stay with me, Ev," encourages Jude. "Mirla will be here soon to look after you."

Evelyn pulls Jude to him and in a low, strained voice says, "Don't let them take Noi, Jude. We still need to find a worm."

Jude looks around to make sure the two standing guard are far enough away not to hear, then whispers, "I did! I had to drop it though to save you, you big lug, but I'll go get it later."

241

Mirla switches off the ignition and allows the boat to drift. Kailee looks up expecting to be at the dive site and approaching the dive boat, but they are several kilometres away and only through binoculars can Mirla see the dive boat.

"What is it?" asks Kailee. "Why have you stopped?"

Mirla stays silent, playing out in her mind what she has planned.

"Mirla, Evelyn could be dying. You must get to him!" pleads Kailee.

"We will when the time's right. You just concentrate on Noi and let me think."

Kailee looks at Noi, held tight in her arms. It's been a struggle to calm her rage at the thought of being returned to her husband and threats to stop it happening.

Meanwhile, Mirla continues to scan the sea around her but never losing sight of Jude's dive boat far ahead.

The lack of action stretches Kailee's patience. "What are you looking for, Mirla? This waiting is not helping anyone!"

Mirla again refuses to answer, but as the sun touches the horizon, now is the time to move.

She turns back to Kailee and Noi as she starts the outboards. "I want you both to stay put and do exactly what I tell you when we get to the boat, understand?"

"Mirla, if Evelyn's shot, then they have guns, and I don't think we have any choice but to do what they want us to do, no matter what you say," snaps Kailee.

Mirla responds under her breath. "I fought these bastards for years. I know what I'm doing."

The skipper of the shooter's boat calls out to Aswar in the tethered cruiser. He emerges from his cabin and focuses his binoculars on where the skipper is pointing. As the approaching vessel is close enough to make out who is on board, a wicked smirk betrays his intentions.

"You!" he calls out to the shooter on the dive boat. "Keep your gun on who's steering that boat. You other two choose between yourselves which of these you want to deal with," he says with a nod towards Jude and Evelyn.

The one speared in the hand aims his rifle at Evelyn, leaving his cohort with no choice but to point his gun at Jude.

Aswar steps onto the dive boat and waits. With the sun beginning to sink below the horizon, he wants to get this over fast, head back to Ambon, then fly to Jakarta.

Mirla idles the outboards and coasts to the side of the dive boat. She looks up at the one aiming his rifle at her and throws him a mooring rope. Surprised, he's undecided whether to tie the boat up or keep his aim on Mirla and the others? He takes a quick look back at Aswar for a hint. Mirla seizes the opportunity to speed up and ram into the side of the dive boat, knocking the shooter off his feet and dropping his gun. Aswar and the other two stay on their feet, but the surprise is enough to allow Jude to grab the rifle aimed at him and thrust it with all his force back while twisting it. It dislocates the finger on the trigger, but not enough to stop getting one shot off that just misses Jude and has the one standing over Evelyn drop to his knees to evade being shot. Evelyn grabs the opportunity to take the lit cigar from his mouth and shove the glowing tip into the man's face.

All the confusion on the dive boat allows Mirla to take out a handgun from the medical kit and aim it at Aswar, who is pointing his gun at her. The skipper of Aswar's cruiser breaks the stalemate by firing into the air before training his rifle on Mirla. For a moment, the temptation to shoot Aswar is overwhelming and worth being shot herself. But Mirla relents and lowers her gun.

"What a pleasure to see you again after all these years," says Aswar, ignoring the painful cries of his men as he steps forward with his gun aimed at Mirla's head. The look in his eyes has Mirla sense he is about to do what she did not. Aswar's ugly face transforms into the smiling, handsome face of Marcus. She is prepared to meet him again.

"Kill her, and I'll kill your baby!" screams Noi, pressing a scalpel taken from the medical kit to her stomach.

The surprise on Aswar's face proves to Mirla that he did not know of the baby, and equally surprising that neither Harper nor her brother told him.

"Bring my wife to me," Aswar ordered one of his men as his skipper kept his rifle aimed at Mirla.

"No!" pleads Kailee. "You don't know what you're doing. She and the baby need..."

"Shut up, Kailee!" snaps Mirla. "It's over!"

"It's just the beginning," calls out Aswar, having accepted that he is to be a father. "I will now have a son to succeed me."

The false belief that he is to have a son does not surprise Mirla. She knows his ego demands it to be. Kailee is unsure what to think, but surprised when Noi drops the scalpel, pushes aside Kailee's arms, and allows herself to be lifted onto the dive boat.

"You see, Mirla Yimenes, I do have a heart," Aswar says, taking the trembling Noi into his arms. "I will take care of her until my son is born."

Noi's fate once she gives birth leaves no one in doubt.

"And don't even think about coming after us," he threatens. "A mother's disfigured face will not hurt my son."

Without looking back, he takes Noi onto his cruiser while ordering his injured and uninjured men to leave their boat and follow him onboard.

Jude rushes to help Mirla aboard and to tend to Evelyn. Kailee follows with the medical kit with tears streaming down her cheeks. "You know what will happen to Noi once he discovers she's having a girl, don't you, Mirla? How can you live with that?"

Mirla ignores her to examine Evelyn's injuries. Jude pulls Kailee close to him and wraps his arms around her as Aswar's boat heads off into the dark waters.

Jude turns to shield Kailee from the sight of Noi sailing off into the distance. As she weeps into his chest, he looks over her head and spots something. "Mirla, I see lights."

Mirla looks to where Jude is pointing. From the direction Aswar's boat is heading, one-by-one, flickering lights appear until there are enough to create an arc closing in on Aswar's cruiser.

"Jude!" Mirla calls out with some urgency. "Get on Evelyn's boat and start it up. Kailee, stop your blubbering. I want you to finish putting on this dressing and stay with Evelyn."

Jude gives Kailee a look that says it's not over yet before jumping onto Evelyn's boat. With the outboards engaged and Mirla joining him, they speed off after Aswar.

The skipper on Aswar's boat turns to him, questioning what is going on with all the lights ahead. Not only forward, but they are now beginning to surround them. The combined light from the flaming torches reveal an armada of fishing boats of all shapes and sizes.

The skipper turns his boat away from the wall of torches to the only opening in the closing circle. Aswar is busy restraining the struggling Noi while his men are unsure of what to do.

"Get us out before they close the circle." Aswar orders his skipper.

"Boss, I can only go where they want us to go," he answers, working the steering wheel so his boat circles within the tightening armada.

Jude is at the wheel as Mirla spots Carlo on one of the many boats. She gets his attention and points to where she wants Aswar herded. He signals his understanding, then passes the order across the ring of fishing boats.

The screen of the onboard satellite GPS lights up Mirla's face as she peers into it. Satisfied she is where she wants to be, she takes out the stowed flare gun.

The Atauro islanders have passed on over many generations their knowledge of what lies beneath the Banda Sea. When Mirla fires the flare into the air, the islanders know precisely what to do.

Under the sudden umbrella of light, the fishing boats complete their circle until Aswar's skipper finds his boat corralled with nowhere to go.

"What are you doing?" Aswar shouts at him. "Don't stop, ram through the bloody boats!"

But the skipper is losing control of his boat as it stutters and lists to one side.

"What's going on?" Aswar cries out in a panic as his boat tilts further. "We're sinking!"

Noi breaks away from Aswar's grasp. A knowing smile brightens her face as fear spreads over Aswar's.

The spot where the fishing boats have manoeuvred Aswar is a no-go zone for the local fishermen and divers. Deep beneath the surface is an active volcano that for years has eased the pressure of an eruption through the continual release of gas. As the gas bubbles rise to the surface, the water density lowers, reducing a boat's ability to float.

As water pours into Aswar's boat through loss of buoyancy, the skipper has lost all control while his men look at each other bewildered.

Aswar scrambles around for a life jacket. "Where are they?" he yells in a panic. "Where are the life jackets?"

But all is too late as water pours in, and within seconds the boat is sinking.

The skipper and Aswar's men help those injured to swim towards the fishing boats, leaving Aswar to fend for himself.

Noi feels the surge of warm energy coming up from the depths. Her strength returns in the comfort of her second home — the ocean.

Not so for Aswar. Deep seawater has forever been his greatest fear. Unable to swim, he panics as he struggles to stay afloat. He looks to Noi for help. His thrashing arms, heavy soaked clothes, and his obesity only added to his problems. His breathing falters, depriving his lungs of buoyancy air as he struggles to keep his head above water.

Noi is in her natural element and stays at a distance from the monster who has stolen her childhood, abused her, imprisoned her and murdered her family. Now is the time to witness the death of Aswar as he begins to sink below the surface.

A splashing from behind makes Noi look around, fearing it may be one of Aswar's men. But it's Carlo and others from the fishing fleet. Protesting loudly, Noi watches as they grab Aswar before he disappears.

"Let him die," she pleads slapping at the water. "I need to see him suffer and vanish from my life."

Ignoring her pleas, Aswar's rescuers pull him aboard one of their boats and joined the others in retreating.

Noi looks around and sees Jude and Mirla in their boat drifting a short distance away. Noi looks around as the flaming lights of the armada sail away. Ignoring calls from Mirla and Jude to swim to them, she takes a deep breath and disappears into the deep dark water. Jude is about to jump in after her, but Mirla holds him back.

After more than a minute and no sign of Noi surfacing, Jude looks to Mirla just as the rear of the boat tips. Both look around as Noi climbs aboard. Her complexion has changed to a healthy glow, but with fury in her eyes.

"Why did you not let him die?" she yells at Mirla. "You had as much reason to see him die as I had."

Mirla pulls her close. "It's not just about you and me, Noi. All the people of Timor-Leste and Atauro have a right to witness their long-awaited justice. It is now in their hands, and you will never again see that man. He will disappear, as will his DNA from your baby." She turns to Jude. "I need to get back to Evelyn, and you need to prepare to recover that worm you told me you found."

247

CHAPTER 59

～･～･～

Manukoko mountain towers over the small fishing village of Maquili on the southeast coast of Atauro Island. A little less than a kilometre up the slope from the water's edge, among a scattering of thatched huts, a small group gathers in a clearing looking over two granite headstones.

One weathered headstone has lichen growing on it, while the other at the head of an open grave is pristine pegmatite with a river of crystals flowing through its depth. Both bear the chiselled surname of Glasson:

Major Alfred Glasson
1915 - 1942

—

Sir Marcus Glasson AO
1942 - 2018

It took months before the coroner released Sir Marcus Glasson's body for burial. The final autopsy report stated the cause of death was massive organ failure as a result of inconclusive findings.

Mirla Yimenes well knew the cause of his death and still harbours two regrets. A broken promise to be with him when he died, and that he did not live to see the result of his sacrifice.

She places flowers at the base of his father's gravestone, then flowers on the coffin supported above an open grave. Noi joins her, putting her baby's hand on a flower as it's placed beside Mirla's.

Evelyn steps forward and among the flowers places an un-wrapped Perdomo Slow-Aged Lot 826 Glorioso Maduro cigar, then steps back and salutes his friend and his friend's father.

Jude is taking the occasion hard and holds back from placing his tribute. It takes Kailee's offer of support to approach the coffin and set his father's Sicura Breitling submariner watch beside the flowers and cigar. He bows his head for a moment of reflection before turning back to six-month pregnant, Kailee. He takes her hand, holding a posy of flowers and proudly displaying a wedding ring on one finger. Together they scatter the flowers over the coffin of Jude's father and the father of a future disease-free world.

In the fishing village below, new headstones have replaced the original wooden crosses marking the graves of Noi's father, mother, and brother. Embedded in the new cross above Noi's father's grave is a small wooden spoon encased in silicone.

The ultimate resting place of Djan Muhammad Aswar is un-known. He was neither seen nor heard of since the villagers took him away eight months earlier, and no-one ever utters his name.

The Indonesian government ordered an investigation into his disappearance, with the findings confirmed by several witnesses that he drowned when his boat capsized in the Banda Sea.

The Islanders handed the skipper and Aswar's men over to the authorities, who ignored their version of events, instead charging them with drug and human trafficking and sentencing them to death.

Sir Marcus' eldest son, Conrad, died as a result of a car accident not long after the incident on the Banda Sea. The crash caused minor injuries and death put down to a resulting heart attack.

Unknown to the coroner, the minor accident forced Conrad's ring hand into the dashboard. His father's signet ring cracked, releasing the undetectable euthanasia drug it carried into a minor cut on his finger.

Harper Glasson gave up reporting on gossip. She left the tabloid paper she worked at, became fond of cheap grunge clothes and less severe makeup, and changed to drinking beer and cheap wine. On the odd occasion she splashed out, Harper would pass a recipe to a bar person for a special cocktail she calls The Carlo.

But Harper has not given up writing. She has secured a publishing contract for her first book, The Miracle Baby, which the publisher is still unsure whether to market as fiction or science-fiction.

Mirla granted Harper permission to use edited scientific data and insisted all names and character descriptions used are false. Apart from that, their relationship remains distant.

On top of what she inherited, as prescribed in her father's Will without contest, Harper received a small parcel of shares in a new company set up to further develop, manage, and market to the world the miracle serum.

Jude returned to the dive site after the 'incident' and retrieved the worm he had dropped. It secured the health of Noi and her baby, which led to registering the dive site and a vast surrounding area as a region of great importance. This gained the support of international bodies who brought into law an exclusion zone barring all mining.

Mirla continues with the research she and Marcus started, confident that more unique deep-sea creatures will give up their secrets to help rid the world of its ills.

While missing her loving partner, she does not continue her work alone. Apart from Jude, her new research assistants Kailee and Noi continue to monitor the growth of both their miracle babies as they mature to an age and a time when they will pass on the serum their babies produce.

Evelyn recovered and continues to run his Sunday Roast Bar with new co-owner Carlo. But his crowning achievement is securing the worldwide distribution of Perdomo Slow-Aged Lot 826 Glorioso Maduro cigars.

Not the end
but the beginning.

Also by Dennis Ogden

SAVING SPADE

WWI has ended but the battle to save a horse has just begun.
"The horses stay!" came the order as men of the Australian Light Horse are being sent home.
Trooper Lewis Dunbar will never abandon his loyal war horse Spade. So begins a perilous journey into the Sinai Desert and his struggles to protect his horse from a mute Bedouin girl, nomadic tribes, and the Djinn spirits of the desert.
The winds of the Sinai whip up a gripping tale that stir the dormant spirits within.
The winds of the Sinai whip up a gripping tale that stir the dormant spirits within.

ISBN-978-0-6480869-0-1 Softcover
ISBN-978-0-6480869-1-8 Ebook

GOOSE HUNT

Briney Ruza is enticed from Australia to Prague by her estranged mother. There she meets ghetto survivor Evzen Kravitz who is in search of a prized possession. Together they uncover much more than expected – including corrupt dealings that fleeced many owners and descendants of property lost to the Nazis and the financing of the neo-nazi resurgence.
Briney has her own personal secrets and the lives of everyone she meets will forever change…or forever be lost.

ISBN-13: 978-0-6480869-2-5 Softcover
ISBN-13:978-0-6480869-3-2 Ebook

OGDEN IMPRINT